# CASTLES
## *in the* SAND

To: Jacie ~ Christmas 2009
From: Grandpa & Grandma CRAIG
       WITH ALL our love!
_____

Hope you enjoy this book. It
is a wonderful story.

# CASTLES
## in the SAND

*Carolyn A. Greene*

Lighthouse Trails Publishing
Silverton, Oregon, USA

Published by:
Lighthouse Trails Publishing
(see back of book for publisher and author contact information)

Library of Congress Cataloging-in-Publication Data

Greene, Carolyn A.
  Castles in the sand / Carolyn A. Greene.
    p. cm.
  Includes bibliographical references.
  ISBN 978-0-9791315-4-7 (softbound : alk. paper)
  1. Christian college students--Fiction. 2. Mysticism--Fiction.
  3. Spiritual formation--Fiction. I. Title.
  PR9199.4.G7343C37 2009
  813'.6--dc22
                                          2009015548

Note: Lighthouse Trails Publishing books are available at special quantity discounts. Contact information for publisher in back of book.

# Contents

*To my beloved praying mother*

*Castles in the Sand* is a work of fiction. However, Teresa of Avila is a real, historical figure (1515–1582). The depiction of her life in this book is based on historical records. Quotes and paraphrases of her writings are taken from her actual written works. The lives of the other characters portrayed in this book are created from composites of true stories. Names and some details have been changed.

## Run

Ponder the path of thy feet, and let all thy ways be established. Turn not to the right hand nor to the left: remove thy foot from evil. Proverbs 4:26-27

NO one noticed the slender girl in the shadows pick up her backpack, tiptoe through the maze of bodies and slip out the back door. The other students were preoccupied as they sat cross-legged on yoga mats while images of Mary, baby Jesus, Celtic crosses, and a winged sun disc flashed across a screen in the darkened room. Two intern youth pastors lay on their backs by the incense station, their eyes glazed as if in a trance. One of them softly chanted a Latin phrase over and over in time to the repetitive beat. The sound man had long since stopped changing the music and lay nearly motionless on the floor beside the control panel.

As the girl exited the room and let the door quietly swing shut behind her, candles flickered and a paper in the hallway floated to the ground. It read:

Thompson Building, Room 109
Welcome Flat Plains Bible College Students
EKSTASIS NIGHT

A WORSHIP EXPERIENCE
7:00 p.m. Friday March 27th
All First Year SPIRITUAL FORMATION Students
Required to Participate
~go deeper~make space for God~

She leaned against the back of the door for a moment, heart pounding. "Okay Tessa Dawson," she whispered to herself, "you either just did the right thing or a very stupid thing. Now run!" While her panicked eyes quickly determined the nearest exit out of the building, she scooped up the paper, crumpled it into a ball, and tossed it into a nearby garbage can before racing down the hall. Her long brunette braids bounced madly behind her as she ran toward the stairwell. Suddenly, she heard muffled shouting in the distance, then footsteps coming down the flight of stairs above her.

Spurred on by fear, Tessa ran toward the nearest door, hoping desperately it would open.

*Locked!* She rushed to the next door and tried the knob.

*Locked!* She could barely breathe.

*Keep going, keep going,* she thought frantically. Turning the corner, she glanced over her shoulder. With furrowed eyebrows, she quietly turned the handle on the lecture hall door. The door swung open. Relief washed over her as she rushed in and quietly closed the door behind her. Inside, the room was deathly silent and inky black. Even the moon's usual casting of long creepy shadows on its walls was missing, for the moon was hidden behind the churning, dark, and ominous clouds that filled the evening sky. Leaning against the nearest wall, the slightly built girl slumped to the floor and rested her head between her knees.

Exhausted and breathing heavily, she sat for a few minutes in the dark, trying to gather her thoughts. She had stayed in room 109 far too long.

*Why couldn't I break away?* she wondered. *Has this place turned into a prison after all?*

Doubts had been brewing in her mind for some time, and now

she realized there was only one thing to do. She must escape. They would soon be looking for her, she realized abruptly with a renewed sense of panic. There was no time to waste.

She groped through her backpack, searching for her cell phone. *Please work this time,* she pleaded, when she finally found it. Her phone had been doing strange things all week. She held down the button with her thumb until she heard the familiar beep. *Finally.* She quickly spelled out a text message, the screen casting an eerie green light on her face:

"Need 2 talk 2 u now"

No sooner had she pressed send and flipped the phone shut than she let out a startled gasp. Her heart skipped a beat. She sensed a presence in the room.

Trembling, the girl tried to jump up, but she fell back to the ground as if an unseen force was pulling her down. Wide-eyed and nearly paralyzed with fear, she shrank against the wall as she watched the lecture hall door slowly creak open. The outline of a man stood in the doorway. A moment later, the silhouette turned away, and the door clicked shut.

*So, they are already looking for me.* She pulled herself up, tiptoed to the door and pressed her ear against it. Silence. She reached for the doorknob and tried to turn it. It was locked from the outside. *Oh no!* Frantically she ran to the back of the room, eyes fixed on the red exit sign. She fell against the broad door handle and stumbled outside, inhaling large gulps of the night air. Her feet felt strangely numb, as if she were in a bad dream. She could barely feel the muscles in her legs as she began a sprint through the puddle-filled courtyard and then across the old soccer field toward the girls' dorm.

It was now raining hard. She probably should have pulled her fleece hood over her head, but keeping her hair dry was the last thing on her mind. For a brief moment, the path in front of her lit up as streaks of lightning zigzagged from sky to ground, like long, white-hot fingers.

*Is this lightning storm God's way of telling me how upset He is with me?*

As she raced toward her dormitory, she continued to cast furtive glances over her shoulder. Was it her imagination, or had she seen the blinds move and the lights go out in the second story window of the old office building she was now running past?

"One one-thousand, two one-thousand, three one-thousand..." She counted the seconds between lightning streaks and thunder.

Her phone beeped. Shivering, she flipped it open as she continued running. It was a message from Gramps! "Teresa, dear, remember 911," read the text message.

"What? That's it?" she cried, fumbling the wet phone, and before she could catch it, the phone slipped from her wet fingers as she slid through a grassy puddle. "No!" she cried out mournfully. Thunder rumbled in the distance as Tessa reached down for her soaked phone. She needed to talk to Gramps!

Suddenly, the girl stopped short and gazed at her surroundings. A fork of lightning illuminated the wet stone-lined path, and like seeing a digital image imprinted in the memory card of her mind, she knew immediately where she was. Right in the center of the outdoor labyrinth. As she stood there, staring in dumbfounded disbelief at her surroundings, she began to experience the oddest sensation. What little strength she had left was now being sucked from her, as though she was being pulled out of herself and into the earth.

"God, if you are really there, help me!" she cried aloud. "I don't want to die!"

She was terrified that this real-life nightmare would end the way her horrifying dream always ended. The dream she woke up from every night, the dream that left her staring death in the face.

Images ran through her mind, like an old black-and-white movie: She was inside a dark, brooding castle, gazing intently at an old, round, carved-wood table covered with dozens of burning candles. Around the table stood brown-hooded figures chanting words she couldn't understand. And a serpent . . . there was always a serpent.

She would awake from the dream abruptly, soaked with sweat, as a voice called to her, "Teresa, you are mine, come out . . ."

Only her parents and Gran and Gramps had ever called her by

her given name. *Is that God calling me?* she wondered every morning. She had been trying to come out. Today she had finally mustered the courage to attempt escape from the suffocating darkness . . . but now this last hour seemed dreamlike. Everything seemed to be happening in slow motion . . .

The next lightning flash shook the ground and jolted her back to the present.

Tessa gathered her wits and raced toward the outside light of her dorm room that she had left on. Upon reaching it, she opened the door and quickly ducked inside, bolting the lock behind her. She slipped off her fleece jacket and and tossed it and her dripping backpack onto her bed. After flicking on the light switch and turning on every lamp in the cluttered room, she sank into the corner of her bed, placed her back against the wall and wrapping her quilt around her, pulling it tight up to her chin. She was trembling, but she knew it wasn't because of the storm. She rubbed her sore arm. There was blood on the sleeve of her shirt.

Tessa needed to talk to someone. Anyone! Even her roommate, Katy, would be a welcome sight—even with her quirky little habits. *Never thought I'd hear myself say that*, thought Tessa.

*Why aren't they back from the missions trip yet?* Tessa looked at Katy's clock radio. It was 8:57. A small handcrafted plaque above Katy's bed read, "Choose Today Whom You Will Serve." Pulling her brown stuffed horse to her face, a gift from Gran the day she left for college, Tessa shut her eyes and softly began to cry. If only she were back at home right now.

Was it really only seven months ago that she had been a *normal* girl who thought about boys and worried about which sweater to wear to class? What had happened to her at this place?

Just yesterday, during her spiritual formation class, there had been another "occurrence"—the worst one so far. At first, she had sensed this strange "thing" only when she was with her spiritual director, Ms. Jasmine, but she was sensing it more often now. Weird, how it had made her feel special at first. Ms. Jasmine had told her it was because she had been granted a unique gifting. But lately, this special "gift" had begun to scare her. It was beginning to manifest itself in public, and Tessa feared it would soon take control of her. She knew something was definitely very wrong here, and she wanted out, and now.

She had felt the familiar tingling begin at the base of her spine earlier this night in room 109—the same tingling that had begun when Ms. Jasmine had first prayed over her. Tessa had felt the warm electric sensation creeping through her, accompanied by a growing lump in her throat . . . but not the kind of lump she would get when she thought of something very sad. This was more forceful. Almost insistent.

As Tessa sat, hiding in her room, replaying the events leading up to this night, she stifled a moan. *Not again* . . . It felt as if something was creeping up into her throat. The intensity was growing stronger, and she fought against it. *No* . . .

Ms. Jasmine's words echoed in her mind: "Some women whom the Lord chooses say it's like they are giving birth to something new and beautiful . . . some call it rebirthing. When you open your mind to the light within, it brings you into the sweet union of oneness with your creator . . ."

Tessa took shallow breaths and weakly flipped her cell phone open once again. It made a terrible crackling sound and slipped like melting butter through her fingers.

"Oh dear Lord, help me!" she cried aloud as she raised her hands to her head and squeezed hard.

Shaking, she crawled to the other end of the mattress and laid her head down for a moment. Was it the thunder outside or her pulse from within that pounded in her head like hoof beats? She closed her eyes and tried to visualize herself running to safety. But this time it wasn't working. There was no drawbridge to cross and no beckoning castle anymore. The castle she had once run to for shelter was turning to sand and crumbling before her very eyes.

Desperate to find her phone, but too afraid to put her hand under the bed, she hung her head over the edge and looked around. Her wet braids made a swishy pattern on the dusty floor. Instead of the phone, she saw only her favorite knitted slippers and next to them a brown paper package with the numbers 911 printed on it. *The package Gramps gave me the day I left for school,* she thought, unsuccessfully choking back hot tears. Tessa grabbed the parcel and pulled it out from its dark dusty hiding place. She quickly tore off the paper, uncovering a book, and wiped her eyes with her sleeve. "Don't want my tears to ruin Gramps' handwriting," she softly sobbed. On the inside of the worn leather cover, it read:

> For whosoever shall call upon the name of the Lord shall be saved. Romans 10:13

Gramps had given her his treasure . . . his Bible. It had been under her bed all these months. Under the first verse, he had written another.

> Neither is there salvation in any other: for there is none other name under heaven given among men, whereby we must be saved. Acts 4:12

"But Lord, what is your name?" she whispered. The lump still gripped her throat as she tried to speak.

"You know My name, Tessa."

*Oh Jesus,* she thought, *help me. How can I be sure it's You? I have been listening to all the wrong voices!*

She forced her lips to move. It sounded more like a quiet whimper than a cry for help.

"Jesus Christ, Son of God, if You are really real, and if You are listening…" she whispered, "help me! If this presence I've been sensing is not of You, then please take it away . . . and save me!" Suddenly, the room turned black and the old Bible fell to the floor with a thud.

## ANOTHER TERESA

THE pale, shivering girl was vaguely aware of being lifted onto a clean sheet and covered with a dry blanket. When she opened her eyes, a blurry face hovered above her. The girl's head was pounding, and nausea swept over her in waves. Slowly, she pulled herself upright on the narrow straw mattress. Suddenly, she cried out with alarm as her big brown eyes continued to stare vacantly.

"Run, Rodrigo! He's found us! Run!"

"Sister Juana, she's burning up with the malaria," Teresa heard a young nun say as she was gently laid back down. Someone was dabbing her forehead with a cool, wet cloth. As if from afar, she recognized the voices of the two nuns who stood at the foot of her bed, praying their rosaries.

Her pulse faint, her breath shallow, the feverish girl closed her eyes, as her memory drifted back to her past, beginning with when she was just seven years old . . .

Holding her little brother's hand, she ran with him as fast as their little legs could carry them, and they made it past the city gate. Suddenly, she felt a large, strong hand grabbing her by the shoulder, abruptly ending their flight. Her uncle had caught up with them.

"Come now, little Teresa, it's time to go home. Your mother is anxious!" he said gently, as he dragged her and Rodrigo back home to their worried parents.

Safely home and tucked into her bed later that evening, she overheard the family members and servants talk late into the night.

"Whoever heard of a noble family having to send a search party into the streets for two precocious children—because of their vivid imaginations!"

"Who would put these foolish ideas into Teresa's head?"

"What could possibly have inspired a seven-year-old girl to run away with her little brother, and to Morocco of all places?!"

"And to face certain martyrdom by beheading at the hands of the Moors!" blustered her irate uncle loudly.

"That is what she desired," sighed another family member. "What do you expect of a child who reads too much?"

As Teresa grew older, only her father understood her love for books and the effect they had on her active imagination. She had inherited her passion for literature from her mother, who had spent many hours of the day in bed reading romance stories. *She is so like her mother*, her father frequently thought, smiling to himself. He often found Teresa alone on the roof of the villa, reading books rather than watching over her younger sisters and brothers in the courtyard below. How she loved those fascinating stories of saints and martyrs.

Twelve-year-old Teresa was profoundly impacted by her mother's tragic death. Her passing had left the young girl feeling emotionally raw and empty. Finally, in quiet desperation one evening, Teresa threw herself on the floor before an image of the Virgin Mary and pleaded with her, "Be my new mother."

Her father kept a watchful eye on his daughter as her extreme devotion to the Mother Mary and her good intentions to live a devoted life eventually gave way to an interest in fashion, perfumes, and hairstyles. Before long, her passion for reading and writing romances was rekindled as her imagination and beauty blossomed. Concerned that Teresa had no mother to guard her virtue, Father sent her away to boarding school at the Augustinian convent. After all, his lovely daughter was attracting the attention of far too many young men.

The first week at the convent was most dreadful for a girl accustomed to the fineries of life. But she soon decided that the harsh conditions served some practical use. At least she was being provided with an education, which was certainly preferable to looking after siblings, she reasoned.

The following year, Teresa fell dreadfully ill. Deemed far too beautiful and charming a girl to be left to die of malaria, the nuns decided to send for her father . . .

Now she lay on this bed, hair damp with sweat from running a high fever, awaiting el padre's arrival. The door slowly creaked open, and the tall, dark-haired man entered the sunny room. Sister Juana and the other nuns moved aside respectfully as Don Alonso Sánchez de Cepeda—smelling of leather, sweat, and horses, his face expressing compassion and concern—removed his hat and sat on the edge of his daughter's bed.

"My dearest Teresa," her father spoke softly, as he wound one of her long dark curls around his forefinger. "The carriage is waiting. I have come to take you home."

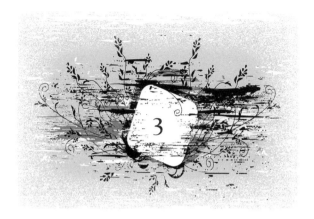

## Bus Ride

And every one that heareth these sayings of mine, and doeth them not, shall be likened unto a foolish man, which built his house upon the sand:

And the rain descended, and the floods came, and the winds blew, and beat upon that house; and it fell: and great was the fall of it. Matthew 7: 26-27

Early September 2008

THE long road wound through the hills, taking her farther and farther from the place she had grown to love. Tessa's legs were cramped and she didn't know how she could possibly last three more hours wedged into the tight space. The stale air reminded her of her last two years in high school and the long school bus rides through the beautiful countryside.

She'd only been gone from home a few hours but already missed her horse. She longed to get off the bus, go back to her beloved mare Sassy, and ride far away from the rolling, yellow-hued hills she'd been staring at out the window. *But that's not gonna happen*, thought Tessa resignedly. Sighing, she pushed one shoe off her foot and pulled her leg up to stretch. Her jeans still smelled like saddle leather and horse sweat from her last ride that morning. *Aaah, if only there was some way to bottle that scent*, she thought with mild amusement.

Nervously, she wound and unwound a long, dark and silky strand of hair around her finger. She'd pulled it from Sassy's shiny mane after she had brushed and hugged her mare good-bye earlier that morning. It could nearly have passed for one of her own.

"I'll be back in time for an early spring ride," Tessa had promised, giving Sassy the biggest carrot from Gran's garden. "We orphans have to stick together."

Sassy had gotten Tessa through some of the worst years of her life. Without barn chores and the sound of that low, happy nicker that greeted her each morning, Tessa would probably have stayed in bed and cried herself to death. The farm had been the perfect place for a grieving girl. She'd been told that as long as she kept her grades up, Sassy was hers to look after and ride whenever she wanted.

Tessa had also grown to love the old barn. At first, she had only seen it as a cobweb-filled building full of smelly manure, but over time she had grown to love its strength, its beauty, and yes, even its smell. Most of all, she had grown to cherish the times she spent there with Gramps, her foster *grandpa*. How many nights she'd had long talks in the barn with him about why bad things happen to good people.

"We don't serve a cruel God who laughs from heaven while hurling lightning bolts at us," he would say, "but bad things happen as a result of living in a fallen world."

*Sure. Easier said than believed.*

When Gramps went in to get ready for bed, Tessa would finish the long talks with Sassy. Gramps always thought he'd left her in the barn to pray, but, honestly, she found praying very difficult after God took her parents.

"I know you understand, Sassy," she'd whisper to the horse, gently stroking her just above the nose where her hair was as soft as velvet. While the mare munched on her evening snack of oats, Tessa would brush her and tell her how much she missed her mom and dad. And when Tessa's tears were spent, the silly mare would nudge her legs, rubbing her head against Tessa's jeans. Sassy loved to have her ears scratched. This little exchange of affection never failed to make Tessa laugh, if you could call it that. It was the kind of laugh a person manages with a lump in the throat and tears streaming down the face. "You were a foster kid once too, ya know. Foster filly, that is." But deep down she knew this dear horse could never understand the pain she had felt when a stranger knelt beside her to tell her that her mom and dad had just been killed in a terrible car accident. How could an animal know the suffering and sorrow Tessa felt—a pain still so raw, even after so many years?

"Hey girl, are you older and wiser than people give you credit for?" Tessa would say as she gently smoothed the gray hairs around Sassy's eyes and nose and patted her warm neck. Sassy was getting up there in horse years, but because Gramps always took good care of his animals, she was still fit and sound at twenty-nine. He had told Tessa the story of Sassy's mother.

"She died a few minutes after her filly was born," he'd always begin. "She was raised by people from day one and has a 'sassy people attitude,' as Gran calls it, and that's how she got her name." There'd been other horses at the farm throughout the years, but Sassy never learned to have real horse manners. "Sassy has never outgrown her teenage years so be sure to treat her like one. Be firm with her. Don't let her get away with sassin' you," he often reminded her.

"You're like me, with a bit of an attitude, but sweet deep down," Tessa told her every night before she turned out the barn lights. "We're the same, you and me."

With affection in her eyes, Gran had often said, "Neither one of you has figured out yet who God made you to be."

*You are wrong, Gran*, Tessa thought. *I know exactly what I am made to do.* As soon as she turned eighteen in October, she would be legally free from the foster care system to do as she pleased. She'd have to wait another year for her legal inheritance, but for now, she would keep her end of her deal with Gramps—to spend nearly eight months at the college. *It'll be more like a prison*, she thought ruefully.

Tessa had been reluctant to go to Flat Plains Bible College, but although she would never admit it to his face, she knew Gramps was right about the friends she had made at Foothills High. They weren't the best influence. She had been embarrassed to tell her friends she was going to a Bible college, especially when they teased her about it. "It's not a convent!" she snapped. "The Browns aren't Catholics. They're . . . they're . . ." She wasn't sure what her foster parents were, but she knew Gran and Gramps were Christians and lived exactly what they preached. She hadn't known anything about God before she met them, but in the last two years, she learned quite a bit about what the Bible said about God. She just couldn't say she knew Him like they did. But she wanted to and was secretly hoping Bible college might answer some of her questions.

That morning at the bus depot, Tessa's attitude had resembled a wind-swept day with bits of sun trying to poke through massive black clouds. She tried to act thankful to Gran and Gramps for all they had done, but it was only a facade. Pangs of guilt tugged at her heart as the old couple took turns hugging her good-bye. "We'll be praying for you every day," Gran had said, hugging Tessa and handing her a small lunch bag.

As she was about to board the bus, Gramps handed her "an emergency package" wrapped neatly in brown paper. "Remember, when you have nowhere else to turn, this is your 911 package. And don't forget our bargain." It seemed like such a silly thing at the time, a 911 package, but though she wouldn't dare admit it to them, it made Tessa feel strangely warm and safe inside.

The bus pulled out of the depot, and she caught the last glimpse of her foster grandparents waving good-bye. Now as she thought of them hours later, she reached down into her backpack and pulled out the bag from Gran. Inside were some cookies wrapped in wax paper that Gran must have baked late last night especially for her. double chocolate chip, her favorite. She took a bite and felt inside the shopping bag—there was something else. Tessa pulled out a homemade pillowcase with something soft inside.

*Gran, you are too much!*

Attached to a furry stuffed horse just big enough to hug was a note that said, "Take care of Sassy II. Love Gran." It was a bay—reddish brown with a black mane and tail—a perfect match to Sassy.

Tears welled in Tessa's eyes. She hadn't meant to be so hard on them. Deep down she loved the white-haired couple who had taken her in after the accident. Jacob and Margaret Brown were Gran and Gramps to everyone, seasoned by thirty years of taking in troubled teens. They had shown her incredible kindness and patience, even though she hadn't always shown kindness in return.

Tessa took another bite and put the cookie back. It reminded her too much of Gran's kitchen . . . sweet and homey. Funny, she had never really thought of the farm as home, until it was nearly a hundred miles behind her.

*Enough sentimentality for one day,* Tessa sternly rebuked herself. *I don't want to show up at Flat Plains Bible College with puffy, red eyes.*

"Well, if you're not going to eat those, can I have one?" a cheery voice rang out from behind her.

Startled, Tessa turned around. A petite, blonde-haired girl peeked out from behind an overstuffed carry-on bag. She pulled off her headphones and smiled at Tessa.

"My name's Elise. Where are you headed?" the girl asked, as they shook hands. Tessa noticed the girl's pretty French manicure and pulled back her hand to hide her bitten nails and calluses.

"Hi. I'm Tessa. I'm on my way to . . ." She was going to say prison but thought she'd better not. ". . . to Flat Plains. Ever heard of it? It's a small hick town in the prairies."

"No kidding! Hey, that's where I'm going! It's my second year there."

"Second year of . . ."

"Bible college."

"Are you serious? Well, it looks like we're headed to the same place then. That's where I'm going!" Tessa grinned as she reached for Gran's cookies.

"Hey, you'll love it! I can show you around when we get there. If we ever get there . . . I've been sitting on this bus for hours."

"So you're not from Foothills then?" Tessa questioned Elise as she handed her the bag of cookies.

"Thanks, I'm starving! Mmmm, these look awesome! Anything with chocolate—my fav! Um . . . no, I'm from Boulder Valley, on the other side of the mountains," she managed to say as she closed her eyes to savor her first taste of the melting chocolate. "Are these cookies ever good. A chocolate-lover's dream! Your mom really knows how to bake!"

"My mom?" Tessa almost laughed. "You mean . . ."

"The couple that hugged you good-bye at the bus depot. Your parents?"

"Uh . . . no. Those are my grandparents. Well, my foster grand-parents, anyway. Gran made the cookies. She's always baking."

"Oh sorry, dumb question. It's these tinted bus windows, you know. So, I don't mean to pry or anything," Elise said between bites, "but does that mean you don't have any parents or grandparents?"

Tessa hated that question. It was one she'd had to answer many times these last few years. She took a deep breath and slowly shook her head, a great sadness etched on her face. Elise was sorry she'd asked the question.

"My mom and dad died a few years ago. Drunk driver. Both Mom and Dad happened to be only children. All I know is my mom's parents were already old when she was born, one of those fluke things or something, you know, so they're not alive anymore. My other grandparents, well, they say my real grandma died when I was little, and I vaguely remember my dad's father. Apparently, he was an ironworker. He kind of got killed when I was little," Tessa added with a sad shrug.

"Kind of got killed?" Elise's eyes were wide. She seemed to have forgotten all about her third cookie.

"Bridge collapsed. He fell and then died of his injuries a year later. I know, it sounds like a soap opera, but that's the truth. And that's the short version of the long story. You know, tragically orphaned girl, gets shuffled around in foster system, finally ends up on farm with nice old couple, gets sent to Bible college. Tune in tomorrow as the saga continues . . ."

"Hey, that's a tough one. Sorry to hear that." Elise looked genu-inely sad.

"Makes for interesting conversation though." Tessa brushed the sympathy off. She'd rehearsed an explanation until she could say it without crying.

"You mean, you have no cousins, no uncles or aunts—no one?" Elise pressed.

"No one. Except for some remote twice-removed second step-cousin on my great-uncle's side that no one was ever able to locate."

Elise was quiet for a while as she thought about the family camp-outs and picnics she'd had at the lake with her cousins that past summer. She came from a noisy home with three boisterous brothers. She recalled that just that morning she had argued with her mom about her father's always letting her borrow the car, even when Elise didn't replace the gas she used. But unlike Tessa, her family had always been there through the good times and the bad, and she'd never known anything else. Suddenly, Elise felt very, very thankful.

"Nah, don't be sorry, I've had it pretty good, I guess. At least I have my own horse . . ."

"Yeah, I see that," said Elise quietly, glancing down in pity at the stuffed horse lying on Tessa's lap. "It's very . . . uh . . . cute," she added with a smirk.

"Oh," Tessa said, giggling, "no, not this. I mean, a real horse. I have a real horse where I live with Gran and Gramps."

"You have your very own horse? For real? What a dream!"

"Yeah, for real. Her name is Sassy, and she's a sassy thing all right."

"Sweet! Here, you'd better take these cookies back. I shouldn't have anymore . . . there've got to be a hundred calories in each, at least!" Elise handed back the bag, dusted off her shirt and took a tiny mirror out of her purse. She pulled the lid off a tube of pink lip gloss and delicately touched it over her lips as she talked. "I love this shade. It's called Orchard Apple, and it tastes like one too. Ever tried it?"

"Uh . . . nope," answered Tessa. The only thing she ever put on her lips was medicated menthol lip balm to keep her lips from cracking after a ride in the elements.

"So you can ride? I always wished I could ride. The only thing I ever rode was a bike."

"Yeah, I ride every day. Well, I did, that is."

All summer long, she had ridden Sassy bareback out to their favorite spot at the back of the property. There Tessa would kick off her riding boots, stretch out in the sun, and read a romance novel while the mare grazed in the nearby meadow. After a good roll in the tall fragrant grass, Sassy usually came and flopped down beside Tessa. Then Tessa would lean on the horse's warm, velvety back and read her book aloud. Nearly every day, the happy pair basked in the warm sunlight together this way, convincing Tessa further that Sassy thought she was human too.

Tessa sighed and leaned her head back. Absentmindedly she wound a thick strand of her long hair around her finger and brushed it across her cheek as she recalled how Sassy's long tail would swish at the flies, hitting Tessa in the face every now and then. It was only a dream now, soon to be a faded memory. That part of her life was probably over, for the time being, at least.

"Do you mind holding my mirror up for a second?" Elise interrupted her thoughts. As she layered more black mascara over her eyelashes, she noticed Tessa watching her closely. "I just switched to blue-black extra long lash. Not sure if it's my shade. Never could close my mouth while I put this stuff on. You too?"

"Never wear it, so I wouldn't know."

"Hmm. I'd go with chocolate brown if I were you, looks good with hazel eyes. But wait a minute . . ." Elise put her makeup away and tilted her head sideways as she examined Tessa's face. "Nah, I guess you're one of those."

"One of what?" Tessa never did like being stared at.

"One of those naturals. You have dark eyebrows and thick dark eyelashes already. Why would you need makeup? You were born pretty."

Tessa felt herself blush. She had never thought of herself as a natural beauty, although people often told her she was pretty. "The weird thing is, my mom was blonde. Guess I got my dark features from my dad. Everyone used to tell me my mom was beautiful."

"Well, look in the mirror, girl, so are you!" Elise encouraged her.

Soon the subject changed to school, boys, and clothes, and the two girls chatted the miles away, oblivious to the other passengers around them. Elise filled her in on everything she needed to know about everyone at Flat Plains. Tessa hoped she would fit in to this new environment. Finally, she grew weary of conversation and pulled out her cell phone to look at the time.

"Wow, look at that, we've been talking for two hours. We'll be there in another hour. Time sure flies when you've got someone to talk to."

"Yeah," said Elise, "well, if you don't mind, I've got some reading I'd like to finish before we hit the big books. And I'm kinda talked out."

"Me too," replied Tessa, reaching for her water bottle.

Elise put her headphones back on, reached into her bag, and pulled out a thick book with a pretty picture of a medieval gate on the front cover. It reminded Tessa of a storybook her mom used to read to her, a story about a princess locked in a castle until a brave prince came and rescued her. But Elise's book did not begin with the words "once upon a time." The title of her book was *Ancient Christianity*.

Elise noticed Tessa looking at the book and smiled up at her. "Just some reading to do with this year's courses . . . trying to get a head start." She winked and smiled.

Tessa stood up and looked around in the compartment above her for a magazine or something to read. *Why didn't I bring along a good book to get lost in?* Then again, she would soon be buried in books and studying for tests.

The long shadow of the bus reached across the road before them like a giant finger pointing the way. Tessa stretched and yawned. She wondered what awaited her when she stepped off the bus. Watching the sun disappear behind the hills fading in the distance, she gazed at the fields of golden grass, imagining she was Senorita Teresa, the beautiful bride-to-be of a nobleman. She saw herself in silhouette ride into the sunset, her flowing dress and Spanish lace veil trailing in the wind, a handsome conquistador following closely behind on his white stallion. Gramps always did say, "One of these days Tessa's imagination is going to carry her away into a daydream." Her favorite dream at the moment was to get through Bible college as quickly as possible and then travel to Spain. She would take her time backpacking through that beautiful country—and eventually end up in one of Spain's renowned stables working with the Andalusian horses, noble ancestors of the famed Lipizzaners of Austria. There she would work, as long as she wanted, with those beautiful, magnificent horses.

Closing her eyes, Tessa tried to imagine a beautiful castle with wild horses grazing all around it. Instead, all her mind could picture at that moment was Gramps back home settling down for the evening in his enormous red leather armchair beside the bulging bookcase. She flipped open her phone and sent him a quick text message to let him know she was almost there.

*If I know Gramps, I'll bet he put a Bible in that package. Sheesh. I'm headed for an eight-month sentence at Bible college. What on earth do I need a Bible for?*

Gran had tried to get Tessa to pack a Bible in her things before she left, but Tessa snapped at Gran, and it wasn't mentioned again. Now sitting on the bus, she felt a twinge of guilt for how she sometimes spoke to Gran and Gramps. But it was a touchy subject. Tessa had always found the Bible a very hard book to understand and didn't see how it was relevant for her life.

She propped up her furry, stuffed pony on her lap, leaned back into the corner of her seat, and drifted off to sleep.

# A Book from Uncle

TERESA woke up in a sweat again, but this time fully aware of her surroundings. It was a warm spring morning, and the birds were singing their happy songs outside the window at her sister Maria's house in the country. She had gotten sick again and they had to bring her here.

She stood on wobbly legs and walked across the cold, stone floor to open the shutters. Oh how her head was pounding! Out of breath from the exertion, she hobbled back to bed and carefully picked up the book she had been reading. Uncle Don Pedro had given her his copy of *The Third Spiritual Alphabet*.

Although she loved reading good books, a girl like Teresa with her effervescent personality, could never have imagined herself interested in learning about such things as "the prayer of quiet." However, her illness had transformed her into a more serious kind of girl. She had grown increasingly weary of those worldly things that had once given her such pleasure. She now harbored secret plans to return to a convent—for good this time. But since Father refused to give his consent to her becoming a nun, she began plans to run away to the monastery at Avila. She decided she would rather become a nun than marry and end by dying in childbirth as her dear mother had. Besides, her beloved brother Rodrigo had set sail for the West Indies, and life at her childhood home would never be the same again. Perhaps it was time to say farewell to girlhood fantasies and pursue a serious life of prayer, as her uncle Don Pedro had been urging her to do.

She closed her eyes and deeply inhaled the fresh morning air. Then she opened the book and began to read:

> Before we begin to explain this Alphabet, it is appropriate to clarify certain considerations that seem necessary for anyone who wishes to attain to God or undertake any spiritual exercise.

> The first is that friendship and communion with God are possible in this life of exile. This friendship is not remote but more sure and more intimate than ever existed between brothers or even between mother and child.

Teresa liked that. Lately, she had felt like an exile, often abandoned on her sickbed to deal with her excruciating headaches alone.

When she read the following, she knew in her heart this message was for her:

> Ordinary things are in the Church for ordinary people, but God has other things for special people, and even the ordinary contains something special.

As Teresa pondered these words, she recalled how she had always been told she was the special one. Perhaps it was time to discover what other things God had for her.

She decided to escape to the Carmelite Monastery as soon as she felt well enough. It would have to be under the cover of darkness, she reasoned pensively. In the meantime, she would devote herself to the mental prayers her uncle had taught her during his visits, and she would spend more time reading the fascinating book she held in her hands.

## First Day of College

September 2008

IT was Indian summer—the type of fall when the warm, lazy summer languishes for weeks, refusing to yield to the cooler days of autumn. As Tessa dodged what seemed like abnormally large and overly abundant grasshoppers that sprang from the grass between the dormitory and the college, her walk across the campus seemed like a mile long. *It certainly is flat here,* she thought. She really missed the mountains and thought about how much she would rather be in the back 350 acres of Gran and Gramps' property. Oh, how quickly she would have traded carrying a heavy bag of books to class for a chance to ride her horse and feel the wind in her hair.

As much as she loved reading, a stuffy classroom setting was not her idea of how best to enjoy books, but she had given Gramps her word that she would stay and put her nose to the grindstone, and so she decided to make the best of it. The harder she worked, the faster time would pass, Tessa reasoned. But she doubted there would be any books in this place she'd care to read, nor people she'd like to hang out with, for that matter. So far, she had made only one other friend, her roommate Katy. And it didn't take Tessa long to discover she was stuck with the campus homeschool *nerd*. At least that is how Tessa viewed her. And she'd never met a girl so excitable and transparent before. Katy was the kind of girl who didn't seem to care at all what others thought about her. And could she ever talk—and talk, and talk. It seemed she never stopped talking. She had heard through the college grapevine that Katy had above average intelligence. *She might be smart,* thought Tessa with exasperation, *but oh what I'd give for a few moments of silence!* Their first conversation, on the first night Tessa arrived, was still fresh in her mind . . .

Tessa's bus had finally arrived at the school, late the previous evening. After checking in with the registrar, Tessa and Elise waved good-bye, as they each went in search of their dorm rooms.

Having double-checked the number on the door with the number on the folder she'd been given at the registration desk, Tessa timidly knocked before stepping inside. Katy, who had arrived early that morning, was sitting on her bed by the window, reading the new school handbook. But before she was welcomed by Katy, Tessa was greeted by an oddly sweet fragrance. The room was filled with the aroma of bubble gum.

"You must be Teresa Dawson. Hello, I am Katarina Buckler, but you can call me Katy." The enthusiastic girl jumped up and vigorously shook Tessa's outstretched hand. Her short, shiny hair and sparkly eyes were the color of rich dark chocolate. She was considerably shorter than Tessa, and not as slender. Tessa detected a faint accent. Russian? French? Tessa wasn't too good with accents. *But she's a fireball of energy,* thought Tessa. *That much I know for sure.*

"My birth certificate says Katarina, which comes from the name Katherine. It means 'pure' in Greek. It was changed in the early centuries from Katarina to Katharina, but now it is the twenty-first century, so I am just Katy. Pleased to meet you." Tessa was amazed—Katy had completed her sentence without pausing once to breathe. Smiling broadly, Katy shook Tessa's hand again and then asked politely, "And who are you? Are you Teresa Dawson?"

"Oh yes," Tessa answered, managing a slight smile. "My friends just call me Tessa. Very nice to meet you. Looks like you've had time to decorate." Tessa's hazel eyes scanned the wall above Katy's bed, examining a large family photo of a row of neatly dressed, smiling children all wearing dressed-for-Sunday outfits.

"Then I shall call you Tessa, yes? We shall be best of friends. Sorry, I tend to talk more than I probably should. A typical Katherine, my mom always says. The first Katherines were very bold. In fact, there is a legend of how my name got popular. A fourth-century martyr from Alexandria was tortured on a spiked wheel and ever since then, there you go, it has been a household name, especially since the Middle Ages. In fact, three of Henry the Eighth's wives were Katherines, and a few empresses of Russia too . . . all bold and—"

"Are you Russian?" Tessa interrupted. Whatever this girl was, Tessa was beginning to wonder whether she could handle sharing a room with such a super-chatty girl for even one semester. Tessa's head was spinning already.

"How did you know? My real mother, she was Russian, and very beautiful I am told . . . and I am talking too much. This is my family now. See?" Tessa's eyes fell on the photo with all the children again. There were so many!

Tessa appraised the girl in front of her. *What a unique individual,* thought Tessa, with some amusement. Between expansive hand gestures, vigorous gum chewing and bubble blowing, Katy was able to continue her non-stop one-way *conversation.*

Curious, Tessa turned her face back to Katy's photograph. She noticed that the children in the picture were all dressed in matching jumpers and color-coordinated shirts, but Katy stood out. The other children were all blue-eyed, blonde-haired, and fair-skinned, but Katy had dark hair and deep brown eyes.

I suppose you are wondering why I am so much . . . taller, yes?"

"Uh . . . yeah. I see that." Tessa humored her. It was almost midnight, and she was really too tired to listen to this girl's life story, but something told her she was about to hear it anyway.

"My parents didn't have any children. So they adopted me twelve years ago when I was eight, and then, *boom, boom, boom.* There you go. They say this sometimes happens, yes? Therefore, these are my little brothers and sisters. And there was a big surprise that happened—number eight is coming in the spring. What do you know? God has blessed my parents with many little olive plants."

"Olive plants?" Tessa asked, bewildered.

"Oh you know, Psalm 128, yes? About the man who fears the Lord and his wife being a fruitful vine and the children like olive plants?"

"Ah, interesting. Well, congratulations." Tessa felt awkward and didn't know what else to say. She thought it better not to mention that they actually had something in common, as in a lack of birth parents. *Don't want to give this girl another tangent to go on about,* thought Tessa. Some things were best kept quiet.

"So this is my half of the room?" She pointed to the bare bed in the corner away from the window. All Tessa could think about was her regret for not spending the extra money to get a room of her own.

"It's extremely dark on that side, yes? I am very selfish to have taken the best spot. If you like, we can trade. However, I do have extra lamps in the closet. Did you know it would be such a small room? Last year I was in a much bigger room on the second floor. By the way, did you know that technically we aren't supposed to be rooming together? You know, freshmen room with freshmen, sophomores with sophomores and all that. They told me in administration this morning it was a clerical error—computer glitch more likely. I told them it must be divine intervention and that God works all things together for good for those who . . . oh, do you want to use my spare lamp? It has a remote control. It's very fancy. I also brought an oil lamp, just in case."

"I'll be OK." What Tessa really wanted was a remote control to quiet the girl down. *Why on earth would anyone bring an oil lamp?* She finally tossed her backpack and Sassy II onto the mattress and began unloading her large suitcase.

While Tessa unpacked and arranged her personal things just the way she liked, Katy proceeded to give Tessa the rundown on all the dorm rules, followed by a detailed description of the courses she was taking. *Well, at least I won't have to read the handbook now,* thought Tessa charitably. *My roommate is a walking, talking encyclopedia of college protocol.*

Tessa tried to put that first meeting with Katy behind her. She even got up extra early so she could quietly slip away to breakfast before Katy woke up and started talking again.

Expecting to be alone in the huge cafeteria, Tessa was surprised to see quite a few other students already enjoying breakfast. *Hmm, early risers, just like me.* She smiled slightly. *I wonder if they have Katy-clones for roommates.*

Standing in line with her breakfast tray, Tessa glanced at the daily menu posted beside the service window. Soup and sandwiches for lunch, and vegetable lasagna for supper. *Good thing breakfast is my favorite meal of the day,* she thought, as she piled her plate with pancakes, a boiled egg, and a lot of fruit.

Wanting to observe her new surroundings without interruption, Tessa opted to eat breakfast alone that first morning. She hadn't even known how hungry she was, until she realized she had eaten her breakfast with lightning speed. Then, slowly sipping her cup of hot chocolate, she soon became lost in thought. She sat there nearly an hour before she was suddenly jolted back to reality as a friendly young guy smiled at her and asked if the seat beside her was taken. Tessa looked around the cafeteria in astonishment. It was now teeming with noisy, excited students. "No, s-s-sit down, p-p-please," she stammered shyly. Then glancing at her watch she added, "I'd better get going. I still haven't figured out where my classrooms are. See ya around."

As Tessa left the cafeteria, she noticed Katy waiting in the breakfast line, chatting animatedly with the guys behind her. She seemed to know everyone.

Now, walking through the college campus and sidestepping the leaping grasshoppers, Tessa noticed with interest that the soccer net and goal posts were being taken down on the far side of the field. In the middle of the field, workmen were digging up yellowing sod, while others carried flat stones from the back of an old pickup truck. *That's strange,* she thought. *Why are they building a stone walkway in the middle of a soccer field?*

Tessa checked her school map and glanced up at the nearest building. This was the Thompson Building, where her first class for one of her required courses was scheduled. She figured Gramps probably would approve of this one—*Classics of Christian Spirituality*, prerequisite to *Spiritual Formation 101*. Sounded like a lot of reading, but she was OK with that. If the class was boring, she would do what she'd done in high school. She would simply grit her teeth, buckle down, and end up breezing her way through it with good marks.

"For Gramps," she said under her breath as she walked into the two-story building. Just under eight months of this and then she would be free! Free as a bird to pursue her dream of backpacking her way through Spain.

Jostled in the busy hallway by a crowd of excited students, Tessa followed the map she'd been given and now stood in the doorway of her classroom. Reluctant to go inside, she stood there for a moment. The realization that she was really, truly committed to this place for a full two semesters struck her with nauseating force. "Just do it," she finally chided herself aloud. No sooner had she stepped inside, than she was greeted with an unfamiliar odor. *Ugh.* The white board at the front of the lecture hall said "Welcome to Fall Spiritual Formation."

*I'd rather be back home mucking out Sassy's stall,* she thought. The barn definitely smelled better than the chemical in those white board felt markers. If she were home, she'd probably be out for a morning ride right now.

She thought she could see the back of Elise's head in the front row, but Tessa wasn't in the mood for talking about lipstick shades. She sighed and found a chair as far to the back of the class as she could. She slid into the seat, hoping to continue the lovely daydream she had started at breakfast: a dream of fresh air, rolling hills, and dear Sassy. Could she make it in this stuffy place?

She supposed she could go along with the rules halfheartedly, the same way she had gone along at the small-town church. It took Gran and Gramps half an hour every Sunday morning to drive to that little church—a precious half an hour—which as far as Tessa was concerned was a waste of perfectly good riding time with Sassy.

The professor's voice brought her wandering mind back to the present.

"... and if you turn to page seven of the syllabus I've handed out, you will see the list of required reading material for this introductory class. You'll be able to get all of these books in the school bookstore. As this is the first spiritual formation class at Flat Plains, you won't find any used books, however. But I guarantee that by the end of the term you will come to believe, as I do, that these books are worth their weight in gold. Either way, keep your books in good shape and you can sell them back to the store at the end of the term—and just so you know, they don't take torn books or ones that have gum stuck between the pages."

*If anyone would stick gum in a book, it would probably be my roommate.* Tessa looked around. It seemed every seat was taken, and to her relief she couldn't spot Katy in the crowd of students.

The students in the class seemed friendly, which put Tessa at ease, and her shyness soon dissipated. As selected students passed out a course requirement sheet, a quiet but cheery chatter permeated the classroom. The girl sitting in front of Tessa, with strawberry blonde curls hanging past her shoulders, turned around and introduced herself as Sonya.

After exchanging introductions with Sonya, Tessa began to browse over the various book titles from the syllabus textbook list. One in particular caught her interest—*Selections from the Interior Castle* by Teresa of Avila. *Hey, great name,* she thought. *I think Avila is in Spain.*

Tessa sketched a horse in her notebook while the spiritual formation professor outlined a detailed road map of the semester that lay ahead. Something about desert fathers and some dead guys called Ignatius and St. John of the Cross. Then she droned on for another fifteen minutes about the relevance of spiritual exercise to contemporary Christianity and attention to self, the world, and our potential for goodness. *Whatever that means.* Tessa took notes, but wrote "blah, blah, blah" in the margin and drew another horse, this one trotting up to a wooden drawbridge that crossed the moat of a moss-covered castle. Noticing the red tassel of a pretty bookmark that Gran had slipped into her new notebook, Tessa skimmed the message on it before placing it back inside.

But now in Christ Jesus ye who sometimes were far off
are made nigh by the blood of Christ. Ephesians 2:13

It was one of those homemade things Gran and her ladies
Bible study group made on Tuesday nights. It was so like Gran
always to be shoving Bible verses at her. Then again, Bible verses
always seemed to show up in the oddest places at the Brown home-
stead. There were even Bible verses carved into the barn walls and
doorposts.

The professor's voice continued as the bell sounded and the
students began to pack their things: "The final paper is due in three
months, and don't forget, attendance and participation are worth 25
percent of your mark. But the most important thing I want you to
take away from this class is that you will learn how to hear the voice
of God. Practicing these disciplines is important for your spiritual
maturity. See you on Thursday."

Tessa liked playing sports, especially basketball, but she had a
feeling this wasn't the kind of exercise the prof meant. Inner life?
She would keep her inner life to herself, thank you very much. As
far as hearing the voice of God, that was not likely. She'd tried that
once. But He didn't say a thing. Even if God wanted to talk to her,
would she really be willing to allow God to take away her freedom
to make her own choices?

As Tessa got up to find the next class on her schedule, Elise ran
over and gave Sonya a big hug. *So it was her in the front row.* The
two girls shrieked and squealed, obviously long-lost friends. They
compared their new clothes and did some peculiar cheerleader hip-
check routine that made Tessa roll her eyes. What had she gotten
herself into?

"Sonya, have you met Tessa?" Elise asked, beaming.

"Yeah, thanks. I just did."

"Hey, you'd better be coming to the newcomers' night tonight
after the meal. There'll be snacks and games, and we'll even teach
you the Flat Plains secret handshake!"

"Secret handshake?"

"Yeah, what we just did! We'll let you in on it!"

"Wow. You guys are just . . . too much. Really."

Tessa thanked them but had already decided that after tonight's meal she would skip the optional social evening and curl up in bed with her new books. After all, she wanted to take advantage of a quiet dorm room whenever she could. Katy would surely be at the social night. All Tessa really wanted was a good night's sleep, which would mean a few more hours of peace and quiet before Katy descended upon her with her latest insights on school, family, life, and God.

6

## TERESA MEETS TERESA

For we are unto God a sweet savour of Christ, in them
that are saved, and in them that perish: To the one we
are the savour of death unto death; and to the other the
savour of life unto life. II Corinthians 2:15-16

AVILA, SPAIN CIRCA 1536

"WAKE up! I beg of you! Juana! Sister Juana Suarez! Wake up!"

It was nearly dawn. The pounding on the heavy wood door of the Carmelite Monastery of the Incarnation at Avila grew more urgent. Sister Juana scurried along the dark hallway with a large candle on her candlestick, the hem of her habit dragging behind her on the cold stone floor. She slid the iron bolt to the side and opened the door a crack.

"Who is calling at this hour?" she whispered.

"It is I. Teresa, daughter of Don Sanchez de Cepeda."

The hinges creaked noisily as the nun swung the door open and a young woman stumbled in, falling to her knees. The nun squinted in the dim light as the girl looked up, her large brown eyes and perfect features reflecting the flickering glow of the candle.

"Teresa? Is it really you? Wait till your father hears of this! He will come to fetch you at once!"

"No Juana," she said, gasping for breath. "I've been reading the letters of St. Jerome and have made my decision. I want to be Teresa of Jesus, and I am here to stay."

OCTOBER 2008

IN the girl's dormitory at Flat Plains Bible College, Tessa had slipped into the homemade, soft flannel pajamas Gran had sent for her birthday. She sat on the floor and leaned against her bed, hugging Sassy II. Her eyes had been glued to a large, hardcover book about women in church history.

"Would you like some gum?" her roommate asked. "It's a brand new flavor, Marvelous Mint Bubble."

"No thanks," answered Tessa, looking up at Katy and wondering if her jaw hinges would wear out before she turned twenty-five.

"So which courses are you taking again, Tessa?"

Tessa pulled a tattered course schedule out of her binder and handed it to Katy. She was actually beginning to like some of the courses she had chosen. The Adventure Discipleship class had been a good pick. It was part of the new spiritual formation program and included an outdoor retreat. And, it was full of guys. Not that *that* mattered, exactly. Tessa smiled. But it sure didn't hurt either.

"Let's see, you've got Earth Care, Outdoor Education, Environmental Ethics, Christianity and Imagination, Women of Christian History, Worship Arts... wow, these are all new. Don't know a thing about them. And they're all part of the spiritual formation program? I am taking classes in theology, evangelism, and international missions. Oh yes, and Greek, and just one little apologetics course. It is too bad we're not in any classes together."

"Yes, it's a shame." Tessa breathed a secret sigh of relief, taking the page back. At least two of her new friends, Sonya and Elise, were in most of her classes. They weren't exactly her type, always concerned about their hair and makeup, but at least they didn't talk a mile a minute, and their friendly attitudes and warm smiles drew Tessa in.

"So who is your favorite professor?" continued Katy, blowing green bubbles.

"Not sure yet." Tessa wanted to read, so she tried giving short answers, without looking up.

"Oh come on. You must have a favorite after four weeks at Flat Plains. Mine is our missions prof, Sam Goldsmith. He's only twenty-six years old, has already been to Africa and South America, and has all kinds of fascinating stories. He has greatly influenced me. In fact, we are going on a missions trip next spring break to South America. Just like the Bible says . . . go into all the world and preach the Gospel. Yes? So tell me, Tessa, who's your favorite professor?"

Tessa put her book in her lap, gave a heavy sigh, and finally looked up for a minute. Maybe if she changed the subject she could actually get some reading done.

"So, Katy, you certainly have a large family. It must be a noisy home. You are probably glad to be at school and get some peace and quiet."

Katy turned her head and looked up at the portrait on her wall.

"Oh yes, the Buckler household is a busy one, that is for sure, yes? Rachel, Rebekah, and Ruth are not as loud as my brothers Joshua, Jeremiah, and Joel. My father, he is the quiet one. He's an engineer and a very intelligent man. And my mom is, or was, a teacher. Actually, she still is. She homeschools all of her children. I finished first, of course. She also writes articles for magazines."

"I see. You must miss them terribly."

Mischievously, Tessa thought if she could just get Katy homesick, Katy might get depressed, curl up in a nice, quiet fetal position, and go to sleep.

"Oh yes, but we e-mail each other every day," she said cheerily.

"Oh." Tessa's shoulders slumped as she realized her plan wasn't working.

"So you still haven't told me who is your favorite professor, Tessa?"

"You know, I've got studying to do here, but if you really need to know, it's probably the one I just met today."

"Today? We have a new professor at Flat Plains? I've been here two years and thought I knew them all. Who is it? I'll bet he's a replacement for one of our counselors, Mr. Daniels, who never came back this fall. That was his last name, but everyone just called him

Daniels. No one said why he left, but it was too bad. He was a very strong Christian man and had so much understanding of the Bible. So who's the new guy?"

"Well, the new *guy's* name is Ms. Jasmine. Our class was just introduced to her today. Jasmine is actually her first name, but that is what she told us to call her, or Ms. Jazz for short."

"Hmm. Haven't seen her yet. Jasmine? That's a creeper vine."

"Huh? What did you say?" Tessa raised an eyebrow. *This girl is so . . . peculiar.*

"We have had a jasmine creeper vine growing up our front porch at home, ever since I was a little girl. You have to watch those."

"A jasmine plant?"

"A vine actually. If I'm not mistaken, I think ours is a winter jasmine. Do you know that the name jasmine comes from Persia?"

"No. I didn't." *Here we go again*, thought Tessa. *This girl and her names. Now it's vines. First, her mom was a fruitful vine, and now Katy thinks she's a vine expert.*

"It's a climbing plant with white fragrant flowers that are used for perfume and tea. Mind you, our winter jasmine has yellow flowers that have absolutely no fragrance, but it stays green all winter. That is what my mom likes about it. She prunes it every spring, after it has bloomed. Actually, we all do. She gives the children pruning shears and shovels and they cut off the shoots and stems . . . they grow wherever they touch the ground . . . a very invasive plant that grows where it's not welcome. Even over fences. In fact, now both our neighbors have several too." Katy doubled over laughing.

"I see." Tessa stifled a giggle. *So bizarre she's actually entertaining.* "So . . . your mom not only homeschools all seven of her children, she is a botanist too?" Tessa joked.

"How did you know? She used to teach at a university but says that students today have all turned into globalist think tanks. But her Ph. D. still comes in handy now and then, yes? Like the time my little brother got a very rare fungal infection from going barefoot when we were traveling and the only cure was a rare plant that grows in the jungle . . ."

"Don't tell me, your mom hacked her way into the jungle with a machete to find the secret cure."

"How did you know? She made a paste and . . ."

Tessa let Katy talk, and she found herself secretly fascinated in hearing about Katy's large, homeschooled adopted family. Even so, she was still feeling annoyed at this girl's constant talking. She soon realized the only way to stop her roommate from talking the whole evening was simply to go to sleep . . . or pretend to anyway.

"Are you going to turn the light off?" Tessa asked, feigning a yawn, while climbing into bed and pulling the covers up around her. Katy closed her theology book and stacked it on the mountain of Bible commentaries and concordances piling up on her nightstand. She flipped off the main light, grabbed her Bible, and hopped into bed.

"Sure. Hope you don't mind if I read for a few more minutes with my book light."

"OK, me too."

They both turned on the small reading lights all the students had been given in their welcome packs. Finally, the room was quiet . . . for three minutes anyway.

"So what are you reading?" It was Katy again.

Tessa was on the verge of losing her patience.

"I'm reading about a girl whose brothers and sisters talked too much, so she ran off during the night to join a convent."

"Really? Read it to me," Katy said quietly, turning her light off. Then she took her warm, chewed gum from her mouth, stuck it on her clock radio, nestled into her pillow, and drew the covers up around her face.

*Brilliant. Maybe if I do the talking, Katy will fall asleep. Quietness at last.*

"Well, it's for my spiritual formation class. Listen to this," began Tessa, proud to see she might actually know something Katy didn't. "There was this sickly girl about my age named Teresa who ran away from her *normal* teenage life to become a nun instead. First, it was just for boarding school, but it turned out she decided to stay. The interesting part was that many of the nuns staying at this convent had private rooms, servants, and wore jewelry and perfume. They even had lap dogs! Mind you, the poorer nuns slept in a dormitory. But they could all receive gentlemen callers and were allowed go outside the convent into the village whenever they wanted."

"Ha. Sounds just like us," joked Katy, remembering how Tessa referred to the girls' dorm as "the convent." They too were allowed to socialize with "gentlemen" as long as it was in a public place. The college students even had their favorite coffee shop in the little town of Flat Plains, which they'd coined "the village." "Anyway, who cares?" She pulled the quilt up over her ears. "Continue," Katy said.

"Well, it seems that any woman who wanted a sheltered life with no responsibilities could escape a life of child-bearing and find a comfortable refuge in a convent in sixteenth-century Spain. St. Teresa changed all that later in her life. But as a young woman, she was sick all the time, and in fact, once they thought she was dead so they poured wax over her eyes and even dug her grave. But she didn't die. She went on to start new convents, where she taught about experiencing the presence of God that she'd learned during her illness."

"Uh-oh," mumbled Katy.

"What? Anyway, while Teresa started out in life somewhat rebellious, she ended up hearing from God. I admire that. Our spiritual formation prof says that contemplative prayer goes back to even before the time of St. Teresa. Apparently, the roots of this prayer go back to Egypt, and the desert fathers and mothers in the fourth cent—"

"What is contemplative prayer?" Katy interrupted. "Do you mean finding a quiet place and thinking about God and talking to Him? Because I think people have always done that, clear back to Bible times."

"Well, not quite. Contemplative prayer is not really about *talking* to God. It's more about *listening* to God. It's a more mature spiritual approach to God and prepares you to hear His voice. It means a deeper way to know God by getting rid of all the mind's distractions and going into a silent place inside yourself, like putting the mind in a kind of stilled state. I don't know a lot about it yet, but I'm learning and—"

Katy sat up and said, "Tessa Dawson! There's nothing wrong with being quiet before the Lord, but what you appear to be talking about is another kind of silence. That's not what biblical prayer is at all! You are speaking of mysticism, yes? And those people you are learning about, they were all Catholic mystics. There's quite a big difference between outer silence and inner silence. Outer silence, like being in a peaceful environment, is fine—that allows you to think more clearly—but inner silence is the absence of thought altogether, and nowhere in the Bible does it tell us to do that. Remember, the Bible warns against vain repetition, which produces the kind of silence those mystics were talking about."

"Well, I know it seems a little . . . you know, Catholic, but—"

"But mysticism goes back *much* further than the third or fourth centuries. We learned about it last year."

"And so? What are you trying to say?"

"What I'm saying is this, this . . . stuff . . . goes back to the tower of Babel!" said Katy with alarm.

"Katy, what are you talking about?" asked Tessa impatiently. She really wanted to ask, "Katy, what are babbling about now?"

"What are they teaching you in that new class anyway?" Katy asked.

Katy shone her reading light on Tessa's nightstand and squinted at the stack of books from her spiritual formation class. "I remember Mr. Daniels talking to us about some of the Catholic mystics from centuries ago. He said the desert fathers had learned mystical practices from those in Eastern religions. He even mentioned some Spanish mystics a few times."

"You know, Tessa, you need to stop reading all these books by Saint What's Her Name and start reading the Bible. I don't want to sound preachy, but I never see you read it."

Tessa glared at her roommate and closed her library book. She almost called Katy "a homeschool nerd," but instead she bit her tongue, turned off the light, and rolled over.

"Her name was Teresa, just like mine," she muttered. "And God talked to her."

"Tessa, God talks to all of us." Katy always had to get the last word. "It's called reading the Bible."

Tessa didn't answer Katy. Usually, she didn't have a problem tolerating Katy and her constant opinions and theories. She'd grown used to Katy's unique personality. In a strange way, she found her presence almost comforting at times. Katy reminded her of Gramps, in having a confidence that seemed completely unwavering, as if there was enough of her surety for both of them. But tonight Tessa felt as though she had more in common with little St. Teresa than she did with anyone in this place.

Closing her eyes, Tessa imagined it was 1534, and the moon shone on her white Andalusian mare as she galloped through the rolling hills toward a beautiful Spanish castle that had beautiful rooms filled with beautiful things. She imagined she was far, far away from everyone who wanted to tell her how to think. She imagined she was like Teresa of Avila who had run away to read, learn, and write books about castles, mansions, and mysterious rooms.

Tessa inhaled deeply, as she had done in class that morning.

The school's spiritual formation professor had been responsible for bringing Ms. Jasmine to Flat Plains Bible College as their new spiritual director. Tessa was immediately drawn to her. Ms. Jasmine was so down to earth. She told them she didn't care about the title in front of her name. Didn't even care if they called her by her first name—in fact insisted on it. She had told the class that if anyone really wanted to know her last name, he or she would have to come and read the nameplate on her office door. What a professor! Tessa still didn't know what her last name was, but it didn't matter. She admired her from the very beginning.

Tessa's mind turned to Ms. Jasmine's promise to soon introduce them to the inner life. Although Tessa felt guarded about anything that came close to her inner life, she was drawn to Ms. Jasmine, including her striking features and platinum hair pinned up the same glamorous way her mom used to do hers.

Ms. Jasmine had placed colorful tapestry cushions in a circle at the front of the lecture hall, and fifteen minutes into her talk the students were encouraged to take one and seek out a quiet place of solitude anywhere on the campus. Once they had found a cozy spot, they were to use the outline they'd been given to practice a listening exercise called *lectio divina*, a "divine reading" that would make them feel closer to Jesus.

"Come back in half an hour," Ms Jasmine had told them, smiling as they filed by to pick up their cushions. She was wearing a classic cream-colored two-piece suit perfectly matched by her pearl necklace and earrings. As she passed close by, Tessa noticed she looked amazingly youthful and attractive for being a middle-aged woman. And Ms. Jasmine had the most beautiful, caramel-colored eyes she'd ever seen.

The listening exercise they were to do seemed simple enough. After choosing a Scripture passage, they were instructed to read it slowly a number of times and wait for a word to "come alive" to them. Then they were to take that single word, close their eyes and repeat it for several minutes. Ms. Jasmine's had read the outline ahead of time to the class. Her voice had a soothing, relaxing effect:

> Sit with your back straight in a comfortable position.
> Notice first the faraway sounds that you can hear.
> Next, allow yourself to become aware of sounds that
> are nearer.
> Then listen closely to your own heartbeat; this is your
> very own rhythm of life.
> As you shut out these sounds, you will hear the sound of
> silence within yourself.
> Listen like this for several minutes . . .
> Write down what you hear God saying to you.
> Remember, he is all around you and in you.

Tessa had found her own quiet spot on a bench in the courtyard, where yellow and red leaves drifted gently to the ground from the tree above. It had seemed weird at first, and Tessa wasn't altogether sure about it. But she read Psalm 15, and soon the word "truth" stood out to her. She straightened her back, closed her eyes, and repeated the word for at least five minutes. It was awkward this first time, because she kept looking down at Ms. Jasmine's instructions, wanting to get it just right. At one point, she thought she had actually heard a voice speak to her. Ms. Jasmine had told them to imagine themselves having a conversation with Christ. "Don't be afraid to listen," were the words she thought she heard, although it was probably just the wind in the trees.

*Why not try it again,* Tessa thought now, as she lay wide awake in the dark. She put her head under her favorite flannel-covered pillow to shut out Katy's snoring, turned on her LED book light under the blanket, and reread a page in what was now her favorite book, *Selections from the Interior Castle,* by Teresa of Avila of Spain. Even the picture on the cover had come alive in her imagination. It was a painting of an ancient castle with a high tower on a green hilltop. Leading up to the castle's stone archways were winding dirt roads that crossed over stone bridges. Tessa's imagination took her back to the storybook her mom often read to her when she was a little girl. Hesitantly, but with anticipation, she opened her new book to the page she had dog-eared earlier and began to read:

> One kind of rapture is that in which the soul, even though not in prayer, is touched by some word it remembers or hears about God. It seems that His Majesty from the interior of the soul makes the spark we mentioned increase, for He is moved with compassion in seeing the soul suffer so long a time from its desire.

*So beautifully written,* thought Tessa. She read it over several times. Now that was beautiful literature, the kind she would like to read in the solitude of a beautiful meadow in a deep, sheltered valley. It was perfect. The word that jumped out at her was "spark." St. Teresa and Ms. Jasmine both talked about the spark within. Ever since her parents died in the crash, Tessa felt as if her own spark had been extinguished. Perhaps she would soon be able to feel the spark come to life again if she could practice being silent like this more often. When she closed her eyes, she could almost see a tiny light growing brighter in the darkness, like a light at the end of a long tunnel. Then again, maybe it was just the lingering glare from her book light. For a moment, she tried to focus on the light. Finally, Tessa quietly turned off the light, laid Gran's bookmark between the pages where she had finished reading, and put the book on her nightstand. At least she had figured out how to make Katy stop talking.

Tomorrow Ms. Jasmine was going to take their SF class outside into the fresh air. They were going to practice another prayer exercise called centering and take the first prayer walk through the brand-new campus labyrinth. Tessa felt as if she was about to step into a new realm, but she wasn't quite sure what it was. Maybe Flat Plains Bible College was not such a stuffy place to be after all. She would text Gramps in the morning. He'd be happy to know she was actually beginning to like this place.

## The Fall Retreat at Quiet Waters Lodge

Casting down imaginations and every high thing
that exalteth itself against the knowledge of God, and
bringing into captivity every thought to the obedience
of Christ. II Corinthians 10:5

November 2008

LOOKING out from her vantage point in the loft, Tessa could
see smoke rising from log cabins between the trees. Winter had set in
early this year for this northern region, and the lake already had a layer
of ice. It looked like a giant cookie sprinkled with icing sugar and the
cabins like gingerbread houses around its edge. The only thing missing
were mountains. Tessa thought she could make out the inlet past Rocky
Point where the largest of several streams fed the lake. Somewhere
behind the trees was the bridge she and the retreat group had crossed
during their nature/prayer walk yesterday—the same bridge on which
she had bumped into the strange and mysterious woodsman.

He came from out of nowhere, or so it seemed. Tessa had been
waiting until the others had gone on ahead and then stopped along
the path, sat and leaned against the old wooden bridge railing to
warm herself in a patch of sunshine. Even though temperatures
outside were low, the students had been encouraged to participate
in this outdoor nature/prayer walk.

"Get alone in nature, and there you will find God in all things," Ms. Jasmine had said. "And you will find your true selves, where the divine spark dwells within each person. Through contemplation, this spark can be ignited."

As Tessa gazed at the trickling water that flowed into the mouth of the lake under the thin layer of ice now formed, she compared the stream to the many spiritual traditions she had been learning about in her spiritual formation class. Just this past week, she had written an essay for extra credit called "Different Streams," about how people from every religious tradition are merging as one, like the lake fed by different streams.

Tessa pulled off one of the gloves Gran had sent her and began to write in her journal: "I now understand how we can learn from all these varying traditions and take what's good from each one. We are all one in His creation. He is the spark, the common ground beneath us all."

Just as she was thinking how pleased Ms. Jasmine would be with her new revelation, there he was. He was wearing a Carhartt vest over a brown plaid shirt and a cap that couldn't restrain his juts of curly black hair from sticking out. He sat on a large rock just past the bridge, reading a book with a black cover.

Tessa was startled at the thought that he had probably been watching her. She closed her journal and put her glove back on. She stood up quickly, threw her backpack over her shoulder, and was set to leave when he spoke.

"It wasn't always like that here," he said.

Tessa didn't want to look at him, much less talk to him, but she had to walk past the rock if she was to stay on the trail. Besides, something about his remark had made her strangely curious.

"What wasn't like what?" she asked. A few steps closer now, she could see white long johns through the holes in his faded jeans. The laces in his well-worn hiking boots were mismatched. One was yellow nylon, one was brown leather. It was difficult for her to get a good look at his face though, no thanks to the cap, the hair, and a beard that had probably been growing for at least a month, But in spite of his grubby woodsman appearance, his clear blue-gray eyes and kind smile gave her a feeling he was trustworthy.

"The lodge. It used to be a Bible camp. You're with them, I can tell. They always have journals now." He nodded at the spiral-bound notebook she held under her arm.

"They?" Tessa wrapped Gran's hand-knit red scarf around her face. She could see her breath in the cold air and hoped he hadn't noticed that she had begun to breathe faster with nervousness.

"The silent retreaters. They spend hours out here sitting on logs and staring at the water and writing. They all have the look."

"The look?" she questioned.

"The faraway look. Like when you're looking at a 3-D picture and you have to gaze past it to see what's in it, or at a tempting piece of fruit hanging in a forbidden tree."

"Oh." She didn't like his attitude. *Just who does this guy think he is?* she thought. "Well, I see you are gazing at a book too."

"Yeah, but the important difference is, this book has already been written," said the woodsman.

"So, what book are you reading then?"

"I was reading something David wrote, Psalm 51, when the prophet came to him after he had strayed. Listen:

> Behold, thou desirest truth in the inward parts: and in the hidden part thou shalt make me to know wisdom.
> Purge me with hyssop, and I shall be clean: wash me, and I shall be whiter than snow.

"So . . . you are out here in the woods . . . reading a Bible," Tessa asked, but it was more a statement than a question, and there was a hint of sarcasm in her tone. She didn't think he was much older than she was, but it was tough to tell because of his beard. Tessa thought the woodsman looked the way a wild prophet from Bible times might have looked. *I wonder if he eats wild locusts and venison stew*, Tessa mused. She was beginning to feel uncomfortable and decided it was time to catch up with the others.

"There is only one way," he said as she walked by, pretending to ignore him. "They are listening to the serpent just like Eve did. It's the same old lie."

A voice inside her head told her to run. And she did. Tessa tried to ignore his voice as she began to run, faster and faster, her boots scattering the crunchy leaves on the trail until she caught up with Sonya and Elise.

She decided not to tell them about the woodsman. Together, they arrived back at camp, just in time for supper. Later that evening, the group drove to the monastery at the end of the lake for the candlelight Taizé service, a special worship gathering modeled after those of a popular monastic group in France. It had been a late night, and the group was instructed to be silent until sometime the following day.

Now, sitting on the loft alone, watching the smoke rise from the cabins on the lake, here in the silence of this room, the woodsman's words echoed in her head. She tried to block him out of her mind.

Thankfully, she was distracted by a few snowflakes that blew past the window, adding to last night's light snowfall that had dusted the ground. Tessa sat on the cushioned window seat watching some chickadees hop around beneath the bird feeder on the wooden deck. The cold wind ruffled their feathers, but they didn't seem to notice.

She took a sip of her hot chocolate and looked down at her paper. It was the second day of the spiritual formation retreat and nearing the end of the designated silence of the night before. She tried to imagine how Katy might manage such a task and instantly burst out laughing, nearly choking on the mouthful of hot chocolate. Ms. Jasmine glanced up at her from the open space below with that annoyed look she got in her eyes every now and then.

When Sonya, Elise, and most of the other students had disappeared into their rooms at the far end of the lodge, Tessa had chosen to stay in the loft. Her mind drifted, as it so often did, to Gramps—how he would love the spiral staircase, built of hand-split pine logs that led to the window seat in this tiny prayer loft. If this were his staircase, there would surely be Bible verses carved into it by now. He had an odd habit of leaving them behind on everything he made out of wood—his doorposts, the gateposts, and even the occasional tree. She remembered watching him from her attic window in the farmhouse one afternoon, as he replaced a rotting gatepost in the fence line. After Gramps had dug out the old post and set the new one into the ground, he took his hunting knife from its leather case, carved something in the post, and then carried on drilling holes for the gate hinges, as if it was all part of his regular fence repairing routine. Later, Tessa had gone outside to see what he had carved. It read, "casting down imaginations" from II Corinthians something—the verse he had read aloud during breakfast that morning after he'd noticed the romance novel Tessa was reading. She remembered how it had bothered her for days. It seemed like a lifetime ago now.

Tessa turned her back to the window. The view from the inside of the lodge was almost as spectacular: Through the pine railing she could see the spacious, main room below her. It was warmly decorated with three huge plush couches positioned around an enormous coffee table made from a redwood slab. Ms. Jasmine sat facing the fire on the couch with the most pillows. On each side of the fireplace were two overstuffed armchairs covered in a moose-and-bear-print fabric. The front of the stone fireplace stretched all the way up to the thirty-foot cedar ceiling. Apparently, the mounted deer and bear head trophies had to be taken down after the Earth Compassion Convention was held here in the spring. They had been replaced with medieval paintings, which Tessa thought didn't quite match the rustic lodge motif, but since the goal of the new owners was to provide contemplative retreats for church groups, she supposed St. Ignatius and St. John of the Cross fit their theme. Replicas were being sold in the lobby to raise money for the new construction project. Ms. Jasmine had her eye on the Teresa of Avila painting and had already called Dr. Johnson, the president of Flat Plains, several times to ask whether the worship arts budget would allow her to purchase it.

The gas fireplace below her reminded Tessa of home. Although warm and hypnotizing, it did not burn real wood like Gramps did in his woodstove, so the smoky wood smell was missing—but in its place a welcome aroma of fried onions and sage was wafting in from the kitchen, probably from the stuffing for night's vegetarian nut loaf dinner.

Quiet Waters Lodge was large enough to feed and lodge the eighty students from the two fall spiritual formation classes attending the weekend. Though the lodge was perfect just the way it was, further renovations were being planned. The architectural designs that a professional artist had recently sketched were on display in the lobby. The drawings revealed some sort of round structure to make more room for future workshops. This domed building on the water's edge was to be called The Quiet Place.

Ms. Jasmine, who knew the lodge well, having attended several staff retreats, also knew the owners. She said they were a Christian couple by the name of Foxe from Muddy Creek Community Fellowship, which was a thirty-minute drive from the lodge and two hours from Flat Plains. Ms. Jasmine had raved about this place for weeks and had already booked three retreats in advance for next year.

Tessa thought she'd better quit daydreaming and get to work. She looked down at her instructions again, but noticed the Quiet Water's brochure she had found in the info rack that morning. It was much more interesting to skim through the fee schedule for other group retreat activities:

$30.00 Chai Tea and Taizé Evening
$40.00 Vegetarian Italian Pizza and Lectio Divina Night
$45.00 The Jesus Prayer Breakfast and Ignatian Examen for Men
$50.00 Teresian Readings with Ms. Bea Still—breakfast and lunch included
$80.00 Silent Sabbath Fast—all day, no meals
$140.00 Children's Listening Prayer Seminar and Guided Meditation (one night)—book now for next year's family campout in our new Listening Cabins
$300.00 GPS for the Soul—Spiritual Direction Retreats
Labyrinth Prayer Walks—FREE—come downstairs and walk our new indoor prayer labyrinth, open 24/7
Coming soon—Christian Yoga in The Quiet Place—book now

The last entry looked interesting. Ms. Jasmine had already introduced them to Christian yoga. Today they were participating in a mini "silent retreat" led by Ms. Jasmine, but Tessa was having trouble concentrating. For one thing, she was haunted by the words of the woodsman. *What does he mean by saying it used to be a Bible camp? It still is!* They were here with their Bible college class reading the Bible, weren't they? She pictured herself going back and having the whole conversation with the woodsman again, this time telling him off. Tessa snorted and shook her head. She was supposed to be doing an imagination exercise but her imagination kept running away.

*Focus*, she told herself, forcing her eyes down at the paper again.

> Invite Christ into your imagination and thoughts during your time of scripture reading. Read Luke 5:12-16.

> Reflect on the story and imagine it as it is happening. Put yourself in the story. Use all your five senses. Imagine Jesus talking to you. What does He say?

> Journal the words He says to you.

Tessa had borrowed a Bible from one of her friends again. They'd all been given a *New Spirituality Bible* in September, but she was forever misplacing hers. This one was a spare that belonged to Elise. Elise was planning to be a youth leader after she graduated in the spring, and she had already been asked to join Merging Force, a popular international Christian youth organization.

Tessa flipped through the *New Spirituality Bible*, which was a compilation of modern paraphrases, and found the book of Mark. She read about a man covered in leprous sores whom Jesus had healed.

They were supposed to get as comfortable as possible when they did these exercises, so she stretched out on the cushioned window seat. Trying to concentrate, she closed her eyes and imagined herself in the Bible story. She tried to picture the village and the man. She even tried being the man. It wasn't working. She was usually so good at imagining, but the problem was, she didn't want to be the guy with leprosy. The other problem was she needed a horse. A daydream was simply no good without one. She sat up, reread the passage, and was more drawn to the end of the story than the story itself.

"Whenever possible Jesus withdrew to places out-of-the-way for solitude and silent prayer," she read aloud. "Oops." She forgot it was supposed to be an afternoon of complete silence and quickly glanced down at Ms. Jasmine again. She was quietly sitting against a pile of plump tapestry-covered pillows with her legs crossed and her eyes closed. Tessa realized the loft where she was sitting was indeed a very out-of-the-way place for prayer. What better place than this for Jesus to meet with her and talk to her? Would this be the day that the spark within would be ignited? The spark that Ms. Jasmine and St. Teresa talked so much about? It was worth another try. If only she could center her thoughts the way Ms. Jasmine did.

Tessa tried again. She inhaled deeply three times. It took awhile, but after doing the breathing relaxation exercises she'd been taught and shutting out the outside noises, she soon found her mind in a very quiet place.

Once there, her thoughts began to drift effortlessly to an out-of-the-way Mediterranean beach where the surf rolled gently on the white sand. The waves lapped at her horse's feet as she galloped bareback, with a delicious, warm breeze caressing her long, flowing hair. She could taste the salty water on her lips as the horse's hooves splashed along the shore. Tessa imagined sliding off her white mare to investigate a disappearing set of human footprints. She followed them before the tide waters could fill them in and soon came upon a huge, barnacled rock by a sandy cove from where she could smell the smoke of a small campfire crackling nearby. A man who had his back to her was playing in the coals with a stick. Curious, she approached the man slowly and was about to say "hello" when he turned around and looked at her.

"I've been waiting for you," he said, smiling. He wore the whitest robe she had ever seen, and his eyes sparkled like bright diamonds.

"Jesus, it's you!" Tessa imagined herself saying delightedly. Or was she imagining it? It seemed so real.

"I have much to tell you, so many things I want you to write down. Can you do that for me?"

Tessa nodded. He told her so many wonderful things that she had to write them down immediately. She rolled onto her stomach, reached over, grabbed her journal and pen from the loft floor, and began writing madly while the words still flowed in her mind.

"There have been too many distractions, keeping you from spending time with me. You are listening to too many voices. Meet with me more often to find out the truth—spend time with me. Be still. It is here in the silence that I am waiting to talk to you. Don't listen to those who are afraid to meet me in the silence. You are chosen. You are the beloved. Everyone could have this, but few realize it. If you come to me and trust my voice, I will guide you.

"Don't be afraid, no matter what people say. I will never utter a false word to you. You can trust me. I am the one who waits for you in the center of the labyrinth—I am in the center of the castle. I will give you delights and favors you never imagined and tell you things that no one else knows. I will be waiting for you next time."

Tears streamed down Tessa's cheeks as she wrote out the words she was still hearing. Suddenly, her pen ran dry. She scribbled on the side of the page but it was no use.

"Oh no!" she said out loud.

She had no choice but to stop writing. Was Jesus actually talking to her? It was so real, she knew it was Him. He had told her not to be afraid. She reread what she had written and noted the phrase that said, "I will never utter a false word to you."

*Wow, only Jesus could say that,* she thought. *These are the words that Jesus said to me! Here in my journal.*

There was a noise in the room below. She looked down. Ms. Jasmine was gone. What time was it?

A faint familiar tinkling sound could be heard moving through the lodge. Ms. Jasmine had brought the bell back from her travels to Asia. She used it often to end prayer exercises at Flat Plains. That meant it was 4:30 and she'd been up here for over three hours already. It hardly seemed like an hour.

The wonderful aroma of onions and sage coming from the dining hall filled the air. Tessa's mouth watered as she climbed down the spiral staircase to sit by the fire and wait for the others. She was in Elise's discussion group, which was to meet here in the main room until dinner time so everyone could share what they had experienced. As much as she anticipated the wonderful dinner, Tessa was more excited to tell Ms. Jasmine that Jesus had actually talked to her. But most importantly, she couldn't wait to go to an out-of-the-way place again and meet Jesus on that beautiful white beach.

## GIFT OF TEARS

IN a quiet little village close to the Sierra de Gredos mountains, a weary-looking robed figure knelt before a statue of St. Joseph in a dimly lit monastery, rocking back and forth while praying quietly...

"I am so grateful for this gift of tears that I do not deserve, even though I do not understand. Perhaps someday I shall know the reason my Lord was so stern and so grave that caused me to vow never to meet with Him again! Had it been a warning? Like the great toad that crawled toward me in the parlor ... was that too a warning which I neglected to heed?"

She glanced behind her, and to each side, and then began weeping uncontrollably, her right hand clutching a crucifix so tightly her knuckles turned white. Her sobbing grew louder.

"Oh these visions! What tortures I have endured ... how can I bear it?" she wailed. "I even gave up mental prayer. I ... I gave it up. I did! First I waited to be free of sin, but they found no fault in me. Not a fault! Yet I was visited again, more visions ... more revelations ... to this most miserable sinner as I."

Behind her, she could hear the group of nuns that stopped a short distance away, pausing for a moment before turning and walking in the other direction.

"Indeed, I have dreaded the time of prayer," she whispered now, lest the others murmur about her even more. "Even Father Francis became afraid of my graces . . . in great distress they insisted I had been deceived by Satan. So I . . . I punished myself, oh I did, I did, in order to resist the effects! To no avail! Father Alvarez said . . . he said it was friendships I must give up, but that changed nothing. Then he told me I must recite a hymn, and I did. That was when the angel came . . . the angel . . . oh, how it pierced me! They told me . . . they said my visions were illusions of Satan and told me to point my finger in scorn at another. I tried to obey them, to no avail, so ridiculous they all are, so now I hold this crucifix in my hand at all times . . ."

She looked up at the statue, wiped her face with her wet sleeve, and held up the wooden crucifix.

"And still they told me my visions were the work of evil spirits! For six years, I was on trial . . . six years! So many prayers and masses said, I grew weary of them all! Yet still the trances and favors have become more violent and frequent . . . oh, I am in distress, such great distress. I am weary, and so tired . . . so very, very tired . . ."

Her voice was weaker now as she shifted her weight from one aching knee to another on the cold, stone floor. "Yet I fear there is more sorrow ahead . . . I fear delusions . . . already they are calling for me . . . more inquiries to tell me I am deluded. How can they be sure *they* aren't deluded and deceived as well? Every one of my examiners tells me something different! Oh! My soul is plunged into darkness! How I long to be alone . . . oh, when will this life ever become more than a never-ending dark night for my soul! I hear them coming even now demanding answers to unanswerable questions. How can I bear it? I want only to be alone. I just want to be . . . oh, please let me be . . ."

Gradually the pitiful sounds of her whimpering subsided as the dreadful footsteps that echoed from the far end of the corridor grew closer and then stopped. She straightened the folds of her habit, held her head high, and with a faraway look in her eyes, turned to face her visitors.

"Sister Teresa," a man's voice said. "Come now, we must ask you more questions."

## THE LECTURE

WINTER TERM 2008

"PLEASE keep your questions for the end of the lecture," Ms. Jasmine announced. "Instead of boring you today, I will use the last part of our class time for your inquiries regarding your marks." She pulled a thick stack of papers from her briefcase and put them on the desk. She nodded disapprovingly at Tessa, who was ten minutes late again. Tessa could already tell the room was going to feel much too warm. Her cheeks and nose were still rosy from her brisk morning walk as she sat down in the front row of the lecture hall beside Elise. She pushed up her sleeves, pulled off her knit hat, and shook the melting snowflakes onto the floor.

Ms. Jasmine removed her glasses, glanced at the clock on the wall, and walked to the white board. Her black high-heeled shiny boots were the kind that clicked loudly with each step she took. She picked up a marker and began her lecture. Tessa admired her black pants and bright pink tailored jacket with oversized buttons that only someone like Ms. Jasmine could get away with. It seemed that anything she wore made her look elegant, even that bright pink lipstick.

"That's gotta be Bombshell Blonde hot pink lipstick by Gigi,"

Elise leaned over and whispered to Tessa. "I have that one, but it looks totally dumb on me. Maybe if I get a psychology degree like she has, I can afford to look like that someday."

Tessa was not in the mood to hear Elise's daily fashion report. She was on pins and needles wondering whether she received a good mark on her paper.

"After today's lecture, I will hand back your papers. You have all worked very hard, and I'm pleased to say a few of you have done excellent research. In fact, several of you have earned such high marks you are being considered for a special, brand-new scholarship which will be announced in the spring."

Tessa had indeed done her research for this paper on prayer. It had been an enormous challenge trying to work with a chatty roommate nearby. If it hadn't been for earplugs and her favorite quiet spot in the library, she could not have accomplished what she had. Tessa had never applied herself so completely to any assignment, but because she liked Ms. Jasmine, she had put a lot of effort into this class. Even so, she thought if anyone in this class deserved a scholarship, it was Elise. Elise did everything well, putting more effort into studying than Tessa had energy for, and always achieved her goals for the difficult assignments she tackled.

"I'd also like to mention that we had a great turnout two nights ago for the outdoor prayer walk, in spite of the snow. Wasn't it lovely? Thank you Elise and Tessa for helping organize the evening."

Ms. Jasmine allowed a few minutes of chatter while she turned and wrote something on the board. It was a time line of the current era, something she often drew during her lectures, although it wasn't too likely anyone could make out the title, as usual.

"Can you read that?" whispered Tessa.

"No," Elise answered, "typical doctor's handwriting. It's just another one of her time lines."

"All right, students," Ms. Jasmine said loudly, drawing a vertical line at the sixteenth-century mark as she waited for the noise to stop. "Let's talk about controversy and the test of time. As you know, some of the early Christians who were contemporaries were known to disagree on many things. Two, for example, are St. Teresa of Avila and St. John of the Cross, yet their writings are considered to be the greatest of all mystical theology. Even St. Teresa's advisors couldn't agree on whether her experiences were from God or from the devil. Some thought her visions were the work of the Holy Spirit, and others remained convinced that her visitations were illusions of Satan. But in the end, the truth came out. Today we see how valuable her writings and experiences are for the church. So in spite of these controversies, the works of many of these misunderstood saints have stood the test of time and are still in print today. You all, of course, know that St. Teresa is a personal favorite of mine."

She turned and made an "x" on the board at the 1970 mark on her time line. "Case in point . . . some of you may have read in your research that not too long ago, St. Teresa was declared a Doctor of the Church by Pope Paul the VI. She was the first woman to be named as a Doctor by the Roman Catholic Church. By the way, ladies, be glad you live in modern times. It took Teresa of Avila several hundred years to get her doctorate. It only took me eight."

As Ms. Jasmine waited for the chuckles and giggles to finish, a girl wearing thick glasses near the front of the room, who Teresa only knew by first name, gingerly raised her hand.

"Yes, Nicky," responded Ms. Jasmine.

"Um, one book I read said something odd," began the girl timidly, her cheeks flushed. "It mentioned that mystics like St. Teresa had erotic experiences during their spiritual peaks. Can you comment on that?"

"Yes, thank you for that excellent question," Ms. Jasmine answered in her usual professional manner. "We can all learn from a fairly new view within psychology and holistic health that an erotic component can be integrated into the mystical ecstasy, which brings about a whole new level of union with the divine. Take for example St. Teresa's experience of ecstasy with the angel that is so beautifully captured in the statue by Gianlorenzo Bernini. Of course, you can imagine that critics opposing mysticism would have an even tougher time accepting this as a superior level of intimacy. I guess it all depends on what one believes. Those of us who understand the mystical state as a state where God is encountered would welcome this deeper dimension of spirituality."

Tessa felt more than a little embarrassed to think about what Ms. Jasmine was implying. She slid down slowly in her chair and looked straight ahead, not wanting to hear anymore about that. It just didn't sound right. They had all read the same book, but she didn't have the courage to ask such a question in front of all the guys. She didn't really want to know the answer, anyway.

"And let me add this," continued Ms. Jasmine. "While I personally do not see the need, there are some contemplative practitioners who offer 'warning,' saying that this kind of prayer is not for the inexperienced novice." Ms. Jasmine made quotation marks with her fingers as she said the word in a mocking tone.

Teresa's ears perked up. A warning? Ever since the retreat she'd been having very good success talking to Jesus during her journaling times, and had even written about it on the student blog. She vaguely remembered seeing that warning in some book she had read. The author had advocated praying a prayer of protection before praying with your imagination, but she had completely ignored it. Now, a brief cold wave of fear passed over her, but she refused to consider it and quickly put it out of her mind. How could she fear the gentle Jesus she met on the beach, and the warm presence she'd experienced only a few nights ago in the prayer labyrinth?

"One well-known contemplative author writes," Ms. Jasmine continued, "that you must offer a prayer of protection to God, lest you come in contact with demons."

Half the class snickered when Ms. Jasmine overemphasized the last word in a low scary tone, especially a group of guys in the back row.

"Thomas, you always have novel ideas. Could you tell the class what you and your friends find so amusing?"

"Uh-huh. That is so paranoid. I mean, if you pray to Jesus, He's not going to send a demon. That's just stupid."

"Exactly right, thank you Thomas. Many of us . . . many of those who have been practicing these methods of silence and contemplation for years also disagree with that statement. Contemplative prayer is not dangerous, and it is for everyone. The Bible says to 'be still and know that I am God.' If we don't silence our minds, how else will we hear Him in our busy lives, amid the constant barrage of noise from televisions, CD players, and a myriad of other electronic gadgets? In order to really know God, you have got to have an inner stillness."

No sooner had Ms. Jasmine finished her sentence, than the ring tone of a cell phone chimed from someone's bag, throwing everyone in the lecture hall into fits of laughter.

"Thank you Amanda. That was perfect timing. The point is, one will hear different views on the subject of listening prayer, but one must always go back to the tried and true, the experiences of the early church fathers and mothers, to whom we owe so much. Why else would their writings still be in print to this day if God did not want us to learn from them? Why would they be given doctorates by the church, even years later, if what they practiced and taught was not from God? Isn't that what you meant, Thomas?"

Thomas nodded his head and leaned back in his chair grinning, proud to have Ms. Jasmine's approval.

"Now, let me ask how many of you are going home for Christmas?" Almost everyone raised a hand. Ms. Jasmine twirled her marker back and forth between her fingers. Her long pink nails made a rhythmic clacking noise on the pen. Tessa couldn't help but think it was to the same beat as, "Oh what fun it is to ride in a one horse open sleigh…"

How Tessa had wanted to go home for Christmas and see Sassy and of course, Gran and Gramps too, but the roads were bad with a blizzard in the forecast, and a plane ticket was out of the question. Besides, she'd had a sore throat and thought it best to stay in Flat Plains and catch up on her assignments. She hadn't been feeling well these last few weeks and could use some peace and quiet, especially if her roommate was going to be away. There were other students staying in her dorm who couldn't afford to travel either, so Sonya had invited them all to spend Christmas Day with her family, who lived only forty miles away in what was rumored to be a very big mansion. When Elise told Tessa that Sonya's home was as big as a castle, that it had many guest rooms filled with tapestries and antiques from Europe, she immediately accepted Sonya's invitation. How could a girl with a weakness for castles miss an opportunity like this?

"Class, can I be honest with you?" Ms. Jasmine asked, a very serious look on her face as the room grew quiet. "When you go home, your families and friends may view you in a different light now that you've learned new things in this class. For example, if they notice you practicing your daily lectio divina readings, they may try to persuade you that the old-fashioned religious ideas they learned are the only right ones. This may even spark controversy within some of your relationships. But remember, the ancient disciplines you have learned were around long before they were. Fundamental Christians who have grown up with a certain narrow brand of religion can't help it—they just don't know any better. If they don't understand, teach them to listen, as you have learned. Remind them that even Jesus retreated to places of solitude and silence to find union with the Father. Tell them that this is why Christmas has come, that the light may be found in each one of us!"

Tessa glanced at Elise. She was closing her eyes and smiling. *Ms. Jasmine is right. Gran and Gramps really are old-fashioned and narrow-minded in many of their views.* Better to spend the holidays here with some of her friends in a modern-day castle.

"I'm sure you are all anxious to get going before the snow gets too deep, but as you leave, come to my desk and pick up your marked papers. I'll stay for half an hour to answer your questions. For those who need to go, have a peaceful and divine Christmas! And be careful if you are driving. It's a blizzard out there!

# 10

## FARMHOUSE

JANUARY 2009

A blanket of fresh white snow greeted Jacob Brown as he woke from a deep sleep and tossed aside his goose-down quilt. His cell phone was beeping.

"It's 6:00 am! You'd think that after being at college for four months that girl would remember the time difference," he complained to Margaret who was in front of the dressing mirror already, pinning up her long hair. He loved to tease her about how he'd married a wife with black hair and ended up with a wife with white hair.

"Last time I looked, I wasn't the only one who's turned white, my dear." But with all the jesting, a deep affection existed between the two that years of love, happiness, hardship, and faith had built. "Now just because you sold your herd of cattle and retired, JB, doesn't mean you can officially sleep in every morning! There are still chores to be done," Margaret reminded him.

She was pleased that their Teresa had agreed to go to the same school where she had met her husband so many years ago. Flat Plains Bible College was founded in the 1950s and had always had a reputation for solid Bible teaching, not to mention the nickname Flat Plains

Bridal School. Without a doubt, the school had earned its nickname. Almost every year, it had seemed that half the student body would end up marrying each other back in those days. Yes, there was no better way to invest their money than to enroll their last foster *granddaughter* there.

Margaret smiled as she thought about how Teresa had faithfully remembered to send them a short text message at least once a week to let them know how things were going. She didn't know it was part of Jacob and Tessa's little agreement, but Jacob felt he should keep his eye on the girl. His lifelong interest in radio and electronics had kept him up to date with the latest technology and served as a perfect disguise for such grandfatherly supervision.

"Tell her thank you for the wake-up call, because a certain old man forgot to get up early and stoke the fire in the woodstove," she chided as she trotted downstairs to make his traditional hot skillet breakfast.

"Yeah, yeah, I'll be down in a minute, my dear," said Jacob, sitting up in bed to read his text message. He had become pretty efficient at deciphering Tessa's shorthand style:

"Mornin gramps, rain today. Learning lots bout prayer in 2nd semestr SF class. Asked 2 b new prayr walk leadr—my favrit! Miss u, giv sass a carot 4 me. Had dream was ridng her 2 castle in avila. Say hi 2 gran—talk 2 u nxt week."

"Learning lots about prayer. I knew we were doing the right thing by putting her there," Jacob mumbled, flipping his phone shut. "And to think, a prayer leader!"

Jacob rose from the bed with a yawn, pulled on his favorite pair of faded Wranglers, and stood by the window for a few moments, buttoning his red plaid shirt. He stared out at the snow-covered foothills as he did every winter morning. These last few mornings his steel-blue eyes had a faraway look. Today, he didn't even laugh at the antics of the small dog racing in circles in the barnyard, barking at the snowflakes. Soon enough, the smell of bacon caught his attention and enticed him to wander down to the kitchen. Margaret never wasted time in the morning. For forty years, she'd been serving him a bacon-and-egg breakfast just the way he liked it, hot and fresh from the skillet before he went outside to do his morning chores. There weren't quite as many animals to look after now, just one old horse, a few laying hens, and Daisy, their old Jack Russell, who waited every morning for that last bite of bacon that Jacob "just couldn't make room for."

While he waited for breakfast, he poured himself some coffee and wandered over to the study, deep in thought.

"You forgot your cream and sugar," called Gran, giving him a strange look.

"Don't need it," he answered.

Where had he heard that name Teresa kept mentioning in her messages lately? Where and what was Avila? He had read that word somewhere before.

Setting down his coffee mug, Jacob pushed the leather chair aside and grabbed the handle on an old wooden chest buried under a stack of books and files. He cleared it off, pulled up the dusty lid, and reached inside past some old Beatles albums. "Why in tarnation are these old vinyl records still in the house after all these years?" he muttered. Sliding his finger across some titles, he paused at an old hard-cover book and pulled it out. He closed the lid, sneezed three times into an oversized handkerchief, and sat down in the big red armchair.

"Why so serious today?" Margaret said as she scooped a spoonful of sugar into his cup and stirred in some cream. She didn't particularly like the look on her husband's face, and she was concerned that for the first time in decades he was drinking black coffee.

"Oh, might be nothing," he answered. "Just digging through that box of junk that girl left behind, that's all. You know, the unusual girl that stayed here one summer, back in the '70s. Remember?"

"You mean the Winters girl? Yes, she was an odd girl. The bacon will be ready in five minutes. Are we still driving to the city today?"

"Yep. I think I'll make a stop at the library too."

The noise of clattering dishes and Margaret's humming in the kitchen soon faded into the background as Jacob sat in his chair and opened the book he held in his hands. The book was called *Life of St. Teresa of Jesus of the Order of Our Lady of Carmel*. Inside the cover was a handwritten inscription:

To Cecilia Winters
March 1944
With affection, Aunt Beatrice

The book was the autobiography of the sixteenth-century Spanish mystic, Teresa of Avila. This particular copy was published in 1904, and it smelled like a musty thrift store. He opened it to the page where someone had placed a bookmark next to a faded picture of a pretty girl wearing a peasant blouse, a long skirt, and yellow flowers tucked into her long, blonde hair. It was in Chapter XX, "The Difference between Union and Rapture. What Rapture is. The Blessing it is to the Soul. The Effects of it."

"Quite the chapter title," Jacob whispered to himself as he began reading:

> I wish I could explain, with the help of God, wherein union differs from rapture, or from transport, or from flight of the spirit, as they speak, or from a trance, which are all one. I mean, that all these are only different names for that one and the same thing, which is also called ecstasy. It is more excellent than union, the fruits of it are much greater ...

As he read, a cold sensation slowly began to spread through his being. It wasn't only because this book had belonged to the girl who stayed at their farm one summer. It was because of the recent text messages he had received from their Teresa. Could it be? He continued to read:

> During rapture, the soul does not seem to animate the body, the natural heat of which is perceptibly lessened; the coldness increases, though accompanied with exceeding joy and sweetness.

Jacob lowered his reading glasses and called his wife. "Uh, Margaret . . . you might want to put that bacon on hold."

"Why?" Margaret called back. "Breakfast is ready." She wiped her hands on her apron, scooped four eggs and six crisp strips of bacon onto two plates, carried them to the table, and turned off the stove. When her husband didn't come immediately, Margaret walked briskly to the study. The alarmed look on Jacob's face took her by surprise.

"Are you feeling OK? Are you having chest pains?" she asked, her brow furrowed as she approached her husband and carefully examined his face with her blue-gray eyes.

"No, no, I'm fine. But listen to this and tell me what you think." Jacob carried on, reading random paragraphs from the chapter:

> A rapture is absolutely irresistible; whilst union, inasmuch as we are then on our own ground, may be hindered, though that resistance be painful and violent; it is, however, almost always impossible. But rapture, for the most part, is irresistible. It comes, in general, as a shock, quick and sharp, before you can collect your thoughts, or help yourself in any way, and you see and feel it as a cloud, or a strong eagle rising upwards, and carrying you away on its wings.

"You're not reading about the rapture of the church, are you, JB?" Margaret interrupted. "It sounds strange."

Jacob shook his head and kept reading:

> You feel and see yourself carried away, you know not whither. . . . Occasionally I was able, by great effort, to make a slight resistance; but afterward I was worn out, like a person who had been contending with a strong giant; at other times it was impossible to resist at all: my soul was carried away, and almost always my head with it,—I had no power over it,—and now and then the whole body as well, so that it was lifted up from the ground.

"JB! I remember hearing this before. It sounds like something that girl was always reciting—what was her first name again? Cecilia Winters' girl. Just like her mother, always talking to dead saints—"

"And about her mother's out of body experiences," finished Jacob. "I asked her once if it was drugs, but she always adamantly insisted it wasn't. I had a feeling it was something far deeper. There was such a strong resistance to God's Word. What was it she would say whenever I shared the Gospel with her?" Jacob squinted as if gazing into another time.

"That she'd already found peace and tranquility," said Margaret. "She came so close to finding it. Only the Lord knows why she was here for the short time she stayed."

Margaret remembered how many times she had told the Winters girl about the Lord, but she had never wanted to hear it. "All she really wanted was to find her mother," Margaret said. But her mother had abandoned her to follow a guru to India, and there joined a religious cult.

"She said her mom had learned to float above the ground," Jacob said, shaking his head, "and the kids teased her, called her mom the flying nun because she wore long dresses and beads and went into meditative trances. From the moment she arrived at the farm, I sensed a deep spiritual oppression in her."

Jacob hadn't wanted the younger foster children exposed to it. There was even a rumor that she came from a line of gypsies who would cast spells on people for money. He had nearly contacted Children's Services, who thought some time at the ranch would help her. She did seem fond of the horse. But just as they thought they were beginning to make progress, one morning the girl packed her bags and left. Jacob remembered it well—it was the day after Sassy was born. Everyone in the house, who was old enough, had been taking turns trying to feed the orphaned foal. Shortly after lunch, one of the girls had brought a note she'd found on a bedroom dresser, a note saying the troubled girl was leaving. Later, they were told the girl had hitchhiked to the city, after crashing a stolen vehicle, and then boarded a bus to search for her mother.

Jacob slid his reading glasses into his shirt pocket and closed the yellowed book. Could the spirituality described in this book have something to do with their Teresa? He tried to shake the foreboding he felt. He had heard that some Bible schools were not teaching the truth anymore, but they had sent her to good old Flat Plains Bible College. Surely, he was overreacting.

"Jacob, tell me, why are you reading this?"

"My dear Margaret, I'm not sure what to make of this quite yet, but I think there is some kind of connection between our Teresa and the spirituality of the ancient mystic St. Teresa. It's just the oddest thing…"

"What is, JB?"

"It's something about the text messages she's been sending since September… it just doesn't sound like she is learning the same things we learned at Bible college, Margaret. I think we should spend some extra time praying for our dear Teresa this morning."

Margaret was puzzled. She wasn't sure what he was talking about, but she'd had the same uneasiness in her spirit. Jacob didn't notice that his hands were cold and clammy until he took Margaret's warm hand that smelled like dish soap and led her to the bench at the wooden kitchen table where two plates of bacon and eggs were getting cold. They sat down together and bowed their heads.

"Our heavenly Father," began Jacob, "we come before You this day to make our requests known, by the precious blood of Your own dear Son Jesus Christ, who died for our sins at Calvary. We thank You for hearing our prayers and graciously granting our requests. Father, today we bring before You our precious Teresa. Please be with her and guard and protect her from the enemy. Keep her from evil this day. We thought we sent Teresa, whom You have loaned to us, to a safe place, but now we are not so sure. We trust You are watching over her, and we place Teresa once again in Your hands. This we pray in the name of Your Son, Jesus Christ our Savior. Amen."

"Amen." Margaret looked questioningly into the depths of the wise eyes she trusted so completely. A tear ran down her husband's weathered cheek. She knew him well enough to know that there was more to this than he was telling her.

## MORTIFICATIONS

"THESE onions are so strong!" complained Sister Carmelita, as she wiped tears and sweat off her face with the long sleeve of her habit. The weather was too warm to be cooking vegetables over a hot fire.

"Not as strong as you will smell if you don't wash your habit soon," chided Sister Rosa. "You know how particular Sister Teresa is about cleanliness."

The nuns on kitchen duty were not supposed to be chatting, much less bickering, but Teresa was nowhere to be seen as they prepared the vegetables for the next meal.

"Where is she anyway?" said Sister Catherine, who had just come in with a basket full of freshly picked tomatoes.

"Maybe she is in a trance," joked Sister Maria. Just last week they had all watched as Teresa had gone into another trance in the kitchen while holding a hot pan of oil. Now accustomed to her trances, their greater concern was the possibility of Teresa spilling the little, precious oil they had left."

"The priests have advised her that the visions are of the devil, and to make the sign of the cross whenever she has one," said Catherine, the youngest nun among them. "She won't be coming into the kitchen for a few weeks. She is fasting and doing penance."

"So that's why she wears a cilice!" chimed in Maria.

"A cilice. What's that?" asked Catherine.

"It's an undergarment made of coarse animal hair. It scratches terribly and makes you very itchy. Pray to Our Lady that you will never be ordered to do mortification and be told to wear one," said Carmelita. "I think slicing onions in this kitchen is torture enough."

The sisters giggled.

"I think it's a terrible thing," said Rosa, a serious-minded nun and the oldest among them all. "Poor Teresa. We must not talk about our dear sister in this manner. If one decides to practice penance, it is only to share the sufferings of the Lord as His bride to be one flesh with Him."

She had personally witnessed Teresa's private confusion over the priests' accusations that her visions were from Satan. Those accusations were the reason Teresa had taken to inflicting tortures and mortifications upon herself. Teresa was just one of many nuns who drew blood in self-flagellation. (The monks did it too, so they were told.) Perhaps she thought that wearing a prickly shirt over her wounds would make her ecstasies disappear. The purpose of such self-inflicted trials was to attain self-detachment, something of which Teresa often talked. Surely, she reaped the benefits of such disciplines, having much more tranquility and self-mastery than the rest of them. "Mortify the flesh and share in Christ's sufferings" was the directive. Teresa's favorite motto was "Lord, either let me suffer or let me die."

On the other side of the convent, Teresa went about her duties in solitude. There was spinning to be done and the never-ending task of sweeping. The convent must be kept organized and spotless no matter how terrible she felt. She would prefer the duty of cooking meals in the kitchen, but today she couldn't bear to listen to the trivial banter of the other nuns. The tight shirt, woven with coarse animal hair, scraped across the fresh wounds on her back each time she stretched her arm to sweep the floor in her cell, and served as a painful reminder of her most recent self-scourging. She would gladly suffer in this way to be one with her Lord—and if it would make the visions go away.

Also deprived of food and sleep, she was weak and faint but she worked in silence. She tried to focus her thoughts to begin to formalize a plan to start her own convents. She certainly would allow less frivolous talk and far fewer comforts since they only served to make the nuns dissatisfied. Her nuns would be required to go barefoot, wear sacks, and live in complete silence and perpetual abstinence, she decided. Someday. Someday she would change the way a convent was run.

The sun was disappearing behind the mountains. The days lasted longer when one didn't have mealtimes to break them up. It would soon be time to light the candles for the evening prayers. She dreaded the thought, but she knew she must be obedient to her confessor. She made sure her flagellum was placed close to the candle so she could use it on herself again tonight after the others had gone to sleep.

CASTLE OF AVILA, SPAIN

12

## Spiritual Direction Session

Lay hands suddenly on no man, neither be partaker of
other men's sins: keep thyself pure. I Timothy 5:22

JANUARY 9, 2009

A small twirling crystal, hanging from a thread on a curtain rod,
caught the sunlight making tiny spots of brilliant colors dance playfully on the walls and ceiling that were painted a deep indigo color.

Tessa's eyes continued to look around the room then rested on a
large oil painting that hung on the wall across from where she sat. The
artist had depicted an extraordinarily beautiful scene of a medieval castle
rising out of the mist. The castle almost appeared to be floating in mid-air.
Tessa loved it. She looked around the room and smiled. She also loved
the way the varying colors in the room were so tastefully coordinated.

Adding to the ambiance, gauze curtains filtered the mid-afternoon
sunlight, providing the room with a gentle warmth that soothed the
soul. Additional lengths of gauze had been strategically hung, dividing
the room into different listening spaces, as Ms. Jasmine called them.

A coffee table held some books and a small, star-shaped vanilla
candle. Its sweet aroma wafted gently through the air, adding to the
aura of peace and tranquility.

Ms. Jasmine was dressed casually today, although her platinum
blonde hair was pulled back into a glamorous roll held together with

a jewel-studded clasp that caught the sunlight whenever she turned her head. Tessa couldn't help but notice how much she reminded her of her own mother.

Before beginning with her usual prayer, Ms. Jasmine had lit the candle and waited quietly for the moment of silence to pass. Tessa always enjoyed these moments of deep breathing, necessary to refocus her thoughts from the outward to the inward.

"We thank you for this mysterious universal gift of prayer that is offered to all who will receive it," Ms. Jasmine prayed softly. "As we sit in stillness and silence, we wait to be infused in the Light."

For some reason, curiosity got the better of Tessa this afternoon. She slowly raised her head, opened her eyes, and watched in fascination as her mentor, or rather her spiritual director, prayed. She noted with astonishment that Ms. Jasmine didn't bow her head and fold her hands to pray the way Gramps always did. Instead, her head was up and her hands were at her side, thumbs and pointer fingers pressed together in a circle. Now as she opened her eyes, Tessa looked away, embarrassed, and pretended not to notice.

"Well. What comes to mind this week, Tessa? What has the Spirit been saying to you?" Ms. Jasmine inquired, her gold bracelets jangling as she rubbed her temples.

"Is it OK if I just read out of my journal this week, Ms. Jazz?" Tessa replied as she pulled a spiral-bound notebook from her backpack.

"That would be delightful," said Ms. Jasmine, crossing her legs and making herself comfortable on the oversized, red-and-gold-tasseled cushion. She leaned against the wall and picked up her cup of steaming hot green tea. "Today is a double session, remember? We have all the time in the world. Begin!"

Tessa opened her journal.

"Oh my stars! Did you draw that horse?" gasped Ms. Jasmine, pointing at Tessa's notebook.

"Uh . . . oh, yeah. I like to doodle sometimes—it's nothing much."

"I had a horse once. Well, she wasn't mine. But she was mine to look after and ride. A beautiful mare . . . she had a foal. A pretty little thing . . ." Ms. Jasmine spoke with a faraway look in her eye as she proceeded to tell Tessa the story of how on one dark night, when the vet had pulled into the driveway, she ran out from the barn crying until she couldn't breathe. She ran barefoot into the foothills shaking her fist at God for taking away the only thing she'd ever loved. She had begged God to save the animal, but He hadn't listened. The mare died, and the tiny foal wasn't expected to survive.

"Early the next morning, I packed a small bag, found the keys, then started the old farm pickup and took off," Ms. Jasmine added in a sad mournful way. "I drove away from that farmhouse and . . . well, no use reliving the past now."

"That must have been a sad time for you. My horse actually belongs to—" Tessa began.

"Wait . . ." Ms. Jasmine cupped her hand around her ear and looked at the window. "Do you hear that? Do you hear bees?"

"Ms. Jazz?" Tessa turned her head toward the window. She couldn't see or hear any bees. The room was perfectly quiet.

"Never mind. It's hot in here. Isn't it hot in here? Would you be a dear and open the window?"

Tessa rose from her cushion and walked to the window. When she tried to open it, it was stuck. She pushed a little harder, and up it went. Instantly a freezing blast of winter air blew the curtains wildly around her face.

"Ah yes, that feels good. Thank you, dear. Now come back and sit down." Ms. Jasmine took a deep breath and leaned against the wall again. Tessa could see the steam rising from her teacup. "Enough horse stories. One can't live in the past. Attachments are merely sources of pain and distraction. St. Teresa knew that. Even the Buddha knew that. Now tell me, where were we?"

Tessa gave Ms. Jasmine a long look, picked up her journal, and sat down. She was quite used to Ms. Jasmine's unpredictable mood swings by now and had even come to expect them. They no longer alarmed her. She always mellowed soon afterward.

How could anyone *not* be mellow in this room? Ms. Jasmine (the most recent faculty addition at Flat Plains Bible College, who had come to the school highly recommended by the Spiritual

Transformation Institute–the most sought-after training center for spiritual formation leaders in North America) had transformed everything. The only thing unchanged in the old prayer room in the Thompson Building was the stained glass window. It was no longer just any old prayer room. It was the Sacred Space. And it was in this room that the more promising students from the spiritual formation classes received personal one-on-one counseling from Ms. Jasmine.

Under her direction, Tessa had been journaling for the past several months. Every morning after a twenty-minute listening exercise, Tessa had faithfully pulled out her pen and notebook and recorded the words she heard Jesus speak to her. It was always thrilling to reread the messages her pen had written, but lately she had become increasingly exhausted by these exercises. *Well, exercise is supposed to make you tired*, she reasoned. Now she read aloud the words Jesus had spoken to her earlier that morning:

"January 9—'When I brought you to Flat Plains you were angry. You thought I wouldn't talk to you, and even if I did, you didn't want to hear me. Now, since we met on the beach and in the labyrinth, you are finally listening to my voice. How pleased I am that you are not afraid to listen anymore.'"

Tessa stopped for a moment and looked up.

"Can I close the window now?" she asked, shivering.

Ms. Jasmine's eyes were closed, her face an expression of serenity. She made a graceful shooing motion with a ring-bejeweled hand. "Fine."

Tessa closed the window and placed her jacket around her shoulders before sitting down. "This is what I wrote today . . . just some of my thoughts," Tessa continued.

"Please go on," said Ms. Jasmine, eyes still shut.

"It was a frosty morning last fall when I first walked the outdoor labyrinth, and my idea of what prayer meant was totally changed. Before walking the labyrinth, I always thought prayer was saying lofty words to God who was somewhere way up there. But what I have experienced as I've been practicing awareness exercises and the listening prayer is that it's only in the silence that I can hear His voice. That first day in the labyrinth is where it started. As we took turns walking, I felt moved, as Jesus met me in the center where He was waiting for me. He spoke to me in that still small voice and told me I was gifted. I wasn't sure at first if it was His voice, but since then I've had an awareness of His presence. It is as if God is in everything around me and in me too."

Tessa looked up for a moment, then continued. "I've also been having the same dream, that I am riding my horse across the drawbridge into the courtyard of a beautiful ancient castle. I can hear someone calling my name, so I explore all the rooms to see who is calling me. Each room is more beautiful, more wonderful than the last, with tables full of food. I have a taste from each table, and go to the next, but I always wake up before I can go up the stairs to the last room, which is locked. I wake up imagining what it would be like in that room, and I know it is the voice of God calling me to the secret room. I try to get back to my dream, but can only imagine..."

*Imagine*... Ms. Jasmine's mind drifted, as Tessa continued to read. She thought about the presentation she had given to the faculty members at the Flat Plains leadership prayer retreat last year. They had seemed mesmerized as she explained the spiritual benefits of praying in a labyrinth. The Spiritual Transformation Institute determined long ago that this was usually the most successful way to introduce Christians to the concept of assimilating breathing exercises and the prayer of the heart into their prayer life.

"Just imagine," Ms. Jasmine had said to the leaders, "getting your students to pray more in one afternoon than they would normally pray in an entire week. Once they try it, you won't be able to stop them from spending time in prayer. The average prayer walk through the labyrinth takes about forty-five minutes, and as you walk, you use both the left and right sides of your brain. This helps to center your thoughts and focus on Jesus. It not only opens you up to God, but also helps give you a new perspective on the depths of the meaning of prayer. Most people say they have a profound experience during a prayer walk and are never the same again. Is your prayer life dry? Do you want to revitalize the spirituality of your students? I encourage you to walk in the labyrinth this afternoon, to see for yourselves if what I am saying is true."

They had all been eager to try it. All, that is, except for two narrow-minded, uptight faculty members. Later that afternoon while the other staff members were walking and meditating along the circular path of the labyrinth, those two resisters had met in the prayer chapel and quietly closed the door. *They were in there at least two hours*, she remembered. Then, later that evening, they'd asked to meet privately with the college president. Evidently, the meeting hadn't gone the way they'd hoped. Both had left the room an hour later, glassy-eyed and shoulders drooping. *They were a picture of despair*, Ms. Jasmine recalled. In September, she'd noted with interest that one of them was no longer at the school.

The other staff members, however, had been much more open-minded to the labyrinth. In fact, their experience had left them mightily impressed. So much so, Ms. Jasmine had received a call from the president of Flat Plains who asked her to assess the possibility of constructing a permanent labyrinth on their campus. Of course, she'd been thrilled to custom-design the large outdoor labyrinth for the enthusiastic staff, especially when they agreed to put her name on the dedication plaque. There had been just one problem. The only available green space had been the soccer field, but since Flat Plains had decided to place more emphasis on their new environmental awareness program and less on their sports program, the vote was eighteen to two in favor of the new plan to build an outdoor labyrinth on it that fall. Indoor soccer would have to suffice.

Much to her delight, Ms. Jasmine had also been invited to accept the recently vacated position of Campus Counselor, in addition to providing assistance with the new spiritual formation class they'd been planning for some time. And now here she was, in this beautiful, newly redesigned room. It was hers, and she loved it.

"Ms. Jazz?"

"Yes, Tessa," she answered quietly, as she shook her head from side to side and opened her eyes.

Tessa shivered. She always had an uneasy feeling when Ms. Jasmine stared right through her like that, but she knew it was an honor to have a spiritual professor of her reputation spend extra personal time with her. Ms. Jasmine had mentioned once in passing that she could charge eighty dollars an hour for private lessons if she was working at a spiritual direction service.

"I haven't told anyone," Tessa continued, "and I'm not sure how to describe this . . . but the last time we did the labyrinth with our class—the winter solstice walk—I felt as if I was in a shower of white light, just like you said might happen to some people. At first I thought it was the snowflakes reflecting the light from our candles, but the light slowly entered my head and flowed down to my feet. I felt as if I was . . . bathed in light. Even though it was below zero and freezing, I felt warm, and time seemed to stand still. I forgot about everyone and everything else."

Ms. Jasmine smiled and nodded. She was pleased to see this girl far more open to enlightenment than the others seemed to be.

"Do you think that was the divine illumination you've been talking about . . . where Jesus meets us in the center of the labyrinth? Is this the place St. Teresa of Avila wrote about? Is this the center of the castle of our souls?"

Ms. Jasmine took a long breath and leaned forward. "Tessa," she began slowly, "you have learned a great deal since you came here. Now here is what I think. I believe these experiences you have been having are definitely divine. I know it is from the Master Jesus, because hearing about your experience fills me with peace and tranquility. It also reminds me of something else."

She took another sip of tea and set the cup on the floor, deep in thought. "Some who have been enlightened like this . . ." She paused, then spoke more slowly with each word, "have called this . . . the middle eye of the labyrinth. God has His eye on you, my child. You are the apple of His eye."

Tessa felt her eyes well up with tears.

"If only more of our students could be so remarkably connected with their Christ consciousness. I am so pleased. Before we end our session together today, we must have a prayer!"

Tessa was good with that. How much she had changed since she first arrived at this school! How much she had matured! God had chosen her and was even speaking to her personally through her daily spiritual disciplines. The spark she thought had died long ago was now being rekindled. Nothing was quite as exhilarating as that. She decided she would open herself completely to all He had to give her.

Ms. Jasmine came and stood behind her. Tessa waited.

"Aren't you . . . going to pray?"

"I already am," Ms. Jasmine whispered, "silently. You may close your eyes and concentrate on the light within you. Praying is a skill we must all learn to actualize. Visualize Christ here in this room."

"Oh. OK."

Tessa thought she could sense a presence moving around her . . . Ms. Jasmine's hands, she presumed, as she could hear the tinkling of her jewelry . . . and then a strange thing happened. She felt a prickly sensation begin in her head and move downward through to the end of her fingertips. Her hands felt warm, and she felt something well up inside her, like a lump forming in the throat, only it came from deeper within.

"Wha . . . what is that?" she asked, startled, not sure whether to be fearful or to welcome this new sensation. Suddenly, she had the same doubt she'd experienced the first time she did a lectio divina reading in the courtyard of the school, when she'd thought someone had called her name, but she had been alone. It was also like the first time she'd walked the labyrinth last September and thought she'd felt a presence when she reached its center and heard a voice saying, "Don't be afraid." Tessa hadn't been sure whether she could trust her feelings, or the voices.

"It's the divine energy of the Spirit's healing touch you are sensing, my dear." Ms. Jasmine always had a comforting answer.

"Ohhh! That's amazing! Ms. Jazz, I was wondering . . . do you ever sense the feeling, like a presence, or that your soul is, like, weightless? Maybe that's a dumb question."

Ms. Jasmine was quiet for a minute, as if listening for the answer before she gave it. "Ah yes, this is what St. Teresa meant when she wrote in the Fifth Mansion of *The Interior Castle* that "as soon as the soul, by prayer, becomes entirely dead to the world, out it flies like a lovely little white butterfly!"

It seemed Ms. Jasmine had memorized the whole book.

"She also spoke of a presence we may sometimes feel is near us, even if we cannot see anyone. 'Is it Christ, or His glorious Mother, or a saint? . . . The soul will recognize which saint has been sent by God to be its helper or companion.' In the same way, you will learn to discern the presence, but you must trust yourself, Tessa. Know your true self. Soak in the peace and tranquility. It is in the center of your soul where He speaks to you."

"Ms. Jazz, didn't St. Teresa pray to Mary? My roommate always says this stuff is so . . . Catholic and can be traced back to Hinduism. I'm not sure what I should say to her."

She didn't see the startled look on Ms. Jasmine's face behind her. "A common misconception," she said nonchalantly. "Your friend will soon learn the truth. We are addressing that this semester in our spiritual formation class."

"She's . . . not going to be taking it. I've seen her schedule."

"It's required."

"She's in the missions program, and they don't require it. Besides, Mr. Goldsmith told her they weren't in favor of—"

"Sam Goldsmith is young and new to the school. He has much to learn." Ms. Jasmine sighed. "I'll have to look into that loophole for next year. How many other students are not getting proper training?" This was exactly the type of problem of which STI had warned her. There were ways to deal with these people who didn't understand spiritual things. She must solve the problem quickly, before it got out of hand. First, she must answer Tessa's question. She walked to the cushion where she'd left her nearly empty teacup, picked it up, turned to face Tessa, and looked her straight in the eye.

"Tessa, dear, we must remember the words of Teresa of Avila." She spoke slowly and clearly. "That dear saint suffered much to learn this great lesson—that Christians who understand the inner life will always encounter obstacles which prevent them from achieving absolute union with God. These obstacles can come in many different forms, some of them evil. The Pharisees opposed Jesus for claiming he had found union with the Father. In the same way, I want you to realize that those who have not been enlightened as you and I have will usually oppose what we are doing. They want to put God in a box. Their faith is based on fear. Do you understand?"

"Uh, yeah . . . ." Tessa felt a little light-headed, almost euphoric. She was trying to remember what Gramps had once told her about the Pharisees, something about them wanting to stone Jesus for blasphemy because He claimed to *be* God, not just that He had found union with Him. It was all so foggy now. Her hands still tingled. This session had seemed strange and scattered, but that wasn't surprising. After all, that was just the kind of person Ms. Jasmine happened to be.

Ms. Jasmine sat down and sipped the last of her cold tea before she recited her usual closing prayer about leaving the castle. She found these double sessions very draining, and they always made her headaches worse. "We're finished for today," she said, massaging her temples. "Have a blessed weekend. Oh, and I'll see you at the labyrinth Sunday afternoon, right?"

The bangles on Ms. Jasmine's wrist jingled as she made the sign of the cross and blew out the candle. The smoke wafted up to the ceiling, catching the last rays of the setting sun before it vanished behind the distant horizon.

LABYRINTH

# ANGELS AND VOICES

SPAIN, 1565

THE cell was cold. There was no table or chair. Only a rough, straw mattress in the corner provided any reprieve for the room's sole occupant. A barefoot nun in a clean but worn habit of coarse serge knelt near the window. The last glimmer of evening light softened the lines on her aging face. Her sparse ink supply allowed no rewriting, but there was no need to reread the lines she had already written. Having commanded her to record her experiences, her confessors would weigh her story on the Inquisition's scale of heresy.

Some said the voices she heard in her head were of the devil. But Teresa was desperate to explain that these revelations she received were from the Lord! It was the Lord who granted her these great favors and visions which she called ecstasy. *They humble the soul*, thought Teresa, *strengthening and helping it to despise this life.*

During these experiences, she seemed to receive a clearer understanding of the Lord's rewards. Yet, she struggled with the fear these visitations also brought. She could no longer resist them or keep them a secret. Not only were the revelations themselves frightening, but visionaries like herself were often burned at the stake. Since her writings would remain in the hands of her Inquisitors for some time, she must choose her words carefully, yet tell the truth.

Dipping her quill in the inkstand, she continued to write about her life, pausing only to rub her arthritic shoulder now and then. This was to be her final writing. She was working on chapter twenty, trying to explain the difference between union and rapture and their effects:

"It seemed to me, when I tried to make some resistance, it was as if a great force beneath my feet lifted me up. I know of nothing with which to compare it; but it was much more violent than the other spiritual visitations, and I was therefore as one ground to pieces; for it is a great struggle, and, in short, of little use, whenever our Lord so wills it. There is no power against His power."

As Teresa wrote, the light grew dim. She lit her candle, then continued to write on the parchment set on the window ledge:

"Further, I confess it threw me into great fear, very great indeed at first; for when I saw my body thus lifted up from the earth, how could I help it? Though the spirit draws the body upward after itself and that with great sweetness, if unresisted, the senses are not lost; at least, I was so much myself as to be able to see I was being lifted up. The majesty of Him who can effect this so manifests itself, that the hairs of my head stand upright."

Deep in thought, she gazed at the candle's flame. How could she possibly describe rapture and detachment with pen and paper? Mere words were not enough to explain the spiritual marriage she had experienced. How could she even speak of the intense pain that accompanied the sweetness of her visions and revelations, the great shocks she would feel when her Lord threw her into a trance, or the indescribable desire, which pierced her soul until it rose above itself. The days that followed such ecstasy never failed to make her feel as if all her bones had been pulled out of joint.

"I have to say that, when the rapture was over, my body seemed frequently to be buoyant, as if all weight had departed from it; so much so, that now and then I scarcely knew that my feet touched the ground. Yet during the rapture itself, the body is very often as if it were dead, perfectly powerless. It continues in the position it was in when the rapture came upon it—if sitting, sitting; if the hands were open, or if they were shut, they will remain open or shut."

But she wasn't the only one. There were others, even in this place, to whom her Lord was granting the same special graces as the ones He had granted her. Others too had experienced raptures so deep that they would appear as though dead or in a trance, sometimes for days.

As she continued to recall her own experiences, she wrote about the priest who told her God had sent her so much sickness because she did no penance and he had ordered her to practice acts of mortification. During one such time of obedience, her spirit was carried out of her body in such a state of ecstasy that she heard words instructing her not to have conversations with men, but with angels.

She described the angel she had seen in bodily form . . .

"He was not large, but small of stature, and most beautiful—his face burning, as if he were one of the highest angels, who seem to be all of fire: they must be those whom we call cherubim. I saw in his hand a long spear of gold, and at the iron's point, there seemed to be a little fire. He appeared to me to be thrusting it at times into my heart and to pierce my very entrails; when he drew it out, he seemed to draw them out also, and to leave me all on fire with a great love of God. The pain was so great, it made me moan; and yet so surpassing was the sweetness of this excessive pain, that I could not wish to be rid of it. The soul is satisfied now with nothing less than God. The pain is not bodily, but spiritual; though the body has its share in it, even a large one."

In the quietness of her room, Teresa had often found herself falling into a deep trance, later pondering the exquisite state of bliss she experienced during these mysterious episodes. However, lately, she found herself losing control. For example, she could no longer prevent them, even when she was in the company of others. They all knew. Some were even sworn to secrecy. But did they know how she had recently grown to fear these times? Increasingly, she struggled to resist these frightening instances when her body was raised from the ground as she prayed. Yet it was no use. She was helpless to stop it.

Teresa slowly straightened and rubbed her stiff joints. She turned to gaze at the crucifix hanging on the wall of her cell as it reflected the candlelight. Her pen rolled across the ledge of the window where she had laid it and dropped onto the stone floor as she grabbed her rosary and began counting the beads, repeating the evening prayer. Immediately, a familiar burning sensation began to grow deep within her, welling upward in surges. It was happening again . . . She grabbed hold of the ledge and began frantically to pray that no one would come through the door and restrain her again.

14

## Jacob Searches for Answers

"Get down from there, Daisy!" Margaret scolded. "You know you're not supposed to be up there!" The dog was up on her hind legs, trying to sneak a chocolate chip cookie from the plate Jacob left unattended beside his armchair.

The microwave beeped. Margaret returned to the kitchen and poured the steaming hot milk into her favorite cup. She added a drop of pure almond flavoring and gave it a quick stir before walking back down the hallway in her fuzzy pink slippers. The *click, click, click* of Daisy's toenails on the linoleum followed closely behind her.

"Must be the first February in half a century that a Stokes seed catalog has lain there unopened in the Brown family household," she said to herself as she went past the study and noticed the large catalog, still in its plastic wrapping, sticking out from under a stack of untouched mail on the oak desk. Jacob was methodically shuffling through some papers. Margaret set down her cup and paused at the hallway mirror beside the study door. She tightened the belt on her terry cloth robe. Satisfied, she reached for her cup and continued to the living room. She stood silently at the window and peered into the darkness.

"Lord," she whispered thankfully, "You are sooo good. Thank You for the warm, safe, and comfortable home You have blessed us with."

She turned and walked to the woodstove, picking up a dropped tissue on the floor. She opened the door of the stove and tossed the tissue inside. During the cold winter months, she often stood there with her back to the hot stove, savoring the warmth it provided. She stood there now for a moment, before making her way back to the kitchen. As she passed the study, she noticed her husband had closed the door and was talking loudly to someone on the phone. She pressed her ear to the wood door. Daisy sat down at her feet and tilted her head.

"That is not true, and you—of all people—should know it, Frank!"

Frank Johnson, the president of Flat Plains Bible College. Margaret knew then that trouble was brewing.

"I've been looking into this spirituality. It's the same thing Buddhists and Hindus practice . . . My problem? What if something one of your students hears in this 'silence' opposes what God's Word actually says? I hear that some of them are being taught to visualize Jesus and have nice conversations with Him—or it—on a white sandy beach! . . . What! . . . Well, that's what I read about today on the Flat Plains student blog. Listen, you are walking on thin ice here—this is not what the Bible teaches about prayer! It is summoning up spirit guides, which God has forbidden us to do."

Suddenly, the door flew open, and Jacob stormed out to the kitchen with the phone to his ear. He didn't even notice his wife standing beside the door, pretending to straighten her hair in the mirror. Margaret picked up her cup and disappeared down the hall, pausing just around the corner as she listened attentively.

"Sure, I know their experiences are real, but that's not the issue. I don't question that. But just because something really happens and feels good doesn't mean it is from God. Didn't Paul say that Satan poses as an angel of light? . . . Well, how does that happen? Think, Frank. Think! Frank, your father knows me. I don't get upset over nothing. Ask him . . . Well, our granddaughter told me the names of some of the authors she is reading. Some of them are dead mystics. Is Flat Plains becoming some kind of school of mysticism? . . . I didn't think so. Well then, why is she reading books written by these people? And exactly who, may I ask, is this Ms. Jasmine person anyway?"

Jacob poured himself another coffee and rapidly stirred in the cream, sloshing some of it onto the counter before continuing to argue and wave his right hand. He carried his cup back to the study, sat down on his leather swivel chair by the computer desk, and listened impatiently to the man on the phone.

"I don't care if she was very popular with the students in the other college," he finally responded, a little too loudly. "And I don't care if enrollment is up this year. Moreover, may I ask why there is an outdoor labyrinth smack dab in the middle of the soccer field? . . . How do I know you have a labyrinth? Well, I'm looking at it on Google Maps right now, that's how. Frank, some folks may regard me as just an old Bible thumper, but I happen to be one who knows how to navigate the Internet . . . No Frank, that is not true. The labyrinth is not just another way to pray. It is another way to teach that all paths supposedly lead to God. It's paganism! We are not to worship like the pagans."

"What's that you said? . . . You have a meeting? Yes, yes, I understand. But I intend to talk to you more about this later, Frank. And I'll want some answers." Jacob Brown hung up the phone with more force than he intended.

"Forty years old and thinks he knows everything. Maybe the poor man is having a mid-life crisis or something," Jacob muttered with dismay, making his way back to the kitchen.

Margaret listened to her husband mumbling in the kitchen awhile longer before she decided to go throw two more logs into the woodstove. She then went upstairs to watch the evening news in bed with her hot milk and Daisy. For the last two weeks, she'd gone to bed alone every night. Jacob had been staying up late in his study, past midnight in fact, researching on-line, and e-mailing "his people," as he called them. He told Margaret he had to be absolutely sure before he did anything. Even so, she was troubled and quietly hoped he wasn't overreacting.

Whenever Margaret asked him questions, he'd get a mournful look in his eyes and simply say, "Just keep praying for our Teresa." In the meantime, she'd taken half a dozen trips to the library and the bookstores, bringing home certain books that he had marked on his list.

That evening, Jacob had brewed an extra strong pot of coffee and parked himself at one end of the long kitchen table, now stacked high with neat piles of books and DVDs. The first book he picked up was called *The Third Spiritual Alphabet*. The owner of the esoteric used bookstore had told Margaret when she'd gotten it that it was the book St. Teresa of Avila had relied on as her guide. Margaret had repeated his words to Jacob when she'd given him the book that morning. Now he browsed through its musty pages, skimming sentences that caught his eye.

"Hmmm . . . the Golden Age of Spanish Mysticism . . . transport of the . . . what? Transport of the soul?" Jacob took a gulp of his coffee. "How can this be?"

The book had other strange-sounding things written in it too. Things about rekindling, spiritual ascension, silence, and the prayer of recollection that invites the exterior person into solitude. According to the author, solitude was where the soul experienced sublime union with God, induced by an exercise that apparently required strenuous mental discipline.

"'Retiring into oneself is preliminary to rising above oneself . . .' What kind of craziness is this?" muttered Jacob. His stomach began churning, and he was feeling a bit queasy. "Mastering the art of solitude, my foot! More like wizardry."

He laid the book aside and picked up another, *The History of Christianity*. Jacob checked the table of contents and turned to the section on the sixteenth century. *Aha, there she is again, this mystical nun from Spain.*

Jacob read about Teresa of Avila suffering greatly from illness. It was believed her fevers and fainting spells were due to tuberculosis. Often suffering from "noise in the head," she turned to the prayer of quiet she had learned from her uncle. Many times Teresa would concentrate so deeply in her devotions and prayer that she felt she was outside of her body. Teresa's health grew worse until the summer of 1539 when she fell into a coma and was thought to be dead. Eventually she recovered, but over the following eighteen years, she experienced many transitory mystical experiences.

Evidently, in her earlier years, Teresa of Avila had experienced periods of something she called "spiritual ecstasy," with the help of a devotional book titled *The Third Spiritual Alphabet.*

"Hmm . . . what exactly is this spiritual ecstasy she's talking about?" wondered Jacob aloud. He rose from the kitchen bench and went to his office, swiveled his chair to face the computer, and Google searched it, clicking on the first site that came up, an online encyclopedia.

"Listen to this Margaret!" he called loudly to his wife, unaware that she'd gone to bed ahead of him. He began to read:

> Definition of Ecstasy: Religious ecstasy is an altered state of consciousness often accompanied by visions. It is characterized by reduced external awareness and increased interior awareness. Ecstatic experiences can be brief, although some last several days. During ecstasy, perceptions of time, space, and self disappear and are replaced with a general feeling of euphoria. These experiences are often recurring in some individuals.

As he started to comprehend the seriousness of the situation, Jacob grew angry. He felt Frank had not been honest with him. It actually seemed he'd been deceptive. "That young so-and-so! We have financially supported that school for thirty years, thinking all along that everything was all right. Goodness, I went to Bible college with his father. I wonder if *he* knows what his son is allowing into that school."

Jacob shut down his computer and walked slowly up the stairs.

"Margaret," he said as he crawled into bed, "we have to get Tessa out of there!"

"I know, JB," Margaret responded quietly, wakened from a light sleep, "but you have to find a way to talk to her that won't frighten her away. She really seems to care about this teacher, Ms. Jasmine. And she's enjoying school. I don't think it's going to be easy persuading her to leave."

The clock on the mantel chimed once. Was it already that late? Suddenly Jacob sat back up in bed.

"Please, dear," Margaret said sleepily.

"Just one more thing," he answered. He slipped on his robe, pushed his feet into his slippers, and returned to the study. As he waited for his computer to come back to life, he tried to remember a word he had read on a Christian research website. He had seen a chart listing symptoms identical to those experienced by St. Teresa and other mystics during ecstasy. If his suspicions were correct, the students of Flat Plains were in far greater danger than he'd first imagined. He found the site again and searched for the chart. The word he was looking for was a word he had never heard before.

"If only I could remember what it was . . . Now where was it?" he asked himself impatiently. "Ah, there it is . . . Kun . . . kunda . . . kund-a-lini."

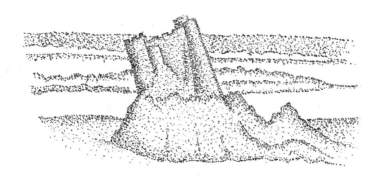

## Symptoms

March 12

"YOU know you will be leaving on Friday the thirteenth, don't you?" Tessa said.

Katy laughed. "Teresa Dawson, you aren't superstitious, are you? Remember, the Lord tells us we are not to be afraid."

"Are you going to bring the orphans clothes or money?" Tessa asked, changing the subject to cover her embarrassment. She watched Katy tightly roll every T-shirt she had and stuff them all into her backpack. She was leaving with her missions class for South America early the next morning.

"We are bringing tons of food, shoes, clothes, and lots of Bibles," Katy replied. "We'll not only be able to clothe and feed them, we can share Jesus with these kids, for sure. 'Go ye into all the world,' as the Bible says." The joy in Katy's heart made her face shine and her eyes sparkle.

Tessa and Katy were opposites, but they did share a common interest. Although Tessa's courses were teaching her to enjoy the silence and stillness, she was also learning to care about the earth's issues. Things like poverty and sustainability. The vivacious, talkative Katy also had compassion for the poor and needy in third-world countries. And of course, they were both orphans. Tessa had finally admitted to Katy one evening that she had lost her parents too. Their stories were very different, but it cemented a common bond between the two girls. Tessa thought it admirable that Katy was going to be working at an orphanage in some faraway village in some faraway country.

"Anyway, you were saying?" Tessa changed the subject again. Katy talked excessively about the Bible. One thing for sure, Tessa knew Katy really believed in what she preached. And sometimes, Tessa felt a twinge of envy—if only she could have faith like that. "When you came in you were talking about something called . . . canaloni? Sounds like some kind of Italian pasta."

"Kundalini. It's the serpent power that is stirred when people who meditate open up their chakras," said Katy.

"Open up their shocks? Say what?" Tessa asked, perplexed.

"No, chakras. Like their spiritual energy."

"Uh-huh. And you know this . . . how exactly?" Tessa raised her eyebrows questioningly. Did Katy really know everything, or did she just believe everything she read?

"Sam, I mean Mr. Goldsmith, our missions professor was telling us this," said Katy between blowing green bubbles. "He has been to India and said this is what he saw, and we might come across it in South America. Gum, yes? Mint flavor. My new favorite."

"You might come across . . . green gum? . . . oooooooh . . . scary!" Tessa replied good-naturedly, with a smile.

"No. We might come across people manifesting the symptoms of kundalini serpent power. Gum, yes?" Katy held out her newly opened pack of gum.

"No thanks."

"No?" Katy continued holding out the pack of gum. Tessa wondered if Katy ever noticed she didn't like chewing gum.

"No thank you, really. So . . . what about this kundalini? You said there are certain symptoms."

"Yes, that is correct. Our professor was telling us about a friend of his named Nathan who allowed somebody on a prayer team to lay hands on him and pray for him. Well, what Nathan didn't know was this person had been involved in spiritualism earlier in his life and was still dabbling in it."

"So what happened?"

"So then, this Nathan person started . . ." Katy's voice grew muffled as she searched under her bed for her camera's battery charger.

"This Nathan person started what?"

"Oh. Here it is. Yes, he started to be fearful, and he began having weird symptoms. It was really bizarre. He remembered that when this guy prayed for him, he felt sparks coming from his head to his hands, and felt something rise up inside him. And after that, he could never get this one song out of his head: 'Hell's . . . Jingle Bells.'"

"That would be 'Hell's Bells,'" Tessa corrected. Her former high school friends had really liked that song. They used to play it on the bus so loudly she could hear it coming from their headphones. But she had never liked the song.

"Anyway, this Nathan was not a Christian at the time, but that experience scared him, so he accepted Jesus Christ and got saved! He realized how wrong he had been, and he repented of these things. Praise be to God! Now Mr. Goldsmith says that Nathan is studying to be a youth pastor."

"So . . . that was in some little jungle village, right?"

"What was?"

"That he got chanted over by some village witch doctor."

"No, it was here in a church."

"Here, in North America?"

"Yes. In a youth group. In a church about twenty miles from here. And so the symptoms he experienced from this laying on of hands were exactly the same as the serpent awakening symptoms that Sam, I mean, Mr. Goldsmith, has been telling us about. It is very common in countries where they practice occultic spirituality, Eastern meditation and yoga, or shamanism."

"And the symptoms are . . ." Tessa sounded increasingly alarmed.

"Here, I will read them to you." Katy reached for a sheet in her notebook, and read aloud from her notes:

> Muscle twitches, prickly feelings, tingling, intense heat or cold, shaking, jerking, feeling a force from within moving one's body in unusual ways or pushing one into postures, hyperactivity, altered eating or sleeping patterns, fatigue, racing heartbeat, chest pains, headaches, numbness in the limbs (often the left foot or leg)—

"Katy, do you always believe everything you hear?" Tessa was surprised at the shrill tone of her own voice. Her heart began beating faster with each symptom that Katy read. "I mean, this *is* the twenty-first century, you know, not the Dark Ages, and things like this may happen in the movies, or in the jungles of voodoo land, but you can't just go around repeating stories you hear about some friend of a friend of a friend and scaring people half to death!"

Tessa snatched the paper from her roommate, crumpled it into a ball, and threw it on the floor before her friend could read anymore. Then she stomped out the room and slammed the door behind her. She hoped her display of anger would disguise her alarm at what Katy had been reading to her.

She didn't dare tell Katy that Ms. Jasmine had been teaching her hatha yoga. Or that the school's spiritual formation class had gone to a sweat lodge to study Native American spirituality where a very friendly shaman taught them mantric chanting. She also didn't dare tell Katy that the kundalini symptoms she had just read were glaringly evident in Ms. Jasmine—and half the SF class for that matter.

LATER THAT NIGHT

TESSA turned the lights on and glanced at the clock again. It was almost 11:00 p.m. and Katy was still at her missions meeting. She curled up under her blanket with Sassy II and shook off her nervous tension as she replayed the morning's conversation in her mind. "Kundalini serpent power," Tessa whispered. "Yeah right. What a bunch of garbage."

Finally, she drifted off to sleep and began to dream again. Tessa dreamed she was riding her horse to the same castle she always dreamt about. A hard and icy rain poured down, and twisted vines had grown over much of the castle walls. Her horse skittishly sidestepped across the slippery drawbridge and into the courtyard. Tessa dismounted onto the muddy ground. The drawbridge heaved upward and slammed shut behind her with a thundering crash. Picking a yellow flower from one of the vine's tendrils, she raised it to her nose to smell its fragrance. Strangely, it had no scent. She slid the dainty wet flower into her hair and ran to the castle's main entry. Removing her dripping cloak, she dropped it on the floor and immediately began searching for a candle. She was wet and cold, and it was getting dark. In the gray, dusky light, she noted that the doors to the first four rooms in the castle's hallway stood ajar. She quickly entered and searched each one . . . but couldn't find a candle anywhere. She noticed, to her dismay, that the doors to the adjacent rooms were all bolted shut. Suddenly, she stiffened. She heard the sound of singing. A lulling, chanting song seemed to be coming from somewhere behind the lengthening shadows.

Looking up the narrow stairwell of the watchtower, she saw light shining under the door of the room at the top of the stairway. She raced up the spiral stone steps, two at a time. Breathlessly, she reached for the iron latch on the door. It felt cold as she turned it. The rusty hinges creaked loudly as the door swung open, instantly flooding the stairwell with bright light. Tessa squinted and then froze at what was before her. Forcing its way through the tower's windows, the vine had grown into the room and was sending its creeping tendrils across its walls and winding them through the rafters overhead. In the center of the room stood a round table covered with candles beside a pot of hot tea. Tessa shivered. Shaking, she reached for the cup of hot tea to warm her hands, but before she could grasp it, the heavy vine suddenly dropped onto her body from the rafters with an audible thud. Tessa screamed. The vine began to move, wrapping itself tightly around her feet.

"Help me!" she shrieked. But no one heard her. She was alone. She felt something wrapping itself around her arms. Tessa watched in terror as she suddenly realized it was not a vine but a long serpent coiling itself around her chest. Slowly, it began to constrict its strong muscles until she could barely breathe. She felt as if life itself was being sucked out of her, and she knew she was about to die.

In the distance, she heard a voice calling, "Tessa, you are mine, come out."

KATY walked into the dorm room after her missions meeting and threw her keys on the nightstand. Tessa was asleep in bed but had left every light in the room turned on. It wasn't unusual for her to fall asleep with her bedside lamp on. Katy was always the last one to turn the lights off each evening, but lately Tessa's lamp was on again in the morning when she woke up. Perhaps Tessa was accidentally hitting the remote control in her sleep, reasoned Katy. Surely, her roommate wasn't afraid of the dark!

Careful not to wake her, Katy tiptoed around the room flicking off all the lights, except the one by her own bed. Tessa mumbled something unintelligible. *Is she awake?* Katy wondered. *I hope so.* After all, it would be nicer to say good-bye to her friend now than tomorrow at five a.m. Quietly she leaned over and shone her book light on Tessa's face and was alarmed to see she was soaked in sweat and moaning incoherently.

"Tessa," Katy whispered, "are you sick?"

Suddenly, Tessa bolted upright, eyes wide open, and shouted, "Somebody help me!"

"AAAHHHH!!" Katy screamed and jumped back. The book light clattered to the floor and went out.

Tessa looked around the room in a daze. She ran her hands over her familiar flannelette pillowcase and reached for Sassy II. It was just a dream. Startled to see Katy standing over her, she cried out, "What are you doing!?" She turned her bedside lamp on.

"What am *I* doing? What are *you* doing? You are the one who scared me half to death! We just watched a video about occultic practices in the deep, dark jungles of —!"

"Jungles . . . vines . . . I . . . I was dreaming." Tessa grabbed her clock radio and turned it toward her. It was just past midnight, Friday the thirteenth, and her pajamas were soaked with sweat.

"That was some scary dream, girl. You will tell me about it, yes?" Tessa sat on the edge of her bed and reached for her water bottle.

"I've been having this same dream ever since . . . ever since . . ." She stopped herself.

Should she tell Katy what had been happening? How could she explain what she had seen two days ago when she had walked into the Sacred Space an hour early for her evening session? Ms. Jasmine's favorite CD had been playing the Taizé chant. The room was dark, except for the single candle that had almost burned to the bottom of its holder. Ms. Jasmine was sitting cross-legged on her huge cushion, the one fringed with red and gold tassels, and as usual, eyes glazed, a cup of Chai tea beside her. The only thing was, Ms. Jasmine was there, but she wasn't. It was as if she had left her body or was in a trance. Tessa had turned and quietly slipped away. Nobody else had seen her. But how could she tell Katy that? And how could she tell Katy that she herself was beginning to have some strange experiences? She was too scared to talk about it, but too afraid not to.

"Katy," she began, sick at heart, "tell me again what you know about that serpent power awakening thing."

## TERESA WRITES THE INTERIOR CASTLE

In my Father's house are many mansions: if it were not
so, I would have told you. I go to prepare a place for you.
And if I go and prepare a place for you, I will come again,
and receive you unto myself; that where I am, there ye
may be also. John 14: 2–3

SPAIN, 1577

"As you wished, I have written everything I know." Teresa
nervously set her papers on the table before her confessors. The
religious directors had ordered her to write about her method of
mental prayer—her interior castle—as a book of instruction for
her nuns. She had been careful to refer to herself in the third person
throughout the book, as she was always under the watchful stare of
her superiors. It had been a difficult task.

"But it has only been two months! You have completed it
already?" the priest said, staring in amazement at the pile of papers
stacked neatly before him.

"I have not only described how the soul is a castle, but also
how a journey into the soul is a series of seven interior rooms, or
inner courts, within the castle that one must pass through by way
of prayer. Each chamber is a different stage of the journey. Read it
and you shall see."

The priest browsed through the first pages while Teresa rubbed the back of her neck. Her joints ached, her head hurt, and she was exhausted after finally completing the most important portion of her written work, so far. It had been an extremely troubling time in her life. During the last two months, her superiors had required this writing, yet she had also been expected to fulfill her regular duties, despite severe weakness. Added to that was the torment of living in fear of the next revelation or rapture that would come upon her without warning.

"So tell me, these first three rooms, or mansions, as you call them," asked the priest, with undisguised fascination, "what stage of the journey do they symbolize?"

"The first three mansions are for those who are just beginning to learn the practice of mental prayer."

"And the next ones?"

Weak from exhaustion, Teresa did not wish to explain. It had been difficult enough writing about these things with the turbulent noise that throbbed in her head: the roaring sound of rushing rivers and oddly, the whistling of birds pulsated continually in her mind. It was most disturbing when she was conscious of her faculties and her soul was not suspended in ecstasy. Whenever an ecstatic experience occurred, she believed it was from the top of her head that her spirit was released and moved out at great speed.

"The last four," she began slowly, trying to shut out the roar of a waterfall in her head, "are for those who have begun to experience the indwelling after having entered the spiritual realm. It is the fourth dwelling that is the turning point, and the one most souls enter. This is where one moves from mere meditation to contemplation. It is an interior awareness when God suspends the soul in prayer with rapture or ecstasy or transport."

"I see," said the priest, stroking his chin. "Here I see you have written about water and worms."

*Must they keep prodding?* She had done as they had asked, and there were chores to be done.

"Yes, like the spring that wells up filling every crevice, so is God's presence to one who reaches spiritual union. But one must be dead to the outward senses and alive to His Majesty, like a silkworm that dies to produce a little white butterfly. So is Divine union in the center of the castle."

How could she explain that although she had only mentioned seven inner mansions, there were many more rooms contained in each one, and courtyards with fountains, gardens, and labyrinths in which one could be consumed?

Teresa grew increasingly uncomfortable and longed to leave. Unaware of her misery, the priest abruptly rose to his feet.

"This will take some time to read," he said hastily, and escorted Teresa to the door.

"I pray it is satisfactory," she said humbly, trying not to reveal the tremendous pain in her head. "It is my strong desire to aid you in serving His Majesty. If the theologians examine my writings and find any error, it is only because of my ignorance. Perhaps I shall be in purgatory for writing this book, but I pray He shall free me from this and pardon my sins."

The priest nodded. "We will examine the work and speak to you soon."

The door closed behind Teresa. Her rough wool habit scraped her bare ankles with each step as she walked quickly down the dim hallway. Pausing before a statue of St. Joseph, she knelt and prayed, "I submit to the teachings of the Holy Catholic Roman Church, may the sovereign Master be praised."

Tired and aching, she made the sign of the cross and hurried back to the convent. Perhaps she could distract herself from the inner turmoil by spinning more wool.

## A Growing Concern

MARGARET'S sewing machine hummed as the bobbin filled up with brown thread. Teresa would love this new quilt waiting for her on her bed when she returned. It matched the colors in her attic bedroom perfectly. Margaret looked up and waited expectantly for Jacob to say something. He had just hung up the phone after a long distance call to another one of his old college buddies. Many of them had gotten married in the local church some forty years ago then settled in the area to work on their family farms.

"Well?" she said, taking her foot off the sewing machine pedal. The quilting could wait.

"It's absolutely true, Margaret," Jacob replied, unaware that he was pacing back and forth over the squeakiest part of the kitchen floor. "The boys over at Flat Plains Church say that last fall two new teachers were hired on staff at the college. One was the new woman who got that labyrinth built in the field. They say this woman goes by the name of Ms. Jasmine. The pastor asked her to give her testimony in their church one evening, and apparently, no one understood what she was talking about, but she had come off sounding very spiritual.

I don't know what's gotten into the heads of the good folks at that church. Sure, half of them fly south to Palm Springs every winter, but just because they aren't around full time is no reason to bury their heads in the sand and tolerate this kind of dangerous deception. That's what it is all right. Where do they think this labyrinth idea comes from?"

"But JB, the Thiessen's have paid for all their grandchildren's tuition. Dorothy's grandson Thomas is graduating this spring. He's going to be a youth pastor! And our church has always been a supporter—there must be some mistake. It's an old and trusted school. I'm sure they run everything past the conference and the board. Don't you think?"

"Well, if that's the case, then apparently we just can't judge a book by its cover anymore or a college by its name. Those days are gone, Margaret. As you know, I've been doing a lot of reading, even before all this started, and it's not just Flat Plains that is plainly falling away!"

Jacob pulled on his winter boots and parka, and pinched together the Velcro on Daisy's quilted jacket.

We're going to shovel snow," he said flatly, as he stepped outside into the crisp winter air. Daisy barked and jumped happily at the falling snowflakes, while following close behind him.

"Don't forget your woolen mitts! Oh dear." Margaret knew he always threw himself into physical work when he had a lot of thinking to do. She hadn't seen her husband look this upset since that unforgettable Thanksgiving Day twelve years ago when someone had stolen ten head of his prized cattle. Even then, he had quickly calmed down when she reminded him that God owned the cattle on a thousand hills. Jacob was not the kind of man who stayed angry for long.

But something told Margaret this was going to be different. She knew deep down that this time, much more was at stake than an investment in earthly riches. This was about eternity. Not only was their Teresa and other naïve students in danger, so was the sacred purity of the Gospel message as revealed in the Bible.

She picked up the phone and pushed the speed dial number labeled "prayer chain."

"Hello, Dorothy? I have a prayer request. A real big one. Are you sitting down? You know the college your grandson Thomas is attending? Yes, the one where we sent Teresa. Jacob and I have some concerns . . . No, no, it's not a campus romance. I wish it was just that. I'm afraid it's something far more serious."

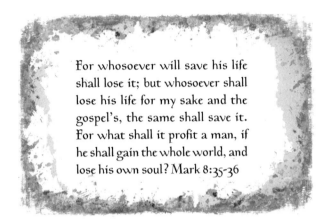

For whosoever will save his life shall lose it; but whosoever shall lose his life for my sake and the gospel's, the same shall save it. For what shall it profit a man, if he shall gain the whole world, and lose his own soul? Mark 8:35-36

## NEW YORK

MARCH 23

SNOW was lightly falling outside the window of an Internet café in New York City as an olive-skinned girl in her early twenties wearing shorts, sandals, and an Argentinian T-shirt quickly typed at a computer.

Dear Mom and Dad,

I will make this e-mail short. Finally got to a computer, and the rest of the team is all waiting their turn after me. We are between flights in an Internet café near the airport.

Just stopping over in New York. That wasn't our plan, but our flights got mixed up and so did our luggage. I lost some things, nothing too important. I know God has planned it this way for some odd reason. We'll be in Seattle tomorrow morning if it stops snowing here. Will be doing a few days of street ministry there.

Mission trip is wonderful so far! I've learned so much! We shared the Gospel—with a translator's help, of course—and led many people to Jesus. They are very steeped in idol worship. They worship statues and pray to the dead, and many are under control of the village shaman. On the last day, Sam led a woman to the Lord. Before that, she had been a very tormented woman, steeped in occult practices and witchcraft. Now, she is overflowing with joy and peace. Saw many more amazing things I cannot talk about until I am home.

Please pray for those who were saved.

Also have been worried about my roommate. The night before I left, she was in some trouble. Please pray for her.

Thank you for the birthday e-card. I still don't feel like I am 21. See you soon.

Love, Katarina

P. S. Give hugs to Rachel, Rebekah, Ruthie, Josh, Jeremy, little Joel, and number 8—hope I get home before she is born.

Katy checked the weather forecast, signed out, grabbed her backpack, and stood up.

"Looks like winter is soon going to be gone," she said to the girl behind her. "OK, you are next, yes?"

## BAD COUNSEL

But when ye pray, use not vain repetitions, as the
heathen do: for they think that they shall be heard for
their much speaking.—Jesus, Matthew 6:7

MARCH 23

"AND so, I'm really not sure what to think anymore about this
spiritual formation training," Tessa said softly. She felt very small and
insignificant sitting in front of the huge desk in the head counselor's
office. The walls were covered with hardwood panels, and on the
one with the credenza pushed against it hung a framed portrait of
a man staring down at her with knowing eyes. The counselor wrote
on a notepad with an expensive-looking gold pen. He had been at
Flat Plains for nearly five years and most of the students respected
him. Tessa had often heard him play the cello in the string quartet
during chapel for Monday meditations. He was a bachelor, but not
the kind the girls would flirt with. She wondered if he ironed his own
shirts every day, as he always wore a crisp white one under his sports
jacket. He had a few odd quirks but was generally kindhearted and
caring. Tessa didn't know why she felt so uncomfortable as she sat in
his office. The counselor analyzed the comments he'd been jotting
down. His notes said this girl had dark circles under her eyes and

seemed very nervous. She had no previous record of drug use and had never gotten into trouble at school.

"Miss Dawson, we realize it's an emotionally and spiritually demanding course. You have probably been working very hard. I see you stayed at school over the Christmas holidays as well as spring break last week to catch up on some course assignments. With the semester nearly over, the pressure will soon be off. Have you talked to your spiritual formation professor?"

"Well, she was the one who recommended that I be mentored by Ms. Jasmine. Naturally, I was excited about that, at first. Now, I'm not sure anymore. So I talked to the other counselor this morning, and she told me that you and Ms. Jasmine are the only people I need to talk to about my concerns."

"Did she now? Instead of speaking to me, have you talked to Dr. Winters first about your concerns?" He secretly wished Dr. Jasmine Winters hadn't been so casual with the students, allowing them to address her by her first name. It was simply disrespectful.

"Well, that's the problem. I'm not comfortable with that."

The counselor leaned forward on his oak desktop and looked at her over his black-rimmed glasses. "Well, apparently Dr. Winters is comfortable enough to have you all call her Ms. Jasmine. Now, could you tell me exactly why *you* are 'uncomfortable'?"

"It's like this. I . . . when I am in a session . . . I mean, when I did the sessions with Ms. Jazz, I mean Dr. Winters, strange things happen, I mean, happened." Tessa started to cry. "I'm sorry, I haven't been sleeping well."

Tessa felt her throat tightening. This wasn't easy for her. At first, in the beginning of the school year, everything was good. Really good, actually, and Tessa had soon become a keen and open-minded student. But later, she'd begun having reservations, even before Katy read her "the list." She couldn't say why, exactly, only that she'd started to feel vaguely suspicious and oddly unsettled about the whole thing. That was probably why she could never muster the courage to take it to the next level. And lately, her resistance seemed increasingly ineffective. She used to have control, but she didn't seem to have it anymore. Had the words of warning, the words she had so carelessly rejected, been right after all?

"What sort of strange things?" the counselor asked, interrupting her thoughts.

"Yes. Well, this may sound very, very weird, but I get a tingling, prickling sensation in my head and my hands, and sometimes all the way down to my feet."

"Has Dr. Winters been letting you drink her Yerba Mate? It sometimes has an . . . effect on certain people."

Tessa shuddered at the thought of the South American tea Ms. Jasmine sometimes drank through a metal straw. She thought the Yerba leaves looked and smelled like a wet horse stall.

"No. You don't believe me, do you?" She reached into her pocket and pulled out a folded, wrinkled paper. It was the list Katy had tried reading to her the other night. Later, when Katy wasn't there, Tessa picked it up, folded it neatly, and put it in one of her books. "I would like to read this to you. These are some symptoms that—"

"That you have?"

"Well, I might have some, but so does my friend Elise and at least half the class. But Dr. Winters has most of these. Can I just read this?"

"Have you been to see the school nurse?" he asked.

"I don't need a nurse!" she said too loudly, and remorsefully looked down at the floor. "Please . . ." she said quietly.

"Go ahead." The counselor leaned back in his chair.

"These are some of the symptoms I am talking about. It's only some of them."

Before coming there that day, she had highlighted certain symptoms on the list with a yellow marker, ones she had either experienced herself or saw or heard about in others, including Ms. Jasmine—especially Ms. Jasmine. She held the wrinkled paper in her clammy hands and began reading the symptoms she had marked:

Hearing sounds like a flute, waterfall, bees buzzing, ringing in the ears, inner voices, mental confusion, difficulty concentrating, emotional outbursts, uncontrollable laughing and crying, rapid mood shifts, fear, rage, heightened awareness, trances, sensations of heat or prickling in the hands and head, feelings of peace and tranquility, ecstasy, dreams or visions of spirit guides, out-of-body experiences, awareness of auras, chakras, healing powers, sensitivity—

"All right, all right. That's enough, I've got the point," the counselor interrupted. He pulled off his glasses, puffed a few breaths of hot air onto the lenses, and unfolded a clean white handkerchief to polish them.

"But I'm not finished. I—"

"Miss Dawson, look, I believe you. A few other students have reported minor things. But everything has an explanation. This is a very old school. Before we rule out the insulation or the lead paint, here's what I think. First of all, you have completed the required reading, am I correct?"

Tessa nodded.

"Then you must know that the ancient Christians who tapped into methods of prayer that the modern church has forgotten also describe many of the same experiences. What if these things, which you say make you fearful, are simply God's graces and favors being bestowed upon you? Rather than having a fear-based faith, we must open ourselves to God's voice. We must not shut the door to new forms of God's communication with us, Tessa. The Bible says, 'Shout to the Lord a new song!' We cannot put God in a box."

He reached behind him and pulled a book from his shelf. The title on the cover said *The Interior Castle*, but Tessa thought this one looked older and thicker than her copy, which was called *Selections from the Interior Castle*. He pushed up his thick-framed glasses and opened it to a page with a folded corner.

"As St. Teresa of Avila wrote, 'Our Lord is just as pleased today as He has ever been to reveal favors to his people, and I'm convinced that anyone who will not believe this closes the door to receiving them herself.' So you see, only those who believe and open the door will be the recipients of His revelations and favors!"

Tessa knew about that. She had written a paper on the Teresian prayer model. "Yes, I understand that concept. But something is not right, I'm telling you. One evening not long ago I arrived early at our mentoring session, and Ms. Jazz was . . . she was . . ."

"Tessa, Dr. Winters is a very spiritually disciplined person, and a fine role model. She does the fixed hours of prayer several times a day, and some people, when they find out, just don't understand. It's a classic case of fearing the unknown. I trust she has been training you to do your prayer exercises as well. May I ask how far you have gone in your quiet prayer time in regard to the inner rooms of the Teresian prayer model?"

"Well, I . . . I could never get past the fourth room," she said, sniffing. "The castle. It haunts me in my dreams. What I thought was beautiful is turning into a bad dream. It's just not lining up with . . ." She stopped in mid-sentence and thought about Katy and Gramps, and how they would often say that something was not "lining up with Scripture." "I guess I just don't know anymore if the voices I am hearing are from God or . . . I'm just . . . I'm very scared."

"Dear Tessa, I think I have just answered your own question." The counselor looked pleased with himself and assured her with a compassionate smile. "Now take a deep breath and listen to me carefully. Close your eyes . . . There, that's right. Now, do you remember how St. Teresa compared the doubts we have to reptiles? Let me read a little more from the fifth chapter." The way the counselor read reminded Tessa of the way Ms. Jasmine read—slowly, methodically, pronounced:

> In the prayer of quiet in the previous mansion, the soul needs to be very experienced before it can be sure what really happened to it. Did it imagine the whole thing? Was it asleep and dreaming? Did the experience come from God, or from the devil disguised as an angel of light? The mind feels a thousand doubts. And so it ought,

for as I said, we can be deceived in these mansions, even by our own nature. It is true that there is little chance of those poisonous creatures entering the Fourth Mansion, but slippery little lizards are small enough to slip in unnoticed. They do no harm, especially if we ignore them, but these little thoughts and fancies thrown out by the imagination can be annoying.

However active those lizards may be, they cannot enter into the Fifth Mansion. Here, neither the imagination, the understanding, or the memory has any power to prevent God's grace flowing into the soul.

The counselor closed the book and placed it on a stack of *Travel Mongolia* magazines. His chair creaked as he leaned back and took off his glasses again. "Tessa," he said, "perhaps you need to enter into the fifth room of the castle and allow God's grace to flow into your soul. You seem too focused on poisonous, negative thoughts, which you simply must choose to ignore. I suggest you contemplate Scripture more often through your lectio divina exercises."

Tessa nodded her head, folded the paper, and stood up. Her ears began to ring again. The book he had read from sounded different from the one she had. Why were they always quoting to her out of books? Gramps usually quoted the Bible, and he seemed to know a lot of it by heart. She wasn't sure if Ms. Jasmine even owned a Bible. If she did, Tessa had never seen it.

She was more confused than ever. Everyone here kept telling her to shut out the noises and go within herself. "There you will find your true self," they'd say. However, her true self was the part of her that was so confused. Gramps always said that God is not the author of confusion. For some reason, Tessa remembered that cold fall day at the retreat when they were instructed to go and find their true selves, and she found the woodsman instead. What was that verse he read? "Behold, thou desirest truth in the inward parts: and in the hidden part thou shalt make me to know wisdom."

She had no idea why she remembered that verse today, but how desperately she longed to know truth and have wisdom right now.

"May I go now?" she asked, rubbing her temples. "I . . . I have a really bad headache."

The counselor nodded and watched her walk to the door.

"Oh Tessa," he said, as if remembering something. "Could you do me a favor and go to the kitchen and pop a frozen macaroni and cheese in the microwave?"

*Macaroni? My life is in a shambles, and he wants macaroni?*

"Sure," she said numbly.

"Oh and Miss Dawson, one more thing," he said as she paused with her hand on the knob. "St. Teresa, your namesake, also said that a venomous reptile cannot live in the presence of divine light. If we are to be Christ followers, we must choose *not* to join the ranks of the spiritually uncivilized who refuse to be enlightened. Please keep this in mind."

Tessa gave a weak, "OK," then opened the door and stepped into the hall. The door swung shut behind her with a precise click. She watched as students walked past her to their classes, chatting and laughing happily as though everything was normal and there wasn't a care in the world. As for herself, she wondered if she was going mad. Nothing made sense anymore.

Back in the office, the counselor glanced at his watch. *Thank goodness she's gone,* he thought. It was nearly noon. Time for the Daily Office, the fixed hours of prayer Ms. Jasmine had taught them at their second staff retreat. He found that even five minutes spent centering down helped him get through a stressful day. Lately, more students like Tessa had begun to ask him too many difficult questions. Not to mention that paranoid old Mr. Brown who had been phoning and giving him a hard time. He was beginning to feel more than a little annoyed.

He locked his office door, put a Taizé worship CD into his Sony player and sat down in his chair again. Glancing up at the chart on his wall, he took a deep breath. He nearly had it memorized but wanted to be sure of the steps, so he read them again:

–Be attentive and open
–Sit still
–Sit straight
–Breathe slowly, deeply
–Close your eyes or lower them to the ground

Then he closed his eyes and slowly repeated the verse of the day from the Sacred Meditation website—

Be still and know that I am God.
Be still and know that I am God.
Be still and know . . .
that I am God . . .
that I am God . . .
that I am God.
That I am God,
I am God,
I am God,
I am God,
I am,
I am,
I am,
I am . . .

The noise in the hallway soon disappeared as Dr. Frank Johnson, head counselor and president of Flat Plains Bible College, shut out the sounds around him and slipped into a peaceful inner silence.

## TERESA'S TRAVELS

SPAIN, 1579

THE snow-capped tips of the Sierra de Gredos loomed above the small carriage drawn by a lone mule. Inside its curtained interior, a small group of nuns huddled together for warmth. Teresa could see her breath even when she covered her mouth with a cloth and coughed quietly. In spite of her graying eyebrows and a few lines, her face was still attractive for someone who had lived in such harsh conditions for many years. The extra blanket she wrapped around herself was not doing much good. An involuntary shiver shook her slim frame violently.

The carriage ride was long. To pass the time meaningfully, some of the nuns recited the rosary as the mule plodded on, pulling the carriage up and down hills through the muddy ruts along the rough path. The faithful beast had done well crossing the river, but darkness would soon fall, and they needed to reach their lodging before nightfall. The nuns were on their way to open a new Carmelite house under the direction of Sister Teresa. In this small convent, the nuns would be under a strict vow of poverty and silence, and would wear habits of coarse brown wool and sandals instead of shoes. Sister

Teresa's plan was to reform them from within into a completely contemplative, cloistered life.

When a wheel hit a large rock, the whole carriage lurched sideways. The nuns were used to the rough ride and held on. Beautiful deep valleys and clean rivers filled the mountain range, but the narrow paths were not always kept clear of fallen rocks.

"We needn't worry, daughters, our driver and his mule know the way. Now, where was I? Oh yes, I went back three times. We must learn persistence through trials. You see, twice as a young girl I had to return home due to my poor health. When my father eventually relented and gave the convent my dowry, I finally took my vows as Sister Teresa of Jesus.

"Have I told you that once I became so gravely ill," Teresa added, "and I was in such a state, they thought I was dead? They had already dug my grave and poured wax on my eyes. Though my soul had been transported outside my body, I awoke after four days but was partially paralyzed. Eventually I recovered, which I attribute to St. Joseph."

Medieval Walls of Avila

Surely, her prayers to the saint had made the difference and not the treatments she had endured at the hands of the village healer. She certainly bore no ill will against the woman who had tried to resuscitate her with dreadful and grisly home remedies that she could not bring herself to mention.

"My health has remained poor ever since," she continued for the benefit of the nuns. "Had I not read *The Third Spiritual Alphabet* as a mere girl of nineteen, I would not have learned about the transport of the soul and spiritual ascension. Only then, through my illness, did I open my soul to God and begin practicing mental prayer."

Teresa paused for a moment before saying, "Oh yes, sisters, the exterior person must learn to find silence and solitude in order to enter into the prayer of quiet. Only when we have become dead to the outward senses and the Lord Himself is perfectly recollected within can the powers of the soul be untied and awakened to God. This is the prayer of union, a delectable death which we can attain here and now in our mortal bodies."

One young nun sat outside the curtained carriage beside the driver. She was huddled in blankets, and listened to them talk. How well acquainted she was with Teresa's trances, which she referred to as the "transport of the soul." She had witnessed some of the most disturbing occurrences in Sister Teresa's life but had been vowed to secrecy. She hadn't been the only one in the choir loft that unforgettable day, waiting for the bell to ring, when they saw Teresa's body rise inexplicably about half a meter off the ground. She'd actually been off the ground! Sister Teresa's body had hung in mid-air, as Sister Anne had later recounted with fresh incredulity! This incident had quite terrified some of them. Since Sister Teresa's body had been trembling as well, Sister Anne had cautiously held her hands under the raised feet of Sister Teresa for the duration of the ecstasy. It had lasted nearly half an hour before she'd sunk to the floor and then stood among them, lucid once again. Teresa had turned to her calmly and quietly and asked how long she had been there, watching. It was then that Sister Anne had been sworn to secrecy, but that kind of secret wasn't the kind that could be kept quiet for very long.

There had been other incidents as well. Teresa's friend, a bishop, once saw her grab the bars of an altar grill during communion to prevent herself from rising into the air, as she cried out to be delivered from her ecstasy. Numerous times, and on different occasions, many others had also seen her raised from the ground. Sister Teresa had always called these experiences "Favors of His Majesty."

Suddenly the carriage turned sharply to the right, the mule pulling them over the bumpy road toward a light that glimmered in the distance. They would have to stay at an inn one more night. Teresa leaned toward the carriage window and parted the curtain to look outside.

"Oh Mother, perhaps we can beg some food to eat, something other than dry figs. That's all we've had to eat for days!" implored one of the young nuns. What she longed for was something of substance, but meat was forbidden in their life of perpetual abstinence.

"Daughters," Sister Teresa announced sternly, "let us not attempt to pamper ourselves, as we have only one more night to sleep at an inn. What grace His Majesty has bestowed upon us to allow this, that while yet in our mortal bodies, we may do penance so we need not suffer as long in purgatory!"

When the carriage finally stopped, the nuns gathered their bags and blankets and prepared to carry them into the inn. It would be good to get out of the cold, no matter how uncomfortable the accommodations might be or how much their hunger pangs gnawed in their stomachs.

"You will write down your experiences, Sister Teresa, won't you?" asked one devoted nun who readied herself to assist Teresa out of the carriage.

"Oh yes, I already have," Teresa answered, grabbing the hand of the young nun. "I was ordered to do so by the Inquisition. So reluctant was I to write about the interior castle . . . until I saw the beautiful crystal globe—"

"A globe, Mother?" the nun asked, a look of bewilderment in her eyes.

"A beautiful globe, in the shape of a castle. Seven mansions it contained, the seven chambers of the soul." She paused between her words, as if in a distracted manner, her eyes gazing into the night as if in a trance. "The innermost one being union with His Majesty, of course… the nearer one gets to the center, the stronger is the light … while outside its gates are snakes and toads and darkness."

The young nun shivered. "Perhaps your writings will be read by others one day . . . but this eve I beg of you to come out of the cold night air."

"Ah yes, my daughter," Teresa smiled faintly, speaking in a detached, faraway voice. "I've been told my writings have been deemed not to be heretical after all. They will be preserved and read, perchance, by others who desire the favors His Majesty bestows upon all those who seek His illumination, peace, and tranquility."

21

## A Difficult Phone Call

MARCH 23—MONDAY NIGHT

TESSA stood outside, shivering in the night air. The field behind the dorm was the best place to get a good signal on a cell phone. She was about to hang up after the fourth ring when a voice said, "Hello."

"Hi," Tessa said in an embarrassingly squeaky voice. "Uh, you don't know me. I'm a friend of Katy's—she gave me your phone number a few nights ago . . ."

"Sorry, I think you must have the wrong number."

"No wait! I mean, please. Katy is in Sam Goldsmith's class at Flat Plains Bible College."

There was a five-second pause of uncomfortable silence. Tessa could hear some shuffling and a cat meowing in the background.

"So you're the one I've been waiting to hear from. You must be Tessa."

"How do you know—"

"Sam sent me a text message ten days ago before he left for South America. He said you might be calling me."

"Well, I just need some advice. If you don't mind, I mean, I have some questions." Tessa felt awkward, but at the same time, she trusted the voice on the other end.

"I think I know your questions. They are the same questions I once had." The voice sounded so self-assured, so confident. "If you want to meet for coffee, I'll be driving through Flat Plains tomorrow."

"Uh, I don't think that will work. I don't have a car," Tessa said as she ran over the next day's schedule in her head. She hadn't actually expected to meet with this person. Maybe she shouldn't have called. *No, don't meet with him!* The voice inside her head shouted.

"Would you like me to stop by the campus tomorrow afternoon?"

"You mean here? At the college?"

"You're thinking you shouldn't have called me, right? Don't listen to those voices. Tessa, if it's what I think, more time is not an option."

Tessa's ears were ringing. She needed to decide. Now.

"OK." She tried to think of a safe spot to meet with a stranger. A safe, private spot out in the open.

Before she could reply, he said, "I'll see you tomorrow, about one o'clock, in front of the Thompson Building."

*Click.* That was all. Some guy she had mixed feelings about meeting, who seemed to know her every thought, was coming here to talk to her tomorrow afternoon. It might make her late for her session with Ms. Jasmine.

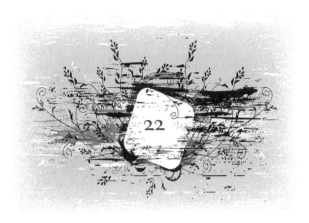

22

# The Light That Was Dark

*Take heed therefore that the light which is in thee be not darkness.* Luke 11:35

"YES, Mr. Foxe," said Jasmine over the phone in Dr. Johnson's office, "they've just arrived here at the Thompson Building in excellent condition, and thank you very much."

"Where would you like these, Dr. Winters?" asked a student who poked his head in the doorway.

"Take them straight down to the main floor to room 109. Use the elevator! And please, be very careful with the prints. They just arrived from Quiet Waters and cost our school a pretty penny."

Ms. Jasmine put the phone back to her ear. "And Mr. Foxe, thank you very much for giving us a discount for next fall's retreat! I can't wait to use your new Quiet Place. Yes, and give my regards to Opal, would you?"

At that moment, Frank Johnson charged into his office holding his microwaved lunch in his well-manicured hands and wearing a very stern expression on his face.

"Jasmine! Where have you been! I come back from spring vacation to find an invoice for two paintings costing six thousand dollars! Do you know what kind of trouble this will bring down on my head? I already have one of our supporters breathing down my neck, and just wait till the board hears about this! And would you mind taking your feet off my desk?!"

"Relax, Frank," said Jasmine as she put her legs down one at a time. She found the odor of processed cheese and macaroni to be nauseating. *The man has no taste for the finer things of life,* she brooded. "So I was out of town for a few days on ... business. Don't worry about it. Your friends, the Foxes, are going to give us a great deal on the retreat facilities next year. Just think! We get to take the entire staff to the new Quiet Place for half price! And they said they'd throw in a free spiritual direction session for everyone on staff here, which they can have anytime, at their convenience. What could I say to such generosity?"

"Uh ... er ... you've made an arrangement with Opal?" Frank looked around and closed the door. "Listen closely, Jasmine," he said quietly. "We have a few big right-wing, conservative supporters with whom we must be very careful. If anyone ever finds out about this, I won't have a job anymore. And if I don't have a job, you don't have a job. Do you understand?"

Jasmine folded her arms and gave him an insolent, defiant glare. It was a look Frank considered most unprofessional for someone of her stature. He had every intention of standing his ground.

"But you haven't even seen the paintings yet!" she protested. "They are a fine investment for the college, and their value will only increase. Just wait until you see them, Frank. I know you will agree!"

"Perhaps we can find a loophole in the books, but just this time," Frank said weakly, losing his resolve. She was always so persuasive. He nervously took off his glasses and pulled out a handkerchief from his pocket. He then opened the bottom drawer of his desk, reached for a small spray bottle, and gave each lens a squirt. How was it possible that this new spiritual director who talked so much about peace and tranquility could make him feel so agitated?

"Ahem. I have practice at one o' clock with the chamber choir. I'll talk to you later." He quickly finished polishing his glasses and walked out, nervously slamming the door behind him. As he did, the portrait hanging on the office wall tilted slightly to the right. Jasmine walked over and straightened it.

"What a dreadfully boring picture," she said out loud to no one. She reached into her shiny black briefcase, pulled out a string of beads, and hung them on the corner of the wood frame. "There, that will do till we redecorate in here too."

As Frank's footsteps echoed down the hall, Jasmine picked up his untouched bowl of macaroni and cheese and tossed it into the garbage. She sat down in Frank's chair again, put her high-heeled boots back up on his desk, pulled out her compact, and powdered her nose. As she reapplied her red lipstick, she thought how much she liked his comfortable and stylish ergonomic chair. It felt rich. In fact, she liked this office very much. Perhaps the chair could stay, but the room needed a face-lift, and she knew just the right painting to add some much needed contemplative ambience.

ON the other side of the building, Tessa pulled a red scarf over her head to hold back her windswept hair and keep the icy northeaster from blowing down her neck. She regretted not having braided her long brown hair early that morning. Just then, a mud-splattered white Jeep with a black top, oversized wheels, and a crooked bumper pulled to the curb where she stood. The driver wore mirrored sunglasses and looked her way for a moment before he stepped out and walked around to her side.

"Your chariot awaits," he said with a smile, as he opened the passenger door and gestured to the front seat with a black-gloved hand. He looked to be in his early twenties, was nicely dressed and clean-shaven, with black hair buzzed to a quarter inch.

Tessa took a step forward and hesitated. "You are . . . Nathan, right?"

"I am. Shall we go?" He sounded so sure of himself.

"But you don't even know who I am . . ."

"I certainly do," he said, his crooked grin revealing a dimple in his right cheek. "Are you coming with me or not?"

Tessa wished she could see his eyes instead of her reflection. She pulled herself up onto the running board, slid into the passenger seat, and buckled her seat belt. Nathan floored the gas pedal, tires spitting out loose rocks from the gravel shoulder all the way to the road.

"Sorry," he said, raising his voice over the cold wind blowing in through the driver's window as they picked up speed on the main road. "I can never get away from that place fast enough."

Tessa wondered why. "I didn't know you'd been here before."

"Do you mind if we head for the town library?" he asked.

"Sure. It's probably nice and warm in there." She hoped he would get the hint and close his window. Wasn't there a heater in this vehicle? She glanced at him as they sped down the road toward Buffalo Avenue and pulled into a fast-food drive through. She wasn't sure if it was his leather jacket or the air from outside that smelled vaguely like the smoky aroma a woodstove leaves behind on clothes. She only knew that his jacket and shoes matched the black Bible cover in front of her on the dash. She thought maybe Nathan was a pastor, although he looked very young.

"Would you rather have coffee?" he asked after ordering two hot chocolates, digging for his wallet in the pocket of his black dress pants.

"Oh no, this is great, thanks very much." Coffee would only make her more jittery. Tessa took one of the hot cups and warmed her hands as they parked across the street from the library. Nathan let the engine idle, took the lid off his hot chocolate, and turned toward Tessa. The steam from his cup was fogging up his glasses. Maybe he would take them off or turn on the heat.

"So, Sam tells me you had some questions."

Tessa took a sip of hot chocolate and burned her tongue. How much had Katy told Sam Goldsmith anyway? She was beginning to wish she had never said anything to her that night.

"To make a long story short," she began, "it all started when Katy told me about your . . . um, your situation. You know, about when you started having those symptoms, the konda . . . kuna . . ."

"Kundalini?"

"Yeah. Um, I'm worried about . . . uhhh." Tessa felt her heart beating faster. "Maybe I shouldn't have called you. I'm just . . . I'm . . ." She looked down and swished the brown plastic stir stick around in her cup.

"You're afraid."

Tessa raised her head. Nathan had taken off his sunglasses and was looking at her with the kindest eyes she had ever seen. Something about him was familiar.

For some reason she couldn't explain, Tessa began spilling her heart out to this complete stranger. For the next half hour, she told him about the experiences she'd had during journaling and in the labyrinth. She told him about the sessions with Ms. Jasmine and her meeting with Dr. Johnson. She even told him about her recurring dream. When the hot chocolate and all her words were gone, Nathan pulled his Bible off the dash and opened it in his lap.

"Wow," he said. "It's even worse than I thought. I don't think Sam even knows just how bad it is."

"Katy might have filled him in by now." Tessa was sure of that.

"Well, they certainly have been going out for coffee a lot."

"Katy? Sam? They've been going out for coffee?" So that was why Katy's cheeks always blushed lately whenever she mentioned Sam Goldsmith.

"Sam's a good guy. I've known him for about three years—met him when he had just started teaching at the college. He was helping his church's youth group organize a missions trip when I showed up. It was my senior year, and I was looking for answers. I'd been partying hard and hanging with the wrong crowd. My best friend got saved and invited me to his youth group. That's when I was prayed over one night, by the wrong person. Parker was a nice fellow, and he'd been hanging out with the youth group, but he'd been mixed up in the occult and a dangerous spirituality all his life. Sam didn't know that part until later. Neither did I. I wasn't saved yet. Apparently, I opened myself up to the wrong powers. Anyway, Parker told me he got visions and messages from angels and I believed him. We went to some soaking prayer sessions at another church, and it got really crazy."

Tessa frowned, but Nathan didn't notice, and continued. "I started having all kinds of weird manifestations, even heard voices. I got real scared one night and went to Sam for advice. He told me the truth about how to be saved, that it's not about having some spiritual experience, but repenting, calling on the name of Jesus Christ, and turning from what I *thought* was the way, and following Him. He said the truth about Jesus is in this book, not in so-called messages from angels or powerful feelings. So I renounced my involvement with the occult, something that Parker never got around to doing."

"Soaking prayer?" Tessa had never heard of it.

"Soaking prayer, listening prayer, contemplative prayer . . . it's all the same thing—man trying to find God through some sort of experience that makes you feel spiritual."

"So did you have any of these symptoms?" Tessa reached into her jacket pocket and pulled out the paper with the kundalini symptoms on it. It was more wrinkled than ever now. Initially, she had resented Katy for reading this to her—now she guarded the list with her life. In fact, this list was the reason she'd phoned Nathan. She needed answers.

Nathan took the rumpled page, unfolded it, and skimmed over it. "Wow. I see Sam has been handing out my list." He handed the paper back to Tessa. "Yes, I am ashamed to say I actually did manifest many of these. Parker had more. So did the teens at the other church where we did the soaking prayer. Makes me sick to think about it now."

"So what happened next after Mr. Goldsmith helped you?"

"After Jesus saved me and set me free, I wanted to be a youth pastor, so I moved out of my parents' home, worked for two years and was saving up to go to college where you are. Then I found out . . . then I . . . uh, changed my mind." He seemed to be choosing his words carefully.

"What did you do instead?" Tessa asked.

"I quit my job, and then I just took off . . . disappeared for a while."

"You took off to where?"

"Well . . ." he said thoughtfully. She could tell he didn't want to say what he was going to say. "That brings me to today. I've been doing some thinking, researching, praying. Maybe God let me go through this time so He can use me to help others. I know you want help, but I don't know if my advice is what you'll want to hear."

"Try me."

"All right. Well, first of all," Nathan paged through his Bible as he spoke, "from what you've said, I think you were attracted to these spiritual exercises because you felt God was far away, and you wanted to *feel* close to Him. But think about it. If you feel far away from God, who has moved? Not God, because He has promised to always be there for the one who calls on Him in faith. And He has said He will never leave the born-again believer."

Nathan turned to Matthew 28. "See? Here Jesus said, 'I am with you always, even unto the end of the world.' It's a promise He will not retract. And even when we don't *feel* close to God, our faith confirms to us that He is with us. And in fact, according to Scripture, Jesus Christ lives *in* us. The Bible says this is a mystery but also is 'the hope of glory.'"

Tessa shivered. Something inside her told her not to listen and that she shouldn't have come here. She remembered the message she had penned in her journal one morning last week: to beware of a tall, dark stranger.

"As far as the kundalini symptoms go," Nathan continued, "be careful, be very careful. What some might call an awakening is, I believe, demonic activity. You must understand that. Sometimes God will allow us to go after things that are not from Him in order to test our commitment. But Tessa, I have to ask you directly, have you ever actually realized you are a sinner in need of salvation and asked Jesus Christ to be your Savior and your Lord?"

"Yes, I have," she said quietly. "But I'm so confused right now." Her legs were restless. They needed to run.

"Tessa, if you have any doubt about the voices you are hearing, maybe that's because they are not from Jesus. If you are His, you will recognize His voice. Listen to this, in John 10 Jesus says, 'My sheep hear my voice, and I know them, and they follow me.' He also said that the shepherd calls His own by name and leads them out. Is He calling you to come out?"

Tessa was cold and uncomfortable, and felt like she was about to lose her composure. "Look, how can you tell me it's not Jesus talking to me! Sometimes I do hear Him, in the silence! If that isn't Jesus, then who is it? Who says that God can't show Himself to us however He pleases? Who are we to put Him in a box?"

Hot tears welled in her eyes and spilled down her cheeks. She felt so stupid for crying. Nathan offered her a crushed box of Kleenex from the backseat.

"OK. Let's talk about putting God in a box. Are we putting God in a box," he asked as she blew her nose, "or has God put us in the safety of the sheepfold? What if He gives us boundaries, but lets us choose whether we want to stay in the safety zone or jump out and do what *we* think is right? What if thinking outside the box puts your mind in the danger zone?" Nathan paused for a moment, then continued.

"It doesn't say anywhere in this book that those who practice certain prayer methods, which aren't really prayer at all, will have access to hidden spiritual truths or messages from God. God has already given us access to Himself. The separating veil between us has been torn once and for all." Nathan was getting all fired up as he turned the worn pages of his Bible to the book of Ephesians. Tessa noticed that certain words were circled and many verses were underlined. Gran's Bible looked like that.

"But we can only get near enough to hear His voice by being silent," she protested.

"No, no, no. Listen to this," Nathan said as he began to read. "'But now in Christ Jesus ye who sometimes were far off are made nigh by the blood of Christ' and this: 'In whom we have boldness and access with confidence.' That means we don't have to do anything to get closer to Him, except believe in what He has already done."

Tessa was quiet. That sounded like the same verse on Gran's homemade bookmark, the one with the red tassel. She had never quite understood what it meant.

"Tessa, can I show you something else? It's why I wanted to bring you here, to the library. It won't take long. Come on."

Nathan turned off the engine, jumped out, and helped her step down to the sidewalk.

"You're freezing, aren't you? I'm sorry. It'll be warm inside."

Warm air greeted Tessa's face as Nathan opened the library door. He led her straight to a section at one end of the library that he obviously knew well. He picked books off the shelves as they walked down two more rows. He then carried them to a back corner by the window to two armchairs and a coffee table and put the stack on the table. They each sat down, and Nathan grabbed one of the books. The first book he showed her was called *Spiritual Medicine for the 21st Century*. He turned to a page with pictures, and told her to read from the top. To herself, she read:

> The seven chakras, or energy centers, are found in the middle of the body within the spinal column. Meditation methods focusing on the chakras are one way to use prana, the most potent flow of energy within the body. This is more commonly known as the rising of the kundalini.

Tessa looked up, and for a moment had a faraway, pensive look. Nathan watched her and wondered if she was beginning to understand this mystical spirituality. Tessa began reading again:

> The spine is the energy conduit through which prana can be channeled to the base of the skull. Experts in kundalini are convinced of its power to heal, but also warn of its power to destroy.

Tessa stared at a drawing of a man sitting cross-legged with a snake coiled around his spine. Underneath the picture was the caption:

> The kundalini snake goddess lies sleeping coiled in her cave, waiting to be roused. She hisses when awakened, stretching from the base of the spine to the top of the head where she meets her consort, the Hindu god, Shiva.

"Nathan, this is terrible!"

"Keep reading, please," he said.

Tessa's lips moved as she skimmed the next chapter about healing energies: "Therapeutic touch, sometimes known as healing touch, also Reiki, is simply a modern day example of prana."

*Healing touch is prana? This is the same thing as kundalini awakening! Is this right?* Tessa shuddered as she remembered the afternoon that Ms. Jasmine prayed for her and told her the tingling she felt was divine energy.

Nathan pulled the book away from her and handed her another one called *The Labyrinth Guide*. The first chapter said the labyrinth was a source of spiritual power and a sacred space, or sanctuary, where one can reconnect with the spirit world.

"A sacred space?" Tessa whispered to Nathan. "Ms. Jasmine has a Sacred Space at the college!"

She continued to read quietly. The author wrote about Eve, calling her the creator goddess, mother of all and said how the serpent was part of her like a coiled umbilical cord. And like the serpent's spiral, the labyrinth connects us to the center of the mother earth goddess, where we will find divinity. Energies are rebirthed in the labyrinth's center, the book said, energies that are used for magic, channeling, psychic ability, and meeting angels.

Tessa sat stunned. Ms. Jasmine had told her once that the feeling rising within her was a kind of rebirthing. Surely, she didn't mean this.

Something else caught Tessa's eye. The book said the coils of the labyrinth correspond with the chakras, and that you can tap into spiritual energies during certain seasons, like the equinoxes and solstices.

Ms. Jasmine had put on a winter solstice labyrinth walk in December.

Tessa stared at the next page about the rituals used by Druids and Wiccans in the labyrinth. Was this for real? She looked at the back cover of the book. A Wiccan high priestess had written it.

"Nathan, I think I've seen enough," she said quietly. *It couldn't be true.* "Maybe Flat Plains is using something other religions use," Tessa protested. "But theirs isn't pagan. It is a Christ-centered labyrinth. Ms. Jasmine calls it 'redeeming the culture.'"

"You have to see one more," he insisted. Tessa looked away and bit her bottom lip as he opened a book called *Journaling* and pointed to chapter twelve, titled "Automatic Writing."

"I'll read it," said Nathan, turning the book around on the table so he could read:

> Automatic writing, or spirit writing, is a form of spiritualism. It is generally the practice of writing a message while channeling information given by the spirit realm. Only those who are able to open themselves up and relax will have messages coming through their pen or computer. Occasionally when the spirit realm completely takes over the human body, automatic writers may find themselves completely exhausted after receiving a message.

"OK, Nathan, OK."

"Just a little more," Nathan implored. He went on:

> To see if you are able to do automatic writing, sit in a quiet place with a pen and paper, relax your muscles, and breathe deeply. As you let the outward noises grow quiet, your thoughts will drift away. As you feel an urge to put your pen to the paper, just begin to write and let the words flow.

"I think I've heard enough now," Tessa said. This was exactly what she had been doing, convinced it was Jesus speaking to her. Had she believed a lie?

"Tessa, this book was written by a New Age medium who channels the messages of Zina, a 2000-year-old prophetess and seer from ancient Rome, and her sister goddesses from the next galaxy. She advises caution when dealing with unfamiliar energy from the 'other side.'"

Tessa laughed. "You're kidding."

Nathan looked at his watch. "I'm really sorry, but I have a job interview at 4:30. I have to take you back now."

*Oh no, it's nearly four o'clock. I'm going to be late.*

They walked back to the Jeep in silence. It had all been too much to take in. If these things were wrong, why was a Christian college teaching them? Surely, the professors wouldn't knowingly deceive hundreds of students.

They rode without speaking. Tessa knew Nathan was thinking about saying something because his right temple and jaw muscle flexed the whole way back to the school.

"Tessa," he finally said, as they reached the school entrance, "you are going to have to make a decision."

"I need time . . ." She hated the way her voice sounded. She was still in shock. Who could she talk to? Sonya and Elise would think she'd lost her mind. Katy would understand, but she wasn't here. Tessa wanted to run away, to some place safe. But where?

"You may be feeling shocked and disillusioned. Maybe you want to pretend we never had this conversation. But don't go back again to what you now know is wrong. And don't run away like I did. If you run anywhere, run to God. His name is 'strong tower.' It's in Him you'll find safety."

As she reached for the door handle, a dozen crazy thoughts raced through her head. How did he know how she felt? Why did he keep talking about running and hiding? Who was he anyway? She didn't even know his last name.

"Wait. Before you go, can I pray for you?"

"Here? Now?" Tessa looked around the campus. No one had ever prayed with her besides Gramps and Gran. Well, Ms. Jasmine had prayed with her, if you could call it prayer. She wasn't so sure now. Never before had any guy prayed with her. Tessa felt uncomfortable, but at the same time, she longed for it with all her heart.

Nathan's prayer reminded her of Gramps. He sounded like he knew God personally. When he finished praying, he squeezed her hand in his and looked at her with his clear, blue-gray eyes. It was a look she knew she would never forget.

"Thank you," she managed to say, as she drew her hand away and pulled the door handle. "I really have to go."

Nathan was about to hop out and help her down, but she jumped out quickly. As she turned to shut her passenger door, she noticed a pair of well-worn hiking boots with mismatched laces on the back seat. One lace was yellow. Nathan leaned over, pulled the door shut from the inside, and rolled down the window.

"And Tessa, remember," he said before she turned to go, "I'll be praying for you. I think you need to either take a stand or leave this place as soon as you can."

"But I . . . I can't just leave," she shouted over the hum of the motor.

"Yes you can. With God's help, you can. But if you stay, check everything with the Word of God. They are all listening to the serpent just like Eve. It's the same old lie."

"What did you say?" she was about to ask. But he had already pulled away from the curb. And suddenly, a picture flashed in Tessa's mind—a young bearded man in the woods by the bridge, wearing boots with mismatched laces. And those blue-gray eyes. Tessa stood there for a moment stunned. Could it be? She put her hand to her neck. "Wait! My scarf! Oh no!" It was the one Gran had knit for her. Her favorite.

Tessa was sick at heart. She looked at her watch. If she hurried, she would only be a few minutes late for her session with Ms. Jasmine. She had to go; her marks depended on it. But she needed time to process everything she had just heard. Somehow, she had to find the courage to say something to Ms. Jasmine. Tessa was sure about this—and Ms. Jasmine was not going to be happy.

## SEATTLE

MARCH 24

THE Flat Plains missions team walked the four blocks to the church where they would sleep their first night in Seattle. Though tired and somewhat bedraggled from their work in Argentina, they each felt a sense of peace in what they had been able to do. Serving at the orphanage and building a home for an Argentinian family had been a humbling experience. The team had seen how little the local people had in terms of material possessions, yet so many of them had seemed so filled with joy. Now, here in Seattle, the group would do another two days of street ministry before flying back to the college.

As they walked past city storefronts, Katy looked into one shop that had crystals hanging in the window and a sign that read, "Healing Touch." An older woman with hollow-looking eyes, sat at the counter. A green gem was glued to the center of her forehead, and sparkles were all over her face. Katy shuddered as she walked by and silently whispered a prayer for her. Katy had seen that same hollow expression in the eyes of a young woman in Argentina the week before. With the help of their translator, Katy had been thrilled to share the Gospel and then pray with her. The following day when Katy returned to work on the house project, she saw the woman again. Most notable was the change in her eyes. This time, they were clear and bright, and she was overjoyed, praising God for sending the tormenting demons away.

One thing was obvious by the look of the storefronts on this city block—Satan and his minions were not confined to South America. The missions team had seen such spiritual darkness and the effects of occultism there, but they knew that same darkness was present in North America.

When the group spotted an espresso café, they crossed the street, chatting excitedly about what they would order. Next to the café was Earl's Electronics Shop. Katy darted inside to replace her camera's battery charger that had been lost in the luggage mix-up at the airport in New York. Browsing around for the least expensive charger, she couldn't help but overhear the big screen television near the front of the small store, blaring the popular *Twila White Show.*

"On today's show, we are privileged to have author and retreat leader Meredith Jones, whose new book, *When Silence Speaks,* has climbed to the top of the best-seller charts. Meredith, that's quite an accomplishment for a stay-at-home mom with three boys!"

"Thank you," smiled a pleasant conservative-looking brunette whom Katy thought looked like a typical soccer mom.

"Also joining us today via satellite will be one of the voices who endorsed her book and catapulted Meredith to overnight success, beloved author and lecturer, Beatrice Still of Bea Still Quiet Heart Retreat Centers. Bea couldn't be with us in person today due to a heart condition. Welcome Bea, is it true you will be ninety-five years old this month?"

"How about that," whispered Katy to herself, raising her eyebrows in interest. "So this is Beatrice Still, the author my aunt never stops raving about. Maybe it's a good thing I'm seeing this today. Thank you, Lord."

". . . and with us in the studio is Meredith's publisher, Stewart West from Mind Body Spirit Books, as well as her spiritual director and mentor Dr.—" The thunderous applause of the audience drowned out Twila White's words as the camera zoomed in on her straight white teeth, just-right lipstick, and her attractive symmetrical face— all framed by that famous head of perfect blonde hair.

"Um . . . hello . . . that will be $12.72 with tax," repeated the girl sitting behind the counter, startling Katy out of her preoccupation with the television show. She'd been distracted, dumbfounded by the near hysteria of the television audience. She looked into her wallet for cash, and finding some, placed it into the waiting hand of the young clerk. Katy watched as the girl with the blue hair and multiple piercings on her face completed the transaction. A thick romance novel with a picture of a winsome looking vampire on the front cover lay spread open on the counter beside her.

"Hey, you don't sell bubble gum here, do you?" Katy asked suddenly.

"Nah. We don't sell gum here."

"If you only knew. I haven't had any gum for ten days . . ." She glanced at her watch, ". . . and about three hours!"

"Hey, I know just how you feel. Got it bad, huh? I can give you a piece of mine. Want one?" The girl didn't smile, but handed Katy a newly opened package of bubble gum. "It's the newest flavor."

"Oh! Oh! It's Marvelous Mint Bubble! Thank you so much," Katy said, beaming as she took out a new stick. "If you only knew! It's my absolute favorite! You have no idea. My friends drink coffee. I chew gum."

"I hear ya," the girl smiled, showing a row of braces with blue elastics. "I'm really not supposed to be chewing gum, but I can't help it."

Katy smiled sympathetically. "Me too. Just like I can't stop talking about God. Do you know God?" she asked.

"God? Oh yeah, he's in the trees and the rocks. He's probably in this bubble gum."

"No way, my friend," Katy said. "God *made* the trees and the rocks, and He loves you! I hope you won't mind, but I'm going to pray from now on that you will want to know Him, as He really is, yes?" At the same time, Katy pulled a small leaflet out of her wallet and handed it to the girl. "This will tell you a story about God's Son."

The girl examined Katy's face, especially her eyes, and tilted her head. "You're a different kind of customer. We don't usually get your kind in here."

"Remember, God loves you!" said Katy with a huge smile.

She held the gum to her nose, deeply inhaling the fresh scent of mint bubble gum. *This is exactly what I need to perk me up*, she thought, *after too many airport stopovers and not enough sleep.*

Preparing to leave the store, Katy glanced back at the overstuffed armchair facing the large plasma television. It was so tempting to linger and watch a little more of the *Twila White Show*. *After all*, Katy reasoned, *the others are just next door at the Java Bistro, and it's probably noisy in there. Anyway, the team knows where I am.* That settled it. She sat down on the black imitation-leather cushion and absentmindedly set her bag on the floor beside her.

"Is it OK if I sit here for a minute?" she asked the clerk. "I'm beat."

"Sure."

Katy leaned back and closed her eyes. Her mouth watered for the stick of gum she still held in her hand. But the proper procedure must be followed. After all, mint bubble gum must first be anticipated and cherished if it was to be thoroughly enjoyed. First, she needed a sip of water to prepare her taste buds for an adventure in flavor. She opened her water bottle, took a long drink, and turned her attention back to the *Twila White Show*.

"And so, Meredith, tell our audience how you came to realize that the seven chakras and the seven Teresian mansions of St. Teresa of Avila go hand-in-hand with that inner voice within the *silence*."

"We call it the territory of the interior soul. St. Teresa called it the seven inner rooms, the innermost room being divine union with God, as you perceive him or her to be. It is only in this center that you will hear with your spiritual ears and see with the eye of your soul. Many who reach this point say they experience a sensation that feels as if their soul becomes detached from their body. Some call this union with the divine, or ecstasy. St. Teresa referred to it as detachment, or rapture."

Katy unwrapped her gum and slowly raised it to her mouth while she stared at the television.

"That's so interesting, so interesting," said Twila White. "You know, Ms. Jones," she continued, leaning in toward her guest, "some would say this sounds very similar to astral travel that we heard so much about in the '70s."

"I'll say amen to that!" agreed Katy out loud.

"Then they need to read my book," replied Meredith Jones, smiling confidently.

"OK, let's hear from one of our other guests who has done extensive research in this area. Dr. Jasmine Winters, is this part of what the Spiritual Transformation Institute is all about?"

Katy's jaw dropped as she leaned forward and laid the piece of gum she was still holding on the arm of the chair, while closely examining the faces on the panel of guests.

"What? Ms. Jasmine?" she muttered, standing up and moving toward the screen for a better look.

"Well, first of all, let me clarify. Today we no longer use terms like astral projection. We have advanced since the '70s and have come into a new understanding of highly spiritual experiences. In fact, we can now scientifically analyze them with current technology. Recent studies of alpha brain patterns have confirmed what the ancients already knew long ago."

The television camera scanned the studio audience, showing close-up images of several smiling women, nodding their heads in agreement. Katy stared in disbelief. Was this really *their* Dr. Winters? Yes, it was. Surely, she'd misunderstood her words. After all, could Jasmine Winters really be telling the nationwide television audience that occultic, out-of-body experiences were beneficial because they could be scientifically verified?

"Could you explain that, Dr. Winters?" asked Twila White.

*Yes, please. Explain that, Dr. Winters,* echoed Katy's thoughts.

"Gladly. The concepts behind the silence are actually very ancient." Ms. Jasmine stretched out her arms to form an imaginary time line. "In fact, Christianity had a rich history of useful prayer methods that were hijacked by other religions." Katy shook her head. What Ms. Jasmine was saying wasn't true. These mystical practices didn't originate with Christianity. *They're much older than that, dear Ms. Jasmine.* Katy thought.

Ms. Jasmine continued. "However, in my travels, I was pleased to discover that these meditation methods are now finally coming back to the church. They are no longer considered only an Eastern practice. You see, by using certain prayer rituals, we can gain direct access to the Divine through silence. Christian mysticism embraces certain meditation techniques that have roots going back to the writings of the desert fathers and other Christian mystics, such as St. John of the Cross and St. Teresa of Avila, who both experienced ecstasy, or what we call weightlessness of the soul today. They all had something in common—they learned the secret of the silent place of God. This is something that my great-aunt Bea has studied for years."

Katy's eyes widened. She didn't realize it, but her mouth had dropped open.

Bea Still's frail voice cut in. "Oh yes, my niece Jazz is right. And as Meredith has said in her book, you don't have to live in a monastery anymore to be a mystic."

"So Jazz—may I call you Jazz too? In case our audience didn't pick up on it, Bea Still is Dr. Winters' aunt." Twila White smiled charmingly at the audience. And the audience smiled back. Katy's heart beat faster—a nauseous feeling in her stomach.

"Great-aunt," Ms. Jasmine corrected, smiling graciously. "I was finally able to connect with my dear aunt, my only living relative, ten years ago after a lifelong search. She had given my mother a book when she turned nineteen, a very old book written by St. Teresa. That book influenced my mother enormously. Then the book fell into my hands when I was a teenager. I never forgot the inscription on the first page, and was eventually able to locate my long-lost aunt because of it. Incidentally, St. Teresa was also greatly influenced by a book, one her uncle gave her when she was nineteen. It was a book on prayer."

"Fascinating! Do you still have the book that was given to you?"

"The original book? Unfortunately, no, it's been lost."

"What a shame. I'm sure it would be a family heirloom. So let's go back to what you said, Jazz, about the terms formerly thought of as New Agey but are now simply re-realized as the *new spirituality* which has been—"

"Rediscovered," Ms. Jasmine corrected again, and as the camera zoomed in for a close-up, the gold pendant hanging on her neck reflected the bright studio lights. At first, Katy thought it was a cross but now recognized it as an Egyptian ankh. "For example, the seven chakras are merely a term used to describe something that Christians have known through the centuries—that God's light dwells in the territory of every soul. All we are doing when we center ourselves and find the stillness is rediscovering our inner wisdom, peace, and tranquility! It's within our true selves! And remember, the term New Age has become, you could say, middle-aged. We need to awaken to the fact that we are in the midst of a paradigm shift that is going to heal our earth and in fact, bring about God's kingdom."

Katy was flabbergasted that she just happened to walk into this store at the very moment that Jasmine Winters was appearing as a television guest on the *Twila White Show*. Dr. Winters was not only her roommate's professor and spiritual director, she was a modern-day mystic who was actively leading undiscerning students at Flat Plains Bible College straight into the occultic roots of ancient mysticism.

As the television audience jumped to their feet with rousing applause, Katy grabbed her bag, pulled out her cell phone, and began texting an urgent message to Tessa while she hurried out the door.

IN the kitchen of a two-story farmhouse nestled in the foothills of the Rocky Mountains, a white-haired woman hummed an old hymn as she rolled out cookie dough on a giant wooden cutting board on the far end of a long country table. She leaned over and turned on the small television, wiping a stray strand of hair off her forehead with the back of her flour-covered hand.

"Welcome back! I'm Twila White, and if you've just tuned in, one of our panel guests today is Dr. Jasmine Winters of Spiritual

Transformation Institute, whose endorsement is on the back cover of the best-selling book, *When Silence Speaks*. Before the break, she was preparing to tell us about a hot new trend in spirituality that is spreading throughout North America to aid spiritual seekers in their life journey. In fact, she is one of the first spiritual directors from STI to design an outdoor labyrinth for a Christian college campus. Dr. Winters, tell us about this project you say is a sign of what you're calling the new spirituality."

Margaret slowly lowered herself onto the creaky bench. The rolling pin rolled off the edge of the table and hit the tile floor, but Margaret didn't even notice.

"JB?" she called.

As the television audience clapped enthusiastically for Twila White, Jacob came hopping into the kitchen, pulling on a pair of work overalls.

"JB," she said. "I think you need to see this."

Jacob approached the small screen, squinted, and leaned in for a closer look. He put his reading glasses on. His eyebrows raised. "Well, I'll be . . . If I didn't know better, I'd say that's the Winters girl! All grown up!"

Margaret nodded. "I would think so, JB, but that was nearly thirty years ago she stayed with us, you know."

"Well, I'll be hog-tied! What is she doing . . . her hair is whiter now, but it always was very blonde. She doesn't look much different, does she?"

"And that's not all that hasn't changed. Sit down, JB. And listen real close. Shhhh, watch now."

Twila White looked at her audience, then turned and pointed upward to a large screen behind her. "Here is a photo of the labyrinth that Dr. Winters designed. And this is at a Christian college, correct?"

"Yes, and a great example of the fact that we have entered the age of a new way of thinking *and* believing. One of the fruits, you could say, of this new spirituality is that all religious traditions are beginning to discover the common roots that they share."

"Margaret," said Jacob, his face turning pale. "I was planning to clean out the barn today. But now I think . . ." He paused and closed his eyes for a moment. Margaret could see he was trying very hard to keep his emotions under control. "I think there's something else that needs cleaning out much more urgently. How many hours did we figure it would take to drive to Flat Plains?"

THE plasma screen in Earl's Electronics Shop showed a close-up of Twila White's famous smile before her show went to a commercial break. The girl with blue hair picked up an unwrapped piece of perfectly good green bubble gum that lay on the arm of the chair in front of the television. She shrugged her shoulders then popped it into her mouth, savoring that first burst of flavor. She sat down on the chair and pulled out of her pocket the colorful tract the strange girl had given to her twenty minutes earlier. She began to read, "For God so loved the world . . ."

Next door, a girl with olive-colored skin and hair the color of dark chocolate stood talking animatedly to what appeared to be a group of tourists carrying backpacks and suitcases. Busy people walking by under their umbrellas didn't even glance up as the group huddled in a circle and prayed right there on the city sidewalk.

24

## DÉJÀ VU

TESSA'S cell phone beeped and then started to flash on and off. She had just left her personal things, including her phone, in the Sacred Space and gone down the hall to the staff kitchen to put the kettle on. The beeping and flashing of the phone was getting on Ms. Jasmine's nerves. Not ten minutes ago, she had sent two students to the water-bowl meditation station in the corner of the room, and it had to be quiet for the curtain was very thin and not soundproof. This was a room where the soul must find silence. She picked up Tessa's phone. "Message received," it flashed. There were two messages in a row. Then another beep—now three messages.

"How on mother earth do you turn this thing off," she muttered through clenched teeth. She pressed a button. Instead of turning the phone off, it opened the first message. It was from that annoying Buckler girl that Tessa certainly didn't need to be hanging around with. Something about the chatty little Miss Buckler bothered Ms. Jasmine. As Tessa's spiritual mentor, perhaps it would be a good idea to read it quickly.

"Urgent Tess! Stay away from your SD! Just saw her on twila white with bunch of new agers. She is one of them, text me back-hurry!"

Ms. Jasmine let out a long sigh through flared nostrils. She hadn't expected anyone in this old-fashioned prairie town to see the show, especially way out here at this Christian school where weeknight television viewing was strongly discouraged. Nervously she glanced around. At the end of the hall, she could hear the kettle beginning to whistle. In the prayer station behind her, two spiritual formation students were concentrating on their visualization exercise. They were instructed to visualize their problems in a pitcher of water, which they poured into a bowl while repeating the Bible verse on the wall, "I am the living water," seven times. The students should have been out of there by now, but they were late getting started. Everyone and everything was getting on her nerves today.

*Well, better safe than sorry*, thought Ms. Jasmine, and quickly pushed delete. She erased the next two messages as well, from some boys—a Jacob and a Nathan. The last thing the girl needed was distractions from the outside. She'd already been acting strangely for a week now. An intense feeling of rage suddenly came over Ms. Jasmine. She pulled a long hairpin from the back of her glamorous head and was contemplating how she could use it to destroy the phone, when she suddenly jumped.

"Why are you holding my phone?" Tessa stood in the doorway carrying two steaming cups.

Ms. Jasmine looked up, startled. "Why, it was . . . it was making funny noises. Very strange noises indeed. The girls, you know . . ." She nodded over to the curtain. "It has to be quiet in here."

"It beeps when I have a text message," Tessa said quietly, eyeing Ms. Jasmine suspiciously.

"Shhh. The girls are meditating," Ms. Jasmine said in hushed tones. "A beep? No. I didn't hear a thing. Were you perhaps hearing the beautiful music the girls were making a moment ago on their Himalayan singing bowls? Sometimes it's so high-pitched, it can sound like a beep."

"Here's your tea—may I have my phone?" Tessa put her cup of hot chocolate on the coffee table. "I used Jasmine tea leaves in your cup this time. That's all I could find in the cupboard."

"Oh my favorite!" said Ms. Jasmine quietly, smiling as she sat herself down cross-legged on a pillow and reached for her teacup. "Thank you my dear girl. And here's your phone . . . oh, oh no!"

Tessa could not believe her eyes as Ms. Jasmine fumbled her phone. It happened so quickly. Yet Tessa watched it play out in slow motion, helpless, as her phone dropped into the cup of hot tea.

"Hurry! Get it out!" Tessa cried, and the girls behind the curtain immediately stopped what they were doing and began to eavesdrop.

"It's all right, never mind," Ms. Jasmine called out to assure them. "Tessa had a wee accident, and we are just drying off her cell phone. Carry on . . . uh, sorry for the interruption."

Tessa grabbed a sweatshirt from her backpack and blotted her lifeline to the world. It still seemed to work, although the screen looked wet inside. How could this day get any worse?

"Now come, sit. You light the candle this time, would you?"

"Uh . . . well, that's what I . . . I wanted to talk to you about, Dr. Winters," Tessa nervously stammered. She was even more upset now. "I was wondering if it was OK if I don't do the session this afternoon? I've been having reservations about—"

"Why would you address me so formally? Tessa, you are already late. Please. Don't test my patience." As Ms. Jasmine spoke, a peculiar look came across her face.

Tessa could feel her pounding pulse in her jugular.

"Ms. Jazz, actually, I've been having some questions. This method of prayer we are learning, some people have been telling me it is not in the Bible, and it might actually bring a person in contact with . . ." As she glanced up from the floor, she noticed that Ms. Jasmine suddenly didn't look very peaceful or tranquil.

"With what, Tessa?" She emphasized each word with a pause.

"With . . ." She struggled to force the words out of her throat. "With a power other than God, and some of the students who have been practicing these methods actually have symptoms very similar to—"

"To what?" Ms. Jasmine said in a low voice as her eyes narrowed. She folded her arms and leaned back. Her pink face had turned pale. "I take it you have reservations about what I am teaching here at Flat Plains."

"It's not that," Tessa lied. What could she say? "I mean, it's about these experiences. I don't know if . . . I mean, I can't talk about it right now."

Ms. Jasmine glanced at the girls who had finally finished their twenty-minute water-bowl prayer exercise. "Girls, that's enough for tonight. We will discuss the Celtic Project next time. You may go now. I'm just starting an important session with Tessa. Isn't that right Tessa?"

Ms. Jasmine's voice sounded odd. Tessa's heart began to race. Her face flushed, and she swallowed hard.

"Well, actually, I'd feel better if they stayed."

"You guys," Tessa called to her friends. The girls, looking somewhat confused, picked up their jackets and turned to walk out the door.

"Good-night Ms. Jasmine," they said, giving Tessa a strange look.

Ms. Jasmine got up to close the door. She locked it and turned to Tessa, smiling.

"Now, Ms. Dawson, please sit down on a cushion. I just want to talk to you about next Friday." She had changed her tone again and talked in a sickeningly sweet, slow voice. "You are still helping me, aren't you? I really need you."

Tessa nodded but couldn't speak. Now Jasmine Winters knew she was having second thoughts. Tessa had forced herself to come. Her intentions were bold, but now that she was here, she felt quite spineless. How could she tell her spiritual director in a nice way that her star student did not intend to complete the last three sessions? Ms. Jasmine had said they were going to be the most important ones of all.

"Tessa, I'm sure you are well aware that participation is worth 25 percent of your mark. I was looking through the prayer journal and noticed you opted out of leading the labyrinth walk last weekend.

I hope this is not a late in the season trend. I am counting on you. Are you with me?"

Tessa felt the strength draining from her bones. She was sitting beside a cup Ms. Jasmine had left on the floor earlier this morning. The smell of soggy Yerba leaves was making her feel sick.

"Tessa," Ms. Jasmine went on, even more slowly as she lit the candle, "your friends, Sonya and Elise, love coming here to Sacred Space and participating in the prayer exercises. They say it's been life changing. Do you know that St. Teresa initially tried to resist the graces and favors that the Lord bestowed upon her? Yes, even she had doubts. Her advisors told her that her revelations were from the devil, but time has proven them wrong. This fear-based mentality was no different from what we are coming against today. If we are to be Christ followers, we must deliberately choose not to join the ranks of the spiritually uncivilized who refuse to be enlightened."

Déjà vu. Where had she heard that before? "Don't be afraid," a familiar voice was telling her. It was the same voice she'd heard the first time she did a prayer exercise in the courtyard, the voice she'd heard the first time she walked the labyrinth, the voice she was unsure about at first. Tessa had a feeling she shouldn't be staring at the flickering flame of the candle. Ms. Jasmine's voice continued to rise and fall hypnotically in the background, like a road winding through rolling hills toward a castle.

"As we shut out the noises, we open ourselves to your favors, your graces, and your presence. Now we enter the castle and let the drawbridge close behind us, shutting out the reptiles of doubt and fear. Here we can breathe deeply in the safety and silence of the inner rooms. Help us to tame the wild horses of our minds and be willing recipients of the light that begins with a tiny spark. Kindle the flame and illuminate our dwelling. Awaken us to the light."

It sounded so nice, so pleasant. Tessa's muscles began to relax. A persistent voice inside reassured her that this was what she needed, not the sleepless nights wracked with fear and concern. She remembered how she would drift off to sleep every night when she was a little girl, when her mom read her stories about princesses and castles.

Maybe Ms. Jasmine and Dr. Johnson were right after all. Maybe she *should* stop fighting these irrational fears and just give in.

Ms. Jasmine continued to lead the guided visualization, but this time Tessa couldn't find the castle or the drawbridge. She couldn't even find the horse. All she could see was a rugged-looking young man sitting on a rock, whose blue-gray eyes looked into her soul, and he said, "Don't believe them, until you consult the Word of God."

Tessa knew right then that she should leave, but her feet felt glued to the floor. What would Ms. Jasmine do if she got up and left? What would Sonya and Elise think if she ran out? What would everyone say if she quit now? She'd be called a freaked-out, narrow-minded quitter. So she sat on the cushion with her eyes closed, waiting for the session to end, and the five o' clock supper bell to ring. *Is this what it feels like to lose your mind and go crazy?* she wondered.

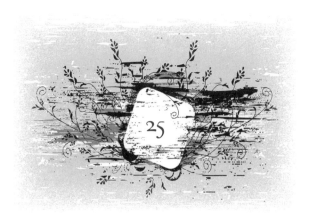

25

# The Debriefing

"ARE you crazy?" the dark-haired girl shouted as she stood up alone in a room full of now quiet students. Sitting in groups on the gymnasium floor of the church, they all turned and stared in disbelief at the pretty girl with the slight Russian accent who had uttered such a disapproving outburst. She continued loudly and boldly, "You are kidding, yes? This Teresa whom you call a saint levitated, hallucinated, and abused herself, and you want us to read and practice what she taught!?"

"Sam," a young man spoke up, "could you please ask your student to sit down and have more respect for our special guest who is leading us in this group exercise?" It was Jonas speaking, the youth pastor of the church that was hosting the event. Half a dozen different missions teams from various Christian colleges across Canada and the U. S. were gathered there that evening. He gently took the microphone from Melanie Byrd, spiritual direction coach from the Center of Youth Transformation, and handed it to a man in a suit who had just hopped up onto the stage.

"It's OK, Jonas," said the man as he turned to face the audience.

"Hello, I'm Dr. Harvey Metzger, and I am the event organizer of tonight's missions debriefing session. I'd like to address this issue, if I may. Contrary to this young woman's objections, our denomination's handbook suggests we can learn from our ancient church fathers and mothers in the area of spiritual formation. That is what this evening is all about—learning from others through dialogue and having a spiritual encounter with Christ."

"Excuse me," continued Katy. "But I'm seeing some major red flags here tonight. Look, anyone can have a spiritual encounter, a spiritual experience. But the devil can, and does, appear to people as an angel of light! He can provide people with a very good spiritual experience if they go looking for one in unbiblical ways. Hey, he can even quote Scripture, if necessary. This is why it is called deception, yes?"

A couple of people looked like they wanted to stop her but didn't quite know how.

The longer Katy talked, the bolder she became. "What you are offering us here tonight is a type of spiritual experience never ordained in Scripture. Many Christians ignorantly suppose that the spiritual realm is a safe and friendly place. But it isn't. The Bible says Satan is the prince of the power of the air! Yes, he is subject to God's supreme sovereignty, but until Jesus returns and sets the world right, God has given the great Deceiver a lot of freedom to deceive those who refuse to be discerning.

"But listen to me, what God offers is so much better than a mere spiritual experience. What God offers us is the life and power of His Son, Jesus, through His Holy Spirit! Instead of teaching who God is from His Word, you say the best way to encounter God is by repeating a phrase over and over. Instead of bringing our requests to the Lord, you want us to repeat a phrase for twenty minutes, which is something the Bible forbids, by the way! What you are offering us is nothing more than ancient mysticism warmed over."

"Young lady, you are way out of line!" blustered Dr. Metzger, louder this time. "I would ask that we all show respect to each other so we don't offend our guest! I am shocked to see such an attitude of fear and lack of civility here tonight. Could you please control your student, Mr. Goldsmith?"

All eyes turned to Sam Goldsmith of Flat Plains Bible College as he stood to his feet, paused for a moment, and gave Dr. Metzger a peculiar look.

"Uh . . . no!" he said bluntly and loudly. "I think we should let Miss Buckler finish, out of respect, sir."

It had all started that morning. It was the day before the missions team was scheduled to fly back to Flat Plains. As their group strolled the streets of downtown Seattle, joyfully sharing Christ with anyone who would listen, Katy had stopped briefly at a store and purchased an interesting book at a fifty-cent sidewalk sale. It was a book about the history of mysticism. During meals, she began skimming through it with keen interest—concerns for her roommate compelling her to search for answers. Ever since she had watched the *Twila White Show*, the whole team had begun praying earnestly for Tessa and for their school.

As planned, their group arrived at the church's gym that evening to participate in the combined debriefing session. The agenda indicated that the session would include a time of sharing and prayer, as well as a devotional time. Their group was a few minutes late and had found places to sit near the middle of the gym just as the worship team had begun to play the second song. It was one of Katy's favorites. She closed her eyes and joined in the worship. *How good to be together with so many believers*, she'd thought. After singing a few more songs, each team began taking turns sharing stories about the mission trip from which they had just returned.

Katy loved hearing the adventures, but she soon noticed something missing from the testimonies of the other teams. They all spoke enthusiastically about serving the poor and putting an end to global problems such as injustice, poverty, disease, pollution, and racism—but there were no stories of people's lives being transformed by the power of Jesus Christ, as her team had seen.

The Flat Plains team was asked to come up last. After they shared about how they had witnessed people being saved and released from the power of Satan through the preaching of the Gospel, the room had grown strangely silent.

But Katy really had known something was wrong when Miss

Melanie Byrd came to the microphone. She'd said something about uneducated people from third-world countries giving too much credit to the devil. Then she'd said they were going to spend some time in prayer. Katy had thought they were going to pray for the lost so she closed her eyes and waited. That's when the lights had been dimmed and Miss Byrd had said she would guide them through a twenty-minute exercise of "praying the Scriptures."

"The purpose," Miss Byrd had explained, "is to lead us through silent meditation to a holy place of union with the Divine." Katy had opened her eyes and had been shocked to read the quote displayed on the large screen:

> The prayer of union is the "chamber" into which our Lord takes us when and how He chooses. But we cannot get there by our own efforts. His Majesty alone brings us there and enters the very centre of our souls.—Teresa of Avila, *The Interior Castle*

Somewhere between the minute of silence to center their thoughts and Miss Byrd's lighting the candle to symbolize their common bond, Katy had jumped to her feet and let out the words that burned in her heart.

When Sam Goldsmith told Dr. Metzger to let her finish, the students stared intently at Katy. She opened her newly purchased book on mysticism and began reading to them, turning it outward to show the pictures to those around her.

"Do you know," she shouted, "that the person who is quoted on the PowerPoint right now, whom the Roman Catholic Church calls a saint, actually levitated and had out-of-body experiences? Look, here is a picture of a statue depicting this nun being visited by an angel that she said thrust his spear into her and pulled out her guts. And here . . . here, look, here is a picture of her hovering above the floor. "

Katy had the floor, and she continued. "This is exactly the kind of lying signs and wonders the Bible warns us about! It says here that St. Teresa of Avila tried to stop her body from levitating. She thought that could be achieved by punishing herself by beating herself with self-scourging whips and spending weeks in self-deprivation. When that didn't help, the other nuns tried weighing her down with stones, but even that did not stop her frequent levitations. The spiritual directors who encouraged and condoned these occurrences in St. Teresa's life were Jesuit priests trained in the mystical spirituality of their so-called inner life and contemplation. Teresa called these experiences 'favors' from God. I call them demonic. Friends, listen to me! Tonight you are taking part in the doctrine of demons, and you need to repent before God!"

Katy knew her cheeks were flushed, and she felt slightly weak-kneed by her effort. Melanie Byrd had stood transfixed, mouth gaping and eyes squinting in undisguised fury as she listened to Katy rant. Suddenly, she turned on her heel and stormed out of the gym. Dr. Metzger excused himself and followed her. The church's youth leader just stood there, looking stunned.

A man's voice rang out. "She's right, you know." It was Sam, now standing beside Katy.

Together they made a striking picture—her soft, dark features contrasted with his blonde hair, rugged good looks, and strong-set jaw. As Katy glanced at Sam, their eyes locked and for a moment, time seemed to stand still for the pair. God was filling them with courage, as if they were martyrs boldly proclaiming their last words before the lions devoured them.

"I've traveled to Spain and stood in the Convent of St. Teresa in Avila," Sam continued. The chapel is decorated with scenes of her levitating. If you don't know what that is, it's when people or objects are mysteriously lifted off the ground. It usually begins with a person going into a mindless trance. Levitation occurs among mediums and can be found in shamanism, Hinduism, Buddhism . . . it's demonic!"

The room was quiet. All eyes were on Sam now. He began to sit down, but quickly stood when he realized he had their undivided attention. His deep, full voice easily carried across the gym without a microphone.

"Oh, they keep relics of her there, at the convent," Sam continued. "Things like her rosary, her ring finger—still wearing her ring—and a piece of her sandal. The exhibit also includes the cord she used to flagellate herself."

"What is that?" called out a curious student from one of the teams.

"Well, we know Jesus suffered once and for all for our sins and took our punishment for us. But some nuns and monks believed that that wasn't enough and that they also needed to suffer for their sins. So they would keep a cord or scourge for self-discipline and frequently use it to whip themselves until their bodies bled profusely."

By the looks on many of the students' faces, they were clearly shocked to hear these things.

"And that's not all," Sam went on. "St. Teresa's heart—which they say is incorrupt—and her arm are enshrined and displayed at the Carmelite convent in the nearby town of Alba de Tormes."

"Ooo...gross!" a few students murmured, making faces as they looked at each other.

Katy was thrilled! She had never seen Sam as zealous for the truth as he was at that very moment. She was proud to be standing at her professor's side. Or was he just a professor to her? At that moment, she realized with amazement that she wanted to be by his side for the rest of her life. She looked at him again with warm, affectionate eyes. Sam wasn't finished speaking yet.

"And about that reading up on the PowerPoint," he pointed at the quote, "if you are a Christian, Jesus already indwells you. The Bible tells us it happened at your conversion, when you were born again spiritually. We don't need a prayer of union in some contemplative silence in order to be indwelt by Him. What you are reading here today is contrary to the truth of Scripture! The prayer exercise Miss Bride was about to—"

"Byrd," corrected Katy.

"What Miss Byrd was about to lead you in . . ." Sam paused to choose his words. "Well, is this what they're teaching you in your colleges, that you need to practice certain prayer and meditation methods to *experience* and know God? What they should be teaching you is how to preach the Good News of Jesus Christ to a lost and dying world. Our Bible schools have always trained and sent missionaries to third-world countries to share the Gospel with people so that many might receive it and be set free from the bondage of sin and find hope for their lives through Christ. Something is very wrong!"

Sam's voice was strong and at that moment, full of compassion. "Can't you see that? We need to get on our knees and pray for boldness to stand against this grievous sin. Or maybe it's time for discerning missionaries from other countries to come into the Christian colleges of North America!"

"Mr. Goldsmith!" shouted a man standing in the doorway. "We have heard enough of your unenlightened resistance for one evening. Anyone from the Flat Plains team may now leave. In fact, I insist you leave, or you will be escorted out of the building by security officers, who have been called in." He pointed to the back of the building. Four men in uniforms stood near the door. "This is nothing more than legalistic extremism—you are an embarrassment to the name of God and a self-centered detriment to a world in need of love and tolerance."

Sam was undeterred. "Haven't you read *Foxe's Book of Martyrs?*" he appealed, raising his voice so all could hear. His voice was urgent. Tiny drops of sweat began forming on his brow, and his hands were cold and clammy. He thought of the apostle Paul, jailed and beheaded for the Gospel, the sixteenth-century martyrs who were burned at the stake, and his friend Philip from Indonesia who had been tortured with a burning log because he wouldn't deny his faith in Jesus Christ. Was this stressful situation even a tiny taste of what those believers had experienced moments before the fires were lit?

"Don't you remember that Christians were burned at the stake for the truth?" Sam continued. "This spirituality is a slap in the face of the many martyrs who went before us, paying a high price when they stood for truth. Don't you see? By its very nature, these demon-inspired practices negate the message of the Cross, yet you have blindly allowed it to enter—"

"Mr. Goldsmith, I insist you leave now, or I will have these officers arrest you immediately." Harvey Metzger returned to the microphone to address the audience. "May I have your attention? I'm terribly sorry, my sincere apologies to any representatives from the Center for Youth Transformation who may still be here. Please remain calm. I think it's time for a song. Would the worship team come up here, please?" He hoped that would break the roll Sam was on. After all, the last thing Dr. Metzger wanted was headlines in the morning paper proclaiming that his church was responsible for some out-of-town college professor being arrested. But he would do have him arrested if he had to.

"I'm sorry too," said Sam, looking down at his missions team. "I think we have seen enough. Let's go." The team members gathered their things and stood up.

A few students from other teams jeered and laughed, but most sat silently as Sam, Katy, and the rest of their team went quietly to the exit at the side of the gym. The door closed behind them. It was dark outside. Dr. Metzger's voice could still be heard over the sound system. "Um... students, please don't get up. Sit back down. The evening is NOT over yet! I said sit down! We are recording this event for our blog! Where are you going! Wait! Please stay seated." His voice had a note of desperation. "I repeat, the pizza is coming in about half an hour. Please come back to your seats if you want pizza!"

As Sam held open the back door for Katy and the other team members, he saw the police officers shaking their heads, then they too left the building and disappeared in their patrol cars. When the last team member walked through the double doors, Sam let the door close behind him and walked over to Katy. "In a small way," he said to her, "this experience was a little like that of the famous preacher from communist Romania, Richard Wurmbrand, who stood and defied the communist church leaders when he boldly declared the Gospel to them. Only dear pastor Wurmbrand wasn't able to walk away as we just did. He was arrested, imprisoned, and tortured for eight years. How could you and I do any less than what we did tonight?"

Katy nodded quietly in agreement.

*Besides*, thought Sam, *had I remained silent this evening, I could never have looked at myself in the mirror again.*

As Sam and his team walked toward the street, he continued pondering what had just happened. Shaking his head in bewilderment he looked at Katy and said, "How can that man talk to those kids about pizza and completely ignore the things we said? I think we should spend a little time in prayer." Looking at a note in his pocket he added, "Looks like our bus isn't coming for another hour anyway."

It was then that they heard a swell of voices coming up from behind them. They'd been unaware that a number of students had followed them out of the building shortly after they'd left.

"Mr. Goldsmith!" a voice called. "We want to hear more. Please!"

Sam turned around. The street light wasn't very bright, but it appeared that the grassy area behind the gymnasium was beginning to fill with people. In no time at all, a crowd had gathered and was now walking toward him.

"Well," he said to them, utterly surprised, "it's not exactly warm and comfortable out here, and it's starting to rain." He looked up at the cloud-filled, blustery sky.

"We don't care! It always rains in Seattle. Just tell us the truth!"

A few others yelled out similar requests. There was an urgency in their voices. Soon, nearly forty students and even a few teachers stood around Sam's small group, pleading with him to speak with them.

Sam motioned the group toward the shelter of a large Douglas fir tree near the church parking lot. He spoke to them for twenty minutes about the roots of ancient-future worship and contemplative spirituality, contrasting it to what the Bible says. It was heavy and hard-hitting. The looks on the students' faces indicated they'd not heard anything like this before. Sam explained that the premise behind this mystical spirituality was the belief that all things in creation were interconnected because God dwelt in all things, including all of mankind, and this indwelling did not depend on the Cross of Calvary. When Sam finally finished, he sat down on the cement curb and put his head in his hands. The small audience was very quiet. Had they not liked what he said?

A girl wearing a baseball cap called out from the crowd. "We had no idea! Now tell us what we can do about it!"

"We need to repent of our idolatry!" came a man's voice from the other side of the small crowd. It was Jonas, the church's youth leader.

"Well, we didn't know. It's our teachers who are the idolaters," called out another young man.

"Yeah, we weren't doing bad stuff on purpose," said a girl, who sounded like she was ready to cry.

"Still, we were dishonoring God," said someone from the back of the crowd, "even though we didn't understand that's what we were doing."

"That's right," called out another. "We should ask God's forgiveness—and we sure better pray for our teachers."

These remarks made a profound impact on the crowd. Spontaneously, one by one, students began calling on the name of the Lord. Some of them were weeping. At about the same time, the rain picked up and began pounding on the pavement. As many as could in the crowd huddled under the tree. Through the conviction and power of the Holy Spirit, students and leaders alike repented and asked God to help them bravely stand up for the truth. Sam, Katy and their friends prayed with them all. Before the group left, several teachers took Sam's hand into their own, and shook it long and vigorously. They all thanked Katy for her courage and her boldness. Jonas was the last to talk to them.

"I'm sorry. I didn't know," he said, his voice cracking. "How can I thank you enough?"

They promised to stay in touch with Jonas and exchanged phone numbers. Sam gave Jonas a strong bear hug and watched him disappear, back into the church.

The Flat Plains team members, though wet and cold, were completely amazed at what had just transpired. They piled into the sixteen-passenger bus that had now arrived for them. While finding their seats, Sam leaned toward Katy and said, "What an evening! Way to go, Katherine the Bold! I am so proud of you." He reached over the front seat and gently punched her in the shoulder.

"Yeah Katy!" the team yelled, almost in unison.

"Yeah God!" another shouted.

As the bus pulled away from the curb, Sam looked back and saw Dr. Metzger and his people standing in the doorway of the church's gymnasium. They seemed hesitant to step out into the rain. Perhaps the downpour had been a blessing in disguise.

"I don't think we've seen the last of him," said Sam quietly. "Dr. Metzger is on the board of directors of our church conference. Boy, I hate leaving Jonas there to face their wrath alone."

"God will take care of him," replied Katy confidently.

All the way to their hotel, the team could hardly contain their excitement over the evening's events. They praised God for His goodness and were filled with hopeful anticipation for what He would do when they got back to their college. They were also very excited when the bus pulled into the hotel parking lot next to a glass-enclosed swimming pool. After sleeping in church basements and youth hostels for nearly two weeks, this place would be heavenly.

"Were you nervous?" Sam asked Katy after the last person had retrieved his luggage from the bus. It had finally stopped raining.

"Nervous? You mean tonight?" Katy slung her backpack over her shoulder, picked up her suitcase, and headed for the stairs. She was chilled from standing out in the rain and was looking forward to a soak in a hot tub with the others.

"You know," she said, pausing on the first step, "I used to wonder if the martyrs were nervous when they were burned at the stake. Now I think I understand what inspired them. We have to stand up for the truth today, like they did. Do you know there is a legend of a fourth-century martyr from Alexandria named Katherine who was tortured on a spiked wheel—"

"Katy?" Sam tried to interrupt. The others had all raced up the stairs ahead of them and were already in their rooms, quickly changing into their swimsuits.

She kept talking, ". . . and ever since the Middle Ages it has been a household name."

"Katarina."

Sam took Katy's bags from her hands, set them on the ground, and held her by the shoulders. He pulled her away from the stairs and gently moved her against the glass enclosure of the indoor pool. It felt warm on her back.

"Katarina . . from the Greek word, *katheros*. It means pure."

The glowing blue light that reflected from the indoor swimming pool shimmered in waves all around them. Katy looked up into Sam's eyes. Why had she never noticed how intense they were? Her heart began to beat very fast. For the first time in her life, Katy Buckler had absolutely nothing to say.

"Katy, Katarina," said Sam, looking deep into the eyes of her soul. "We are leaving in the morning. Tomorrow night we'll be back in Flat Plains, and you will be going back home to your parents' house the next day, correct?"

"Yes," she whispered. She wondered for a moment if he could hear the thumping of her heart the way she heard it pounding in her ears.

"And soon you will no longer be my student, correct?"

"Yes."

"Katy, this morning the Lord led me to Psalm 35 where I read, 'Take hold of the shield and buckler, and stand up for mine help.' Katy Buckler, do you know the Old Testament meaning of 'take hold'?"

Katy felt as if the earth had stopped rotating beneath her feet and that if she breathed she would fall right off. She had the odd sensation of barely being able to get her next words out.

"It means," she said softly, "it means to bind bonds strongly . . . to tie fast. Yes?"

Sam knelt down on one knee before her. He took her hand in his and looked into her eyes that were the color of dark melting chocolate.

"Katarina Buckler, will you marry me?"


As a dozen or so college students grabbed their towels and headed down to the indoor pool, one of the girls glanced out a hallway window and remarked to her teammates, "If I didn't know better, I'd say that was Sam Goldsmith out there kissing Katy Buckler's hand."

As they raced to catch two open elevator doors, they all roared with laughter at what seemed a preposterous comment.

"Wait a minute," said one of them. "Where *is* Katy?"

"I don't know," said another. "Has anyone seen Sam?"

26

## FRIDAY MORNING

What a friend we have in Jesus
All our sins and griefs to bear.
What a privilege to carry
Everything to God in prayer!

MARCH 27

"JB kissed me good-bye and hopped into our old Ford pickup and reminded me to pray for him. Then he drove away. He didn't even bother to pack a suitcase!" said Margaret.

"Is he positive about this?" asked Dora, a lady with pleasant, suntanned wrinkles. "These are very serious accusations to be making. After all, Flat Plains has been a trusted Bible college for over fifty years!"

Many of the ladies in Margaret's Friday morning prayer group had just returned from Palm Springs earlier that week. Now, as Margaret calmly told her story, they were stunned to hear about the things being taught at the school their donations had supported for so many years where many of the ladies' grandchildren attended. Deep concern was reflected in their expressions.

"Yes, Dora, Jacob is very sure," answered Margaret. "He's been researching for over a month now, day and night, and there is not a shadow of doubt that this woman has been teaching a spirituality that is rooted in ancient paganism."

"Oh Margaret. I have always trusted JB's judgment," said Sherry, the church's librarian. "But as you can imagine, this is a huge, shocking revelation to come home to!"

The ladies in Margaret's Bible study group carried their Bibles and teacups to the kitchen and gathered around the long farm table in the Brown's house.

"Well, if it's as you say, Margaret, I don't think there's anything better we can do this morning than bring it to the Lord in prayer." Ninety-year-old Betty was always the most outspoken one in their group. She was also the one who always prayed about *everything*.

"Yes, Betty, you are right," agreed her cousin Emma, dipping her oatmeal cookie into her hot tea. "We should have been praying about this a long time ago. Margaret, you should have told us sooner."

"To be honest, I . . . I didn't know whether you'd believe me," Margaret said quietly as she passed a plate of home-baked cookies around the table. "I can hardly believe it myself."

"Margaret, I feel terribly convicted," said Dora, the youngest in the group. "Some of us have been eating dates under palm trees and lounging by the pool in southern California all winter long while this has been going on at home. I feel like I've had my head buried in the sand!"

One by one, these physically frail but spiritually strong saints of God took turns reading passages from the Bible, often reciting Scripture verses by memory. And through it all, they prayed—their humble, earnest prayers rising like incense to the very throne room of their holy, sovereign God.

That afternoon, Sherry and Betty phoned all their friends, who in turn phoned all *their* friends. By evening, hundreds of concerned people were praying fervently for Jacob Brown, Teresa Dawson, and Flat Plains Bible College . . . and they were praying that God would bring to light those things hidden in darkness.

Jacob drove all the way to Flat Plains in one day, stopping only for fuel, and once for a bite to eat and some coffee. Deep in thought and praying frequently, the miles and hours passed quickly for him as he prepared himself for the confrontation to come.

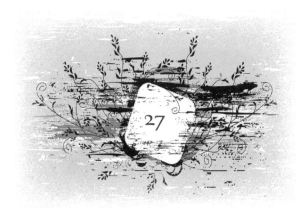

## The Woodsman

OUTSIDE a small cabin at the edge of a lake, a woodsman in a Carhartt vest and cap firmly wedged his axe into a chopping block and gathered a load of freshly split firewood into his arms. Dark clouds began rolling in as he carried the wood into his cabin and dropped the logs into a box beside a warm, crackling woodstove. He tossed two nice pieces of alder into the cook stove, turned on the radio, and filled a cast-iron kettle with water.

The weather announcer warned that two big weather systems were about to clash in the area, bringing on a violent spring storm. The woodsman stood at his window, and as he watched the sky turn black, he was thankful for the roof over his head and a cupboard full of provisions. His cabin was small but sturdy, and its builder had carved the foundation right into a rock. He was prepared for snow, sleet, rain, or whatever the approaching storm might bring.

"Guess I was a little hasty, shaving off my winter fur for the spring," he said to the gray tabby on the ledge staring out the window and twitching her tail. "Yeah, I know, I don't like it either. They call it The Quiet Place, but it's just a westernized Ashram where the Foxes teach their eastern-style meditation." He shook his head and sighed at the round tent-like structure across the lake that looked like a giant marshmallow. He wondered if it would hold in this storm.

"Well, kitty, it's a good thing I quit working at the lodge when I did," he said, stroking her soft fur. "I'd hate to be the one to clean it up when it all collapses. Since it's built on a pier, the structure will be very unsteady, especially during the spring thaw. Expect the lake to be a mess, ol' girl."

He hung up a pair of dress pants and a shirt he'd picked up at the cleaners that afternoon and put away his folded laundry. When the kettle began to whistle, he poured the water slowly through a small sieve filled with coffee grounds into a mug. Then he sat down on a wide willow rocking chair, kicked off his worn hiking boots, and warmed his feet by the stove. While the man was slowly sipping his black coffee, deep in thought, the cat suddenly jumped onto his lap, languidly stretched her body, and kneaded his legs with her claws.

"Aren't you being friendly today? Good thing I'm wearing my long johns." The woodsman laughed. His furry friend had been hanging around the cabin for a few months, and it had taken no small amount of patience and fish heads to gain her trust. After the cat poked a few more holes in his jeans with her sharp claws, she curled up in his lap, closed her eyes, and purred contentedly. He gently stroked her warm back and smiled at his little companion. "Sometimes it takes a while to figure out where we're safe, doesn't it?"

He could relate to that. That's why he was here, hiding from the world and trying to figure things out. But it wasn't always this way. For his first two years after high school, things had been good. He had found a job working at the camp across the lake, doing maintenance work during the day and attending their Bible studies in the evening. *Those were wonderful days*, he remembered with a forlorn kind of fondness. He had grown so much in his relationship with the Lord during that time. Yes, things had been good. Then the Bible camp was sold to another Christian organization. And when the new owners had arrived last year, it didn't take him long to realize they had big plans for big changes. They had still planned to host retreats, but rather than offering Bible studies and opportunities to worship God in song, they now offered programs that included things like mantra meditation, lectio divina and Christian yoga. They had even hired an artist to paint a "Christ-centered" labyrinth on the floor of the fireside room in the basement. How shocking to see churches, Christian schools, and seminaries sending their leaders there for retreats. The last straw for him came about three months after the Foxes had arrived on the scene. The day indelibly etched in his memory was the day that the Flat Plains Bible College faculty had come for their annual staff retreat. The newest member of the staff was a woman who called herself a spiritual director and who actually convinced the rest of the staff to walk the new labyrinth.

The young woodsman had had enough personal experience with that kind of mystical, esoteric spirituality to know a bad thing when he saw it. He'd come out of all that and found the Lord—well, the Lord had found him.

That day the Flat Plains faculty had come, he been amazed that only two of their professors had recognized the inherent danger in the contemplative practices. He remembered how shocked his friend, Sam (one of the two "trouble-making" professors from Flat Plains), had sounded when he had called and asked for a lift back to the school. Sam had wanted to remain at the college to be salt and light, but the other professor resigned from his position immediately and left that very same day.

"And that's when I quit my job at the lodge," he said softly aloud, looking down at the sleeping tabby on his lap as if she somehow understood. "And that's also why you and I are living on lake trout and beans."

Soon, the wind chimes outside the cabin window began playing their delicate song louder and louder. He picked up his telephone, dialed the number again and got the same recorded message he'd been hearing for three days: "The person you are calling cannot be reached." He put the phone down and took a gulp of coffee. He remembered the frightened eyes of the beautiful girl with the long brown hair. He had not been able to forget her. Had she recognized him that day in town? His beard was gone by then. Had she noticed his surprise when he saw her again? *He* recognized her instantly. She looked exactly as he remembered her looking on that chilly autumn day when he first saw her standing on the bridge with her red scarf. She had come from the retreat center.

That was the day Nathan had started to pray for Tessa. Their meeting had confirmed what he believed God had been pressing on him for months—that it was time for the woodsman to deal with his disillusionment and his concerns, and get busy doing something constructive about the problem that had begun across the lake but was now spreading farther than he had ever imagined it would.

But right now, at this moment, all he could do was sit tight in the safety of his cabin and trust God to get the beautiful girl through the spiritual storm surely raging inside her. Only the Lord could break the stranglehold of the lies that held her in bondage.

Outside, thunder began to rumble in the distance and raindrops started spattering on the metal roof overhead. Sitting in his chair, he removed his cap, bowed his head, and began to pray. Cradled in his hands was a hand-knit red scarf.

Meanwhile, across the lake at Quiet Waters Lodge, no one heard the loud creaking and groaning above the din of the fast-approaching storm. Moments later, the strong, cold March winds began to heave The Quiet Place from its floating foundation.

28

## Ekstasis Night

Remember therefore from whence thou art fallen, and repent, and do the first works; or else I will come unto thee quickly, and will remove thy candlestick out of his place, except thou repent. Revelation 2:5

MARCH 27—FRIDAY EVENING

ROOM 109 in the Thompson Building was decorated much the same as the Sacred Space, but being a double-sized room, Ms. Jasmine had opened the divider and had done her best to make it more elaborate. This was going to be her evening.

"This is my favorite prayer station, Thomas," said Ms. Jasmine excitedly to the student council president as she gave him a quick tour of the room. This was Thomas' final year at Flat Plains, and he was an intern youth pastor at a community church in a nearby town. If she could get him interested in spiritual formation, maybe she would be invited to speak in his church.

She led him past a large cross that was leaning against some wooden crates and over to a heavy green curtain that hung from the ceiling. She pulled it aside to let him have a peek. In the corner were candles of various heights and sizes surrounded by bowls of various shapes. Some were filled with water, some with stones. A golden chalice had been placed beside a bread-filled basket on a small wooden altar.

"It's just one of many Sacred Spaces we've made for this evening's prayer journey. The candles will all be lit in a few minutes. Try to imagine the ambiance," she urged enthusiastically. "The cup will be filled with the fruit of the vine for dipping the bread during the Eucharist."

"Interesting art," the young intern pastor said, noticing the new pictures Ms. Jasmine had hung on the wall. "Uh, did you say Eucharist?" His expression told Ms. Jasmine he would need some time adjusting to this word. Dr. Johnson had warned Ms. Jasmine that there would be some students who would raise their eyebrows to new ideas in spirituality. But hopefully that would all change very soon.

"Pardon me, did I say Eucharist? I meant communion...it's...ah, it's the same thing." The last thing she wanted to get into tonight was a theological debate over the Catholic doctrine that Jesus was actually present in the bread and wine during Mass. She quickly turned Thomas' attention back to the artwork. "These works of art are prints of the paintings hanging at Quiet Waters Lodge. This is a print of St. Teresa of Avila and this is of St. John of the Cross," she stated, pointing to each one reverently. "The church today has lost so much richness that it needs to rediscover....." Ms. Jasmine's voice trailed off as she reached into her bag, pulled out her cell phone, and began punching numbers.

Tom looked up and smiled at Tessa as she jogged through the door in her track suit. "Tessa, hi!"

"Uh, hi, Tom," Tessa wondered if he'd be a good one to talk to. He was going to be a youth pastor after he graduated. She wanted to pull him aside and ask him, but Ms. Jasmine was standing right beside him.

Ms. Jasmine looked Tessa up and down, a disapproving expression on her face.

"You're late," she scolded. "Didn't you get my messages?"

"But I'm right on time, and . . . I didn't get any messages, Ms. Jazz. My phone, it hasn't been—"

"Oh forget it!" she snapped. "I want every candle lit. And here, go fill the chalice with grape juice, and hurry back! It's almost time."

"But the fire regulations . . . Dr. Johnson said to remind you that if—"

"Never mind the rules." Ms. Jasmine handed Tessa a lighter and told her to get going.

Tessa looked at the open bottle Ms. Jasmine had just given her.

"Uh, Ms. Jazz?" Tessa said stunned.

"I've already taken the cork out. Now get going."

"But, this isn't grape juice." Tessa remembered the familiar aroma from the night of the accident. It made her sick. She remembered her parents going out the door that evening. Her mom was beautiful. They were going to their favorite restaurant to celebrate their anniversary and were leaving twelve-year-old Tessa with the baby-sitter. A few minutes after they walked out the door, the sound of a sickening crash and a thud sliced through the night air. Tessa ran to the intersection half a block from her house. As the sirens got closer, a man stumbled out of a car with a crumpled hood and poured the rest of his bottle into the storm drain. Shocked, Tessa stood nearby, the smell of alcohol filling her nostrils. When the ambulance arrived, they had to use the jaws of life to get her parents out of their car. By then, it was too late . . .

"Everything will be fine. Just hurry up!" Ms. Jasmine's voice jolted her back to the present. "And there's more in the fridge for refills—would you keep an eye on that?"

"I just don't understand why we are using real wine," Tessa said with a confused expression.

"Honestly, Tessa, you worry too much!" Ms. Jasmine said as she rushed off.

By the time Tessa lit the last candle, room 109 was beginning to fill up with people. She handed the butane lighter back to Ms. Jasmine who was smiling and graciously welcoming students as they walked through the door. "Welcome to our first experiential worship night." They were mostly students Tessa knew from her spiritual formation class, but there were about half a dozen faces she didn't recognize.

Ms. Jasmine turned to Tessa. "Here, it's your turn. While I dim the lights, keep handing these out to everyone who comes in. Why are you so deathly pale? And what on earth are you wearing?"

"Dr. Winters, I wanted to tell you earlier . . . I don't know if I can stay here. I . . ."

"What?" Ms. Jasmine shouted over the sound of the music. Someone had turned the volume up high.

Ms. Jasmine was beginning to get another one of her bad headaches, and her favorite *Soaking in Silence* relaxation CD wasn't scheduled to be played until the last half hour of the evening.

"I said, I don't think I can stay here."

"What did you say?" Ms. Jasmine stepped closer.

"I'm sorry. Please, Ms. Jazz, I . . ."

"Tessa!" Ms. Jasmine grabbed Tessa's arm and pulled her into the hall. She stood so close that Tessa could smell her breath. Not only did Ms. Jasmine's eyes pierce her, so did her long red fingernails. She spoke sternly and slowly. "Read . . . my . . . lips. I have to go to the microphone now, and introduce these students to experiential worship. Then, I expect you to lead the students through the prayer stations exactly as we have practiced. Remember, there are newcomers here tonight. The president of this college is dropping in sometime during the evening as well. Our presentation has *got* to run smoothly. Tessa, I'm depending on you to do your very best. And one more thing. You should know that it's now a toss-up between you and Elise as to who gets the thousand-dollar Rising Star scholarship from Spiritual Transformation Institute. Remember, this is *my* night."

Then Tessa found herself standing alone by the door, rubbing her arm where Ms. Jasmine's nails had torn her skin. She pressed on the sleeve of her shirt to soothe the burning sensation. With a forced, artificial smile, she waited for the last stragglers to arrive, mechanically greeting them as they came. Elise and her roommate were among the last ones to show up.

"Tessa," said Elise, a look of pity in her eyes, "are you feeling OK? You look really pale. You wanna borrow some of my makeup? Let's see, all I've got is some pale pink blush, but at least it will make you look less pasty. On second thought, maybe you should go see the campus nurse. You don't look too good."

"I'm fine, really." Tessa didn't want to talk to Elise. Following that dreadful session in Sacred Space last Tuesday, Tessa had caught up with Elise and confided in her. She had expressed her concerns, but apparently they'd fallen on deaf ears. Elise hadn't said much. In fact, she had totally ignored Tessa since then. Some friend.

*What is happening to me?* Tessa wondered mournfully. A month ago, she had been so excited that Ms. Jasmine had chosen her to be the assistant for this evening's presentation. Ms. Jasmine had even doubled the number of spiritual direction sessions with her, to make sure Tessa understood everything. She often said that Tessa was her best student, and was pleased she was growing in her skills and giftings daily. Tessa had always been quick to accept Ms. Jasmine's every word. But all that had changed, ever since the night before Katy had left.

Annoying, talkative Katy. She sure wished she could talk to her right about now.

It was 7:04 p.m. when Dr. Jasmine Winters stepped onto the stage and took the microphone. Dazzling under the spotlight, hers was a commanding presence with her smooth platinum hair falling straight down the back of a long, scarlet, medieval-looking dress with flowing sleeves. Colored lights danced on the walls, reflecting brilliant purple off the beautiful amethyst stone that hung at the end of her pearl necklace. Tessa remembered that Ms. Jasmine had shown her the stone during one of their sessions. It had been a gift from her great-aunt. Looking at her now, most people might have thought she looked like an angel from heaven as she stood under the lights. But just which kind of angel, Tessa was no longer sure.

Unexpectedly, she remembered Katy's words of warning, words that had made her so angry at the time. It had been a few weeks ago. Tessa had excitedly told Katy about the things she'd been experiencing during her quiet times as she journaled the words Jesus was speaking to her.

"Tessa, I don't care whose voice you think you are hearing. Be careful! Don't you know even Satan disguises himself as an angel of light? The Bible warns us not to be surprised if his servants also disguise themselves as servants of righteousness."

Tessa's brow creased and her face turned somber as she watched Ms. Jasmine motion for the microphone to be turned louder and the music turned down.

"Good evening everyone," a smiling Ms. Jasmine began in a low, somewhat sultry voice. "My name is Jasmine Winters, and I'd like to welcome all of you here tonight. Some of you are visiting. We'd like to welcome the youth group from Flat Plains Church. We are glad you came out."

After the whistling and cheering died down, she continued.

"Now, all of you who are in our first year of spiritual formation have been to our Taizé night and our labyrinth walks, but you may not have heard about the latest worship experience called Ekstasis. Tonight will be the culmination of all we have learned, and will continue to learn, but with a new twist where ancient meets new! Tonight Flat Plains takes its first step up from the flat plains and into the new ancient-future worship. My assistant, Tessa, and I will lead you through the spiritual practices this evening. "

Dr. Winters pointed a manicured hand toward Tessa. All eyes turned to the pale, slender girl at the back of the room.

"Smile Tessa," said Ms. Jasmine. Some of the guys whistled. "I also have good news and some bad news. The bad news is that the prayer walk we were going to do on our outdoor labyrinth is going to be rained out. The good news is that we have set up alternative prayer stations here in this room. In fact, the worship arts team has brought in a portable canvas labyrinth that you will find on the other side of the room divider. By the way, after today, the labyrinth kit will be available for sign-out in our school library, in case any of you interns out there want to introduce it to your youth groups." Ms. Jasmine looked at Thomas as she spoke. He nodded, looking pleased.

"We'll get started in a moment, but first I do want to mention that you are welcome to come and receive ashes on your forehead before you start the prayer stations, to celebrate Lent. So now, we'll begin the Ekstasis worship night with Techno Monk. Then we will guide you in a Taizé chant, then through the prayer stations, and then end the evening with a soaking prayer session. I guarantee you will love how we end this evening! I am certain it will be an unforgettable experience for us all. And now as our DJ turns on the strobe lights, let the music take you outside of yourself!"

Immediately, as if on cue, the ceiling lights were turned off, the popular Techno Monk beat was turned up, and a strobe light began to flash. Tessa quietly leaned against the wall at the back of the room while the students cheered and began dancing and jumping vigorously up and down, like in a rave or mosh pit. She wanted to leave, but she was too distraught to move. A battle raged inside her. The mood was enticing and the hypnotic beat drew her, but strangely she also had the oddest sense that she was not supposed to be there. If it weren't for her recent concerns about Ms. Jasmine, she knew she would be jumping to the beat along with all the others.

Tessa was feeling sick and confused, hot and cold all at the same time. She was beginning to feel panicky and didn't know what to do. *Maybe if I stay for the first half hour, Ms. Jasmine won't notice if I slip out later.* Then Tessa heard a familiar voice telling her to stay, and something began to surge up inside her. It was that feeling again, and it frightened her. But this time, she also heard another voice—"Tessa, you are mine. Choose me and come out." Strangely, she wasn't afraid of that voice.

She remembered Nathan's words, "Is He calling you to come out?"

IN the old farmhouse, the clock on the mantel chimed seven times. On the floor in front of the woodstove a small brown and white dog lay snoring beside a pair of fuzzy pink slippers. The only other sound in the cozy farmhouse came from the kitchen, where a white-haired prayer warrior sat at the end of a long table with her head bowed. Her hands were folded on a worn-out book as she quietly spoke.

"...and You know where our Teresa is right now, dear Lord, and so I ask that You speak to her and show her the right path to choose. Give her ears to hear, and guide and protect her steps. Shine Your light where there is darkness. Protect her tonight, in the name of Jesus, and may this be the day she makes a decision for You."

She dabbed her soft cheeks with a crumpled, wet handkerchief.

"And Father, I thank You for hearing our requests and answering them, according to Your will. I also ask that You guide Jacob tonight.

Fill him with Your wisdom and boldness. Send help to him, and may his judgment shine like the noonday sun. May he fulfill the works that You have prepared for him to do."

When Margaret finally said "amen," she heated some milk, tossed three logs into the woodstove, slipped on her warm pink slippers, and went up to bed.

Downstairs the clock on the mantel played its comforting midnight melody and chimed twelve times, just as it had done for forty years.

MS. JASMINE rang a small bell into the microphone. It was time to start the next phase of the worship experience. Tessa had been standing against the wall like a frozen statue during the first three Techno Monk songs. Now as the Taizé chants began, she felt like a prisoner of war, trying to resist mind-control techniques and as though she were caught in a bad dream from which she could never wake up.

Students began to approach her, asking about the correct order of the prayer stations. She numbly handed them each a direction card from the stack she had printed the week before and pointed to the first instruction on the list—

Number One
Go to the cross

The cross. It was made from an old, rough wooden beam that some-one from the worship arts class had found on a junk heap. She hadn't seen it until today. As Tessa continued to go through the motions, handing out cards like a robot, she couldn't help but stare at the rustic piece of wood. It looked so much like the hand-hewn support beam in the solid barn that Gramps had built—the one she had gazed at so often on long winter evenings while she lay stretched out on hay bales nibbling carrots with Sassy. The verse Gramps had etched into that one was from the book of Proverbs, and now it came to her mind with full clarity:

The name of the LORD is a strong tower: the righteous runneth into it, and is safe. Proverbs 18:10

Time seemed to stand still as Tessa looked around the room. When the presentation on the PowerPoint began to play, her mind felt foggy. It was the DVD she had helped make with the worship arts team for their Christianity and Imagination project to set the background mood for the next worship phase. Sonya and Elise were among the preoccupied students who sat cross-legged on yoga mats while images of Mary, baby Jesus, Celtic crosses and an Egyptian winged sun disc flashed across a screen in the darkened room. Two intern youth pastors lay on their backs next to the incense station, their eyes glazed over as if in a trance. One of them was Thomas, who was chanting a Latin phrase over and over in time to the repetitive beat. The sound man had long since stopped changing the music and lay nearly motionless on the floor beside the control panel.

Suddenly she realized something was very wrong with this picture. Nothing lined up. Nothing lined up with what Gramps said, with what Katy said. They wouldn't be here, doing this kind of stuff, because this was all wrong. Ms. Jasmine was wrong, Dr. Johnson was wrong. "Oh Lord, show me what to do. Please help me."

Something inside Tessa told her to go.

It was time to make a decision.

Ms. Jasmine had looked over at Tessa a few minutes earlier and given her the oddest look. Tessa didn't know it, but the expression on her face revealed what was happening inside her—her eyes were wide and her jaw was clenched. Suddenly she felt that presence—the one she'd first felt at the labyrinth and the one that sometimes engulfed her when she was going into the silence. But this time, it wasn't the same. It felt constricting, suffocating... evil. She had to get out of the room. She would wait until Ms. Jasmine was looking the other way, then she would make a dash for it. It felt as if her life depended on it.

No one noticed the slender girl in the shadows put on her jacket, pick up her backpack, tiptoe through the maze of bodies and slip out the back door. There was only a whiff of smoke from the candles that flickered as the door quietly swung shut.

## 29

# In Like a Lion, Out Like a . . .

*And they rejected his statutes, and his covenant that
he made with their fathers, and his testimonies which
he testified against them; and they followed vanity, and
became vain, and went after the heathen that were round
about them, concerning whom the LORD had charged
them, that they should not do like them.* II Kings 17:15

MARCH 27—EVENING

A steady beat boomed in the distance as Dr. Frank Johnson walked
into his dark office and set a stack of student essays on his desk for
marking. Suddenly, his chair moved. He jumped back, startled.

"Hello there."

"Who the devil is there?" said Dr. Johnson startled and angry.
He took a few steps to the door and flicked on the light.

"Oh no, I'm not him, I can assure you. I am Teresa Dawson's
grandfather," Jacob introduced himself as he swiveled the chair to
face the president of Flat Plains Bible College. Even if Jacob hadn't
recognized him from his picture on the college website, he could
have spotted the family resemblance. It seemed like only yesterday
he had chummed around with Frank Johnson Sr. in Bible college,
and now here he was, confronting his middle-aged son.

"You must be Frank Johnson."

Jacob held out his hand. Dr. Johnson shrugged and reluctantly shook Jacob's hand.

"Oh, let me guess. Mr. Brown, caretaker of the foster girl whom you refer to as your granddaughter. That explains the old pickup with the canopy I saw in the parking lot. So, what can I do for you? You do know that the term isn't over yet, don't you?"

"Actually, I was doing some reading," said Jacob calmly, holding up a paper.

"You drove all the way to Flat Plains to do some reading?" Dr. Johnson said, mildly sarcastic. "Where'd you get that?" he asked, eyeing the paper Jacob held in front of him.

"I'll answer that if you tell me where you got *that*," Jacob pointed to a string of beads that hung on a large portrait of the school's founder, Isaac Thompson.

"What! That's not ... those are ... uh—"

"Your rosary beads?"

"Those aren't mine! Even if they were, I don't have to answer to someone who snuck into my private office."

"Someday, we will all have to answer to God," Jacob said cryptically, "especially teachers—who will receive a stricter judgment. Frank, this is a Protestant, evangelical Bible college."

"You don't have to tell me what kind of college this is! Now tell me where you got that piece of paper?" Frank demanded.

"I just thought I'd help you clean up before all the visitors arrive next month for graduation." Jacob held up the paper he had ripped off the bulletin board in the hall, still keeping it out of Dr. Johnson's reach.

"It's not what you think!" protested the president, bracing himself for a debate. He took a deep breath and tried to relax the muscles in his neck while Jacob carried on—

"And what is that loud beating I hear?" Jacob asked.

"Oh ... that? Why ... uh ... oh yes, I believe that must be band practice. These old walls really echo, you know." Frank hoped the old man wouldn't get too curious about the noise.

"Let's see, I think I was just at the part that said ..." Jacob cleared his throat, then began reading:

Spring Labyrinth Walk
A prayer of stillness is offered when entering the labyrinth.
We bow to the earth. We reach to the sky;
We embrace our true selves. And bless the earth.
Wake yourself up to wisdom within

Jacob pulled off his reading glasses and leaned back in Dr. Johnson's chair.

"Tell me Frank, did you know Isaac Thompson?" he asked, pointing a finger at the painting.

"Never met him," Frank answered dryly.

"Well, he taught me pretty much everything I know about the Bible. He was a man of God. And if he were alive today, he would be asking why a college founded on the precepts of God's Word is teaching its students an unbiblical spirituality?"

"Mr. Brown, we've been over this on the phone. Dr. Winters designed the labyrinth, and she came to us last fall with high recommendations from the Spiritual Transformation Institute. She is—"

"That transformation center she came from has a history of promoting New Age meditation techniques," Jacob said. "Don't you understand? The labyrinth is something I'd expect to see at a New Age festival or . . . or an eastern meditation center."

"But . . . students are spending more hours in prayer than we ever dreamed of!" Frank argued. "As part of their spiritual formation, the labyrinth offers spiritual fulfillment to an emerging generation that has new questions, new doubts—"

"There are no more questions today than there were thousands of years ago!" Jacob sighed and lowered his tone. "Look, King Solomon said there is nothing new under the sun. You want to offer your students spiritual fulfillment? They will only find it through a close, faithful relationship with Jesus Christ, one that is founded on His Word, the Bible, not in a labyrinth! Not through centering down with mother earth, but through the blood of Him who was sent to by the Father so that we might be saved."

"Yes of course, and that's why it's a Christ-centered labyrinth.

The New Age stole spiritual practices like the labyrinth, and we can reclaim them for God. Christ is the divine illumination within each one of us . . . when we find our true selves—"

"Divine illumination! Frank, I beg you, consider the words of Christ when He said He is the way, the truth, and the life, and no man comes to the Father but by Him. He came to save us *from* our true selves! What you are teaching here is humanism, it's esoteric philosophy . . . it's . . . it's occultism."

"Mr. Brown." Frank paused, closed his eyes for a few seconds, and took another deep cleansing breath. "This dialogue is going nowhere. May I remind you that this is not the way of today's Christ follower. Here at Flat Plains we have begun to look at the old doctrines you have mentioned, in fresh, new ways. For example, the views of other cultural traditions and other models of a non-violent atonement. You obviously don't yet understand the deep spirituality we are teaching here! We are moving away from the narrow-minded ideology and dogmas of former generations."

"Narrow-minded?" Jacob asked. His eyebrows rose as he examined the man who stood before him. "Tell me Frank, what does Scripture mean when it says 'narrow is the way, which leadeth unto life, and few there be that find it'?"

"Oh sure, the way is narrow, but that doesn't mean narrow-minded," answered Frank sharply.

"What is that supposed to mean?" Jacob went on. "Frank, do you believe that Jesus Christ is the only way of salvation?"

"Of course, but there are many different ways of interpreting that. Jesus means different things to different people and to all their various traditions, but that doesn't make one view more correct than the other."

"Oh, Frank," Jacob sighed. So this is what it had come to. Here he was, in the office that had once belonged to his beloved mentor and Bible professor, in the exact place where years ago, he had accepted Jesus Christ as His Savior and Lord. Jacob could never have imagined that the day would come when he would have to ask this question of the president of Flat Plains Bible College: "Frank, do you believe Jesus' death was the final sacrifice for our sins?"

"While the college still holds to tradition, there are many valuable views we can gather under the umbrella of—"

"Frank, answer the question. Let me reword it for you. Was Jesus Christ's sacrificial death the full and complete atonement for our sins?"

"Well, a sacrifice, yes, but Jesus was not a substitute for sin. He merely confronted the system of religious sacrifices—"

"Dr. Johnson!" Jacob was shocked, but Frank didn't blink an eye. "Did Jesus die so that sinful man could be reconciled to God?!"

"While Jesus' death was a very real thing, he didn't die *for* the sins of the world—he was killed *because* of the sins of the world. The system killed him. Jesus' life and death provided humanity with a perfect model of servant-leadership. You know, dying to self, laying down one's life, that's what I mean. We can follow His example in our own lives. He had the perfect consciousness that all humanity should strive for. But to say he had to die as some sort of substitute for the sins of others . . . well that is just not so. A loving God would never make His own son die in such a violent manner. That's just, just . . . well, it's barbaric."

For the first time since the conversation between Jacob and Frank began, Jacob sat speechless. Frank paused, then added, "We encourage our students to read all the theories, like those detailed in books you can find in any Christian bookstore . . . all are valuable to the table around which we gather."

"I was afraid of this," Jacob interjected. "Do you realize, you are actually denying the atonement?"

"While we value the traditional view—"

"You don't value God's Word! You've replaced the truth with a lie!" Jacob's fist banged on the desktop, accidentally hitting the edge of a plastic dish and catapulting it, and its lukewarm contents, through the air. Dr. Johnson, too deep in his own thoughts to jump to safety, bore the full brunt of Jacob Brown's wrath. Disgusted, he pulled out his handkerchief and attempted to wipe sticky macaroni and cheese sauce off his newly dry cleaned pant leg.

"Mr. Brown, there's no need to resort to violence! I . . . I am truly shocked at what you are insinuating. I am going to speak with Dr. Winters right now. She's a very sincere Christ follower and would love to answer your questions regarding the labyrinth. Unfortunately, at this very moment she's in . . . she's in a . . . a meeting." Dr. Johnson slowly backed up, then turned to go.

"I'm not questioning anyone's sincerity. It is possible to be sincerely wrong." Jacob hadn't meant to raise his voice, but he was losing his patience. "While you are looking for Dr. Winters, would you please locate my granddaughter and tell her that her grandfather is here to see her? I haven't heard from her in a week and would like to know what is going on."

Frank Johnson was doing his best to remain calm. The last place he wanted this man to follow him to was room 109. The older generation just wasn't ready for the new spiritual practices they had introduced to the students. This was exactly the trouble-making sort of person Dr. Winters had warned about. He was the paranoid kind of resister who feared change so much he would interfere with and even hamper the progress they had made.

"I will tell her . . . if I see her. You may wait here," he said, trying to look calm as he turned the door latch. Dr. Winters would not be pleased to hear about this.

"Quite the storm over Flat Plains tonight," Jacob said, peeking out the blinds of the office window on the second floor as the lightning flashed. "First week of spring too, and you know what they say about spring. Comes in like a lion and leaves like a—"

*Boom!* Thunder rumbled through the walls, drowning out the steady rhythm that came from the main floor below in room 109. Dr. Johnson paused briefly in the doorway, as if he had something else to say. Instead he walked out the door, his shoulder brushing the light switch off before he briskly walked down the hall, leaving his visitor to wait in the dark.

"Leaving like a snake, in this case," Jacob mumbled, finishing his sentence. He reached in his coat pocket and pulled out his cell phone. "Well, well, what have we here?"

How long had his phone been flashing? Teresa? He hadn't heard from her all week. Did she know he was here? He flipped open the phone and read the text message.

"Need 2 talk 2 u now." That was all it said.

He had come to find her tonight. Wherever she was on this campus, he was sure she needed help. The best advice he could give her was found in the Word of God. He thought of the Bible he had wrapped in paper and sent along with her and hoped she'd been reading it instead of the *New Spirituality Bible* he had noticed sitting on Frank Johnson's desk. The things Tessa had mentioned had concerned Jacob deeply and made him wonder if she had received any solid Bible teaching at this college at all. From what he had seen so far, in the short time he had been here, things were much worse than he'd originally thought.

Suddenly he was overcome with grief. This was his fault. He'd sent her to a school he'd trusted based on the school's biblical integrity and former reputation. The last time he had been at Flat Plains, things had been very, very different.

"Lord, what should I say? How do I tell her about this deception?" he prayed, his voice cracking. He had already been talking to God all the way here. Quickly he spelled out the only answer that would help her.

"Teresa, dear, remember 911."

*Surely she will catch o*n. It was all he had time for right now. He would have to find Teresa later. Jacob pushed send. "Lord, please protect our girl tonight," he prayed, hoping she wasn't present at the Ekstasis Night in room 109 that he'd read about on the Internet.

Jacob stood up, parted the blinds, and looked out the window again. A flash of lightning lit up the night sky, followed by a ferocious clap of thunder. The campus became visible just long enough so he could see the outline of the labyrinth in the distance. He shook his head. A lone figure was outside on this stormy night. Was someone actually walking the labyrinth in the rain?

Jacob watched as headlight beams slowly turned into the long driveway from the road. He glanced at his watch. It was almost nine o'clock. "Lord, Your ways are perfect and just. Do as You will tonight, but save this school from the enemy, and save our dear Teresa."

*Bang!* Another lightning strike, a little too close for comfort. In the flash, Jacob could see a convoy of vehicles approaching. It was led by one rather large 4x4 driving into the school's parking lot.

"They showed up. Praise God. They showed up! And it's high time."

# THE ELDERS

*And Nadab and Abihu, the sons of Aaron, took either
of them his censer, and put fire therein, and put incense
thereon, and offered strange fire before the LORD, which
he commanded them not. Leviticus 10:1*

A dozen men walked quietly down the hallway, turned, and
stopped at the first door on their left. Their coats were soaked through
at the shoulders from the rain. None of them were very happy about
leaving the homemade apple pie and ice cream behind at their Friday
evening songs and dessert fellowship night. Still, they were far too
curious to miss this mysterious, emergency meeting. Not much in
the way of intrigue ever happened in Flat Plains.

"Art, are you sure this is where JB said to meet? It doesn't sound right."

The stocky one wearing the Levi jacket and John Deere cap
answered "Yes, it says Room 109. This is it."

Art turned the knob and cautiously pushed the door open. The
smell of smoke and incense assaulted their senses as they slowly filed
into the room with bewildered expressions. One man nearly tripped
over a cushion laying on the floor. Another almost knocked over a
painting on an art easel that read, "Stations of the Cross." As their eyes
slowly adjusted to the dimly lit room, they noticed that motionless
students lay everywhere, seemingly unaware of the their arrival. Most
of the students' eyes remained closed while repetitive Gregorian chants

played in the background. Several girls sat in a circle, their eyes also closed, while one young man read something to them from a book in a monotone voice. Others sat cross-legged by themselves on mats. One young lady was rolling on the floor. The new arrivals recognized a few teenagers from their church who were too deep in concentration to notice the gentlemen standing there, staring in absolute disbelief. Candles and icons were sitting on various tables on the sides of the darkened room. A sign above a table strewn with paint brushes and paper read, "Worship Art Station." Above another table read, "Pray with Salt Crystals." On other tables were containers filled with sand or stones, and on the walls hung dark paintings of somber looking monks and nuns. And what was that statue over there? The mist machine Ms. Jasmine had rented to create the right mood spilled fog out of a cauldron-like container onto the floor, making it difficult to tell.

"What is all this?" one man whispered.

"What are these kids doing?" asked yet another.

"Are they on drugs or something?" asked Art in a hushed tone.

One of the men coughed loudly to get someone's attention. Just then, a woman in a long scarlet dress peered out from behind a dark curtain. There were ashes on her forehead in the shape of a cross. In one hand, she clutched rosary beads and a golden cup; in the other she held an empty wine bottle.

"Gentlemen, may I help you?" asked Dr. Winters. She smiled tentatively, trying to conceal her trepidation.

"Yes, ma'am," said the tallest man who was wearing a suit and tie. He motioned to his wide-eyed friends, standing with their mouths agape. "Pardon me, but my associates here would like to ask you a question, if it's not an inconvenience."

Despite her trepidation, Ms. Jasmine couldn't control the instant flare of anger she felt, and she was unsuccessful at hiding her irritation. "Sure. But as you gentlemen can see, the students are in the middle of a worship experience."

"Well, that's exactly . . . that's what we were wondering about," said Art. "My friends and I here have ourselves a problem. Do you know where we can find Dr. Johnson?"

## RESCUED

THERE were voices outside, and someone was pounding hard on the door.

"Teresa Dawson! Let us in!"

Tessa crawled across the floor in her dark room, pulled herself up, and opened the door. She shone her reading lamp into two concerned but smiling faces.

"Gramps?" Tessa could hardly believe her eyes. "I'm so glad to see you. But what are you doing here? And Katy? Wow, am I ever glad to see you too," Tessa blurted out, totally confused. "Oh, and did you notice? The power has gone out."

"We know! It's the storm," said Katy matter-of-factly. "Just wait a moment. Let me find my oil lamp," she continued, heading straight for her closet. Gramps and Tessa could hear her shoving boxes around in the dark, but she finally found what she was looking for. Soon the room was glowing warmly from the light.

Tessa smiled to herself. *And I always thought she was a nut for having an oil lamp in her closet.*

"Tessa! You don't look so good," Katy said as she brought Tessa into the light. "You've lost weight in the last two weeks and look at those dark circles under your eyes! What is going on down there in room 109 anyway? I saw students going in and out of there carrying candles. Ah . . . with this blackout, it's obvious, yes? I heard the fire alarm. And why are all those pickup trucks in the parking lot?"

"Oh Katy! My chatty Katy is back!" Tessa dropped Gramps' hand, which she had been clinging to since she saw him, then threw her arms around Katy, hugging her hard. "You're here! Oh, it's so good to see you both! I was praying for help, and look who God sent to me! I've been so wrong. Katy you were right all along . . . I've got to talk to you both about what's been going on here. You won't believe it, Gramps!"

"I know. I know all about it, Teresa. I do have Internet access, you know," Gramps said. He hugged her, and it made her feel warm and safe.

"You've read about this on the Internet?" Tessa searched his eyes.

"Yes, Teresa. I've been researching the things going on here. Gran and I have been very concerned, and we have been praying for you. I finally sensed the Lord urging me to drive out here this morning. I'd like to take you home with me tonight. Even though you've been officially released from the foster system . . . as far as Gran and I are concerned, well, you will always be our granddaughter. You can stay with us for as long as you like. Will you agree to leave school a couple of weeks earlier than originally planned? I think I can get it arranged for you to finish the term online from home."

"Will I agree!? Oh, Gramps, you have no idea what an answer to prayer this is!"

"Excuse me, but speaking of prayer, I think we should all stop what we're doing and spend some time in prayer right now," interrupted another voice from the doorway. "Approaching the door, I overheard the last part of your conversation, and I really think we need to pray."

"Mr. Goldsmith? What are you doing here?" Tessa asked, as Sam stepped into the golden light of the lamp.

"Uh, Tessa," said Katy. "Sam knows everything. In fact, the whole missions team now knows about what's going on, and we've been praying for you and for the school. So let's continue to pray tonight, as Sam suggested."

"Yes!" replied Tessa and Gramps in unison. They reached for each other's hands, and the four of them stood in a circle. They prayed for Tessa, for the staff, and for the students of Flat Plains Bible College. When it was Tessa's turn, she asked God to forgive her for being so blind and to help her follow Him and trust Him from then on. When the last "amen" was spoken, Tessa realized that for the first time in months, she no longer had an oppressive fear hanging over her. She felt free. The storm that had raged within her was over, even as the storm outside had subsided and the lights came back on.

"Oh how can I ever thank you? All of you!" Tessa cried joyfully, as she hugged Katy again. "And thank you for giving me Nathan's number—you have no idea . . . He is so kind."

"It's OK. Really. When you didn't respond to my text messages from Seattle, I thought you were still mad at me."

"Messages? What messages?"

"Girls," interrupted Gramps, "you can have a few minutes to talk later. But right now, you should get started packing up your things, Teresa."

"All right, Gramps." Oh it felt so good to hear him call her name. "Hey Katy, can you help me?" Katy nodded. "And while we pack, I want to hear about your missions trip." Tessa looked at Katy with new eyes—she realized, Katy was a true friend.

"Oh yes," said Katy happily. "I have lots to tell you. But first, I must let you know that I'm going home tomorrow. Mom had the baby. Another girl!"

"Aw, Katy, congratulations! You have a new little baby sister." Tessa smiled gently.

"And guess what else? I'm bringing Sam home for the weekend."

"Wha . . . ? Why? Why are you bringing your professor home to see your baby sister?" asked Tessa, totally confused.

Katy looked at Sam questioningly.

"Go ahead," he replied grinning from ear to ear. "Tell Tessa the good news."

"Tessa, Sam isn't just my professor anymore," Katy began shyly. "He asked me to marry him, and I said yes. We're getting married!"

Well, Flat Plains Bible College had never witnessed such an explosion of joy, as on that night.

When the excitement subsided somewhat, the two girls began boxing up their things. They both chattered excitedly, Katy recounting the experiences of her missions trip to Argentina and Tessa recounting her struggles of the last few weeks.

While Katy was fastening the latch on the last suitcase, Tessa looked over at her and smiled. What a true friend she had found in Katy. Tears welled in Tessa's eyes, and she praised God again for His amazing love and faithfulness to her. She then remembered the prayer she had said earlier in the evening, asking God to help her if He was real and if He was really listening. He answered her prayer by sending Gramps and Katy to rescue her. It seemed nothing short of a miracle that they showed up when they did. She knew now that God *was* real and that He *was* listening. She was so happy, she felt as if her heart would burst.

*And if my heart were to burst*, she thought playfully, *that would be all right. It would mean I'd really be going home.* And for the first time in her life, the thought of dying didn't scare Tessa one little bit, and the thought of living at peace within herself gave her a sense of great joy.

## Soaked

*And the priests went into the inner part of the house of the
LORD, to cleanse it, and brought out all the uncleanness
that they found in the temple of the LORD into the court
of the house of the LORD. II Chronicles 29:16*

THE rain had finally stopped. A warm Chinook wind blew the
clouds away and a three-quarter moon lit up the campus path.

Loud angry voices could be heard from the far end of the courtyard as two figures walked toward the girls' dormitory.

"... and so he comes back to the school ... engaged to one of his
students!" It was Dr. Johnson's voice, and he was with Jasmine. "The
outrage! And right now, they're holding hands and skipping up to his
office to 'put some things in order,' whatever that means. I don't like the
sound of it. He'd better not be leaving like his friend Timothy Daniels
did last year. Left me high and dry without a counselor! It's mutiny, I
tell you! This is not good, Dr. Winters! Having these types of so-called
Christians on staff —may as well hang a black cloud over our school!"

"You think *that's* bad! What about *my* night? First you send me
dimwits to set up the music. I told them to play Techno Taizé Monk
Chants, and what do they bring? The Tenor Mennonite Men's Choir.
The good news is, I had a backup CD in my office. The bad news is, my
helper ran away and sent in the spies. Great! Just great! A whole line-up of
farmers praying at me in the name of Jesus as if I were the devil incarnate!
They said we may as well be in the Dark Ages with all the candles that

were burning. What a herd of legalistic fundamentalists!"

"*Candles!* So that's what set off the fire alarm!"

"Yes, that's when the fire alarm went off, and everyone started leaving—with my expensive organic beeswax candles—and left me standing in the dark! And it seems no one knows how to turn the lights back on in that ancient Thompson Building. Everyone just ignored me!"

"But Dr. Winters, the entire campus was without power. It wasn't just the Thompson Building. Don't you know there was a storm? Lightning hit the main power pole. We are running on the generator for now and only have limited back up and emergency lights. You *must* know," he added, noticing her clothes. "...you've obviously been outside...you're soaking wet!"

"Yes. Yes, I am wet, Dr. Johnson," Jasmine spat through gritted teeth. "Evidently, the smoke from all the candles set off the old smoke alarms and the next thing I know, the malfunctioning sprinkler system goes off and starts soaking the place. How ridiculous!"

JACOB and Tessa, stacking the last of her luggage by her dorm room door, could overhear the end of the conversation of the two faculty members who were approaching the dorm's walkway. Jacob turned to Tessa and said in a low voice, "The way I see it, this is all very ironic. The Ekstasis Night was advertised on the school's website as an ancient-future worship evening, ending with a soaking session. Get it? Soaking session!" And Jacob shook his head and laughed at his own wit.

"Oh, Gramps!" Tessa giggled. How much she had missed his dry sense of humor. She was really beginning to see things from a new perspective—even Gramps and Gran—and it pleased her immensely. She picked up one of the remaining bags to carry to the truck, took a few steps, and froze in her tracks.

Dr. Winters and Dr. Johnson stood directly before her.

"There you are, Tessa, the servant whom I trusted, the one who brings me tea and sits at my feet." Ms. Jasmine smirked. "We've been looking for you. Is this disastrous evening all your doing?" Ms. Jasmine's voice was smooth but full of resentment. She grabbed Tessa's arm, the same one she'd grabbed earlier in the evening and made bleed. "Well, *is* it?" she demanded again.

She began to dig her long red nails into Tessa's arm, when suddenly someone stepped between them and broke Ms. Jasmine's hold. "Just one moment ma'am," came a firm, strong voice. Frank Johnson and Ms. Jasmine found themselves face-to-face with Jacob Brown, who had just stepped out of Tessa's dorm with the last suitcase. Frank stepped back, but Ms. Jasmine's feet were glued to the ground as she stared unblinkingly into Jacob's steel-blue eyes.

It took about ten seconds before it finally registered.

*Could it be,* she wondered, astonished. *Could it really be?* The last time she'd seen those eyes was a long, long time ago. It was the day before she had run away from her last foster home.

"Mr. Brown? Jacob Brown from Rocky Mountain?"

"Ms. Winters. The years haven't changed you too much."

"Wha . . . what are you doing here?" Disconcerted, she turned her gaze toward the parking lot where she could see the outline of an old pickup truck. "Still driving the same old vintage Ford?" she whispered softly, but loud enough for Jacob to hear.

"Yes, I am," he answered.

"Amazing," Ms. Jasmine said, shaking her head.

"Amazing indeed. After you drove off in it that day, the truck needed a lot of body work to get it back into good condition. Somehow, I'd always hoped you'd come back one day with some regret in you and pay for your mistake."

"What!" Ms. Jasmine looked back at the old man again.

"Nah, just kidding. You don't owe me anything. It's all forgiven."

Ms. Jasmine and Jacob stood staring at each other for a few moments without either saying a thing.

Jacob felt genuinely interested and concerned. *When all this is straightened out with Teresa, maybe Margaret and I can have lunch with this young lady and try to help her.* "As I recall, you were just a bit younger than Teresa when you made your decision to run away. . ." Jacob's voice trailed off as he turned to close the dorm door behind him. Then he gently took Tessa by the elbow and together they began walking toward the parking lot.

"My . . . my decision?" Ms. Jasmine stammered, following behind.

"We all have choices." Jacob stopped and turned to her, a look of sadness etched on his face. "You have chosen to run after a spirituality that the Bible warns against. Listen, it's never too late to repent and turn to Him. He has always been there waiting for you. But there could come a time when it is too late. 'My spirit shall not always strive with man,'" Jacob quoted from the Bible. He had spoken the same gentle words to her the night before she'd run away, twenty-nine years earlier.

"How dare you speak to me that way! You talk to me as though I'm some lost little girl! Are you aware of who I am, of my highly respected status in the spirituality community?" Ms. Jasmine stomped her foot on the sidewalk.

"Yes, I am aware of who you are. And someday I hope to talk to you longer, Jasmine, but right now," Jacob said softly, "I'm taking my granddaughter home."

"Your . . . your granddaughter?" Ms. Jasmine looked at Tessa, shocked. "*You?*" Turning to Frank Johnson, Ms. Jasmine demanded incredulously, "Dr. Johnson, he can't do that. Can he do that? Tell him he can't do that!" Ms. Jasmine's shrill voice carried clearly through the night air.

"Dr. Winters is correct. You . . . you can't just take Tessa away like that, before the school term is complete." Dr. Johnson stammered. "She will lose all her marks and —"

"I can, I will, and I am. She is not yours. She belongs to her heavenly Father, and what she needs right now is time with Him, not points with you. And as for her credits, we'll see about that. When the truth comes out about what has been taking place here, about what these students . . . well, we'll just see about marks and credits."

Jacob threw a blanket and a pillow into the front seat of the cab of the truck before adding, "Oh, and by the way, Frank, I just talked with the elders from the church down the road. As you probably know, they are also on the college board. After their little visit to room 109 earlier this evening, they decided to hold an official, impromptu board meeting in the school cafeteria. They voted to bring in some tractors and equipment to scrape those large stones off the soccer field and reinstall the soccer goalposts as soon as the ground thaws. There's even room in the budget to hire someone to haul away those stones and lay some new turf. And if you think you might try to reverse the decision, don't bother. The vote was unanimous."

Immediately and unexpectedly, loud cheering erupted from a growing crowd of young men standing in the moonlight nearby. "It looks like some other 'fuddy-duddies' are joining us," Jacob said to Frank, pointing over in the direction of the young men.

"But those rocks!" Ms. Jasmine wailed. "Those aren't just any old rocks. They were hand-picked stones! That's my labyrinth! I designed it! Do you know how hard I worked to get that in here? They can't do that! Dr. Johnson," she said indignantly, "have you no spine? Tell him they cannot do that!"

"Oh, one more thing," Jacob said as he placed the last of Tessa's things into the cargo bed. "The elders' wives have offered to restore and redecorate the prayer room." Jacob closed the canopy lid on the back of the truck and locked the handle.

"Wait a minute here! The prayer room—that's my Sacred Space! It is redecorated... you CAN'T DO THIS! Why are you undoing all my hard work? I... I won't allow it! I'm a highly educated, highly intelligent, and famous person, you know? Don't you realize who I am?"

Ms. Jasmine, enraged, turned her attention to Dr. Johnson and hurled further barbs at him in a most unprofessional manner. His own anger rising, Dr. Johnson turned *his* attention back to Jacob.

"Mr. Brown! Do you have a theology degree? Have you written books on spirituality? Do you have any Ph.D.s in psychology? Do you have any idea who my superiors are? Mr. Brown! You will be sorry you came here and interfered—very sorry indeed!"

Growing weary of the two-man circus act playing out before him, Jacob sighed and said, "Go talk to the board, Frank. You'll find them waiting for you in your office." Then he reached inside a large toolbox on the back seat of his truck and tossed Frank a flashlight. "Here, you might need this. Think of it as a going away present."

"Oh. Wait a minute," said Tessa. "I almost forgot something."

She rummaged through her large purse and found a dog-eared book with a picture of a castle on the cover. She pulled out the bookmark, slipped it into her pocket, and skipped back to Ms. Jasmine, standing in the moonlight.

"Here Dr. Winters. I won't be needing this anymore." She handed Ms. Jasmine her copy of *Selections from the Interior Castle*. Calm and unintimidated, she looked straight into Ms. Jasmine's eyes. "This 'new' Teresa won't be influenced by the 'ancient' Teresa or her crumbling sand castles ever again."

Turning away, Tessa was filled with a peaceful assurance that Ms. Jasmine no longer held any power over her. As she stepped onto the pickup, she paused and looked back, suddenly feeling a great sadness that her tutor appeared to be so blinded to truth. She slipped inside and squeezed Gramps' hand. "Let's go," she said quietly.

They drove away through the main gate. Tessa's eyes filled with tears as she stared with pity at the shrinking figure of Dr. Winters in the side mirror. The doctor's red lips were moving, but Tessa couldn't hear what she was saying. Her wet, dyed blonde hair no longer looked so angelic, but her cheeks, smeared with streaks of dried black mascara, did make her look like a mime whose mask had melted away. Ms. Jasmine's brand of peace and tranquility had proven to be nothing more than a thin and fragile mask. And what Tessa had seen beneath that mask that evening had not been pretty.

After driving in silence for several minutes, Tessa finally spoke. "Oh, Gramps. You've made them so angry. Dr. Johnson is a very influential man. And Dr. Winters is powerful too . . . only I don't think her power comes from the Lord . . . Aren't you worried?"

As they left Flat Plains and turned back onto the old highway that would take them home, the right turn signal clicked on and off in time to "Grace Flows Down." Tessa hadn't heard that song in months. Right then, it sounded sweet and beautiful to her ears.

"My dear Teresa," said Gramps, looking at her with a twinkle in his eyes as they continued along the narrow two-lane road, "when God cleans house, no one can stand in His way. Besides, if the Lord is for us, who can be against us?"

## FINDING HOME

MARCH 28

"DAISY, let go of the broom . . . please!" Tessa laughed as she affectionately scolded the little dog who seemed far too happy to have her back home. Tessa had finished mucking out Sassy's stall and sprinkling it with clean straw. She couldn't remember a time when such a chore had given her so much delight. As she tidied up and swept the barn floor, she couldn't help but think how the practices she had been involved in at college reminded her of a dirty stall. She shuddered as she thought of Ms. Jasmine's so-called sacred space.

After dumping the wheelbarrow full of manure out behind the barn, Tessa scrubbed out the water bucket, filled it with fresh water, and measured half a can of oats for Sassy. Finally, she gave her beloved mare a good brushing and picked out her hooves before bringing her in for the night from the paddock.

"There you go girl, all nice and clean."

Sassy nickered as Tessa threw two flakes of hay into her stall for her supper. Sitting down on a straw bale with Daisy, Tessa sighed and smiled a happy, thoroughly contented smile. It was so good to be back home in the sweet-smelling barn with hay stuck in her hair and horse dirt on her hands. She breathed it all in, enjoying the soothing sounds of the horse's munching and the gentle clucking of Gran's bantam hens roosting for the night. When Sassy stuck her head over her stall door, oats falling out of her mouth to check on her best friend, Tessa giggled.

"Oh Sassy, go eat your oats, you silly girl. I'm busy right now." Then she quietly said to herself, "The old Tessa spent a lot of time talking to her horse and not enough time talking to her God."

She opened the Bible that Gramps had given her to I John, laid it on her lap, and read aloud.

"'If we confess our sins, He is faithful and just to forgive us our sins, and to cleanse us from all unrighteousness.' Wow. That's amazing."

Against a soothing symphony of melting snow dripping off the barn roof and tumbling down the rain gutters, Tessa did a lot more reading and thinking. And talking.

"Oh God, can we go back to the first time I tried to pray in here? Remember? When I asked that if You were real, to prove it? Well, I believe You are real now."

She got down on her knees by the straw bale and wept until her eyes ran dry. Daisy's stubby tail wiggled as she licked Tessa's salty cheek. Tessa remembered what Nathan had said about the necessity of renouncing the wrong things he had done when he got saved.

"And Lord, I totally reject all the things I became involved with that were not of You. I am so sorry. Please forgive me for listening to the wrong voices. From now on, I want to follow You and know You, the way Gramps does . . . the way Katy does. I want to have a close, personal relationship with You, like they have." As Tessa prayed, the sound of the dripping snow running off the barn made her think of the hard layers of sin, hurt, and sorrow that felt like they were melting and running off her heart at that moment.

"God, remember when I first came to live here, how Gramps and Gran helped me understand that we're all sinners and need a Savior? And that Sunday afternoon when I prayed with Gramps after that evangelist spoke in church, and I accepted Your gift of eternal life? I knew that gift was because of what Jesus did for me on the Cross, that He somehow took the penalty for my sins, so that I wouldn't have to.

"But it wasn't long after that, I got mixed up with the wrong crowd at school. Some of my friends, well, you know how they mocked my faith, and I just wanted to fit in. Everyone kept telling me that Jesus was just one of many paths to You. And You know what my science and philosophy teachers taught us about You . . . and so I started to doubt Your Word. I actually believed that people knew more than You, Lord. I was so confused."

Tessa talked to the Lord so differently now. For the first time in her life, she understood what it meant when people said they had a personal relationship with Him. She could hardly believe she could say the same thing now, and mean it. *Surrendering, trusting* . . . oh, what lovely, real words they had become! Tessa continued pouring her heart out to this new Friend, who was also her Lord and God.

"And so, God, when I went to Flat Plains, I guess I was searching for spiritual answers, and so I trusted my professor, and I believed the teachings of someone like Teresa of Avila. That's when my life really got messed up. Scary messed up. Oh, heavenly Father, please forgive me for not completely trusting the things in Your Word, for rejecting the Bible's warnings and the advice of godly friends who really do love me. I've been a fool! Lord, thank You for leaving the ninety-nine sheep and searching for me. Thank You for bringing me back safely to Your sheepfold."

It wasn't just the smells and sounds that made the barn the most peaceful place Tessa had ever been in. The barn had always been peaceful, but for the first time in her life, Tessa's heart and mind were filled to overflowing with the calm and peaceful assurance that she finally belonged to Someone, and that He loved her.

Wiping her runny nose and her tears with her jean jacket sleeve, Tessa really understood, for the first time, something incredibly powerful and wonderful. She was not an orphan anymore. She was a child of the King.

MARGARET was sitting in bed, snuggled in her pink terry-cloth bathrobe, sipping a cup of warm milk. Jacob told her she looked beautiful with her hair down and brushed that way. She was glad to have her husband back home. The Lord had answered all her prayers and more. For forty years, she and Jacob had read the Bible together before going to sleep every night, except for the last month. But that was all behind them now. This evening, Jacob chose something from Romans. Margaret closed her eyes and listened to Jacob's gentle voice:

> For as many as are led by the Spirit of God, they are the sons of God.

> For ye have not received the spirit of bondage again to fear; but ye have received the Spirit of adoption, whereby we cry, Abba, Father.

> The Spirit itself beareth witness with our spirit, that we are the children of God.

"Isn't that beautiful, Jacob? Just like our Teresa." Margaret smiled.

"Margaret, it's no coincidence that our pastor will be preaching on this passage as we go through Romans 8 tomorrow morning, and that Teresa will be with us," said Jacob as he closed his Bible. He'd bought it last year to replace the one he had given to Tessa, and already the gold was wearing off the edge of the pages. The floor creaked as he stepped out of his plaid slippers and looked outside from his bedroom window. "She's still out there," Jacob said as he walked over to the bed.

"Jacob, maybe you should go out and talk to her."

"No need, my dear," he said warmly. "We had a very nice talk last night on the long drive home. I think she has Someone more important to talk to tonight."

"But out there? It's so chilly tonight."

"Now Margaret, remember, the One she is talking to chose to

be born in a stable with animals. I couldn't think of a better place to meet with Him."

"You're right, JB. And have you told her she can stay here as long as she likes?

"Yes, she knows she is free to stay or go, but I did see a sparkle in her eyes when I mentioned that The Rock is hiring right now for the summer. It would be a perfect job for her. She could bring Sassy."

"JB, you are a genius! What better place for her than a Christian dude ranch! And you will tell her that boy called long distance, won't you? What was his name again? Nathan? A nice boy, and so polite. He said he had something that belongs to her."

"I'll tell her," Jacob said, "tomorrow after church."

"And what about the lawyer who just called this week about the will from that distant relative on her great-uncle's side that no one had ever been able to locate? When are you going to tell her about those things?"

"The will can wait a bit. Right now, she needs to find God's will for her life."

"Yes, of course . . . There's something I'd like to talk to you about Jacob. I have been thinking that maybe we need to legally adopt this girl. Somehow, I think it could make a real difference in her life, knowing we were really, truly hers. And since we have no children of our own, someday she could inherit the farm."

"I like that idea Margaret." Jacob sat down on the bed next to his wife and patted her soft hand before turning out the light.

LATER that night, Tessa tiptoed upstairs to her attic bedroom and slid between the flannel sheets of her bed under the cozy new quilt Gran had sewn for her. She turned out the lamp and breathed in the pleasant smells of the farmhouse. The chimney pipe that went through her room made its familiar crackling noises. Downstairs, the old clock on the mantel chimed eleven times. Daisy lay curled up and snoring on the throw rug at the foot of her bed—or was that Gramps snoring from the room below? Home sweet home! Everything was true and right here.

She lay awake for a while, just listening. Listening, and remembering—how happy she felt when she was a little girl as her mom read her favorite story about the handsome prince who rescued the beautiful princess from the castle tower.

Then, for the first time in months, Tessa fell into a deep, uninterrupted sleep. She dreamed she was on a white horse, riding in the clouds and wearing fine white linen. She was following a Prince who was wearing a crown on His head and riding a magnificent white stallion . . .

Beside the bed on the nightstand, the moonlight shone on an old Bible opened to a page where a tattered, homemade bookmark lay. . .

> And the armies which were in heaven followed him
> upon white horses, clothed in fine linen, white and clean.
> Revelation 19:14

# EPILOGUE

TESSA DAWSON has a new job at The Rock, a Christian dude ranch in the Rockies for troubled teens, where she gives riding lessons and leads Bible studies. She is saving up to go to a small missions school on an island off the coast of Spain and plans to tour Europe afterward, with a stop at the famous Spanish Riding School in Austria, home of the Lipizzaner.

KATARINA BUCKLER is writing a discernment manual for Bible college students. She will be teaching a class at Flat Plains Bible College called The Truth about Spiritual Formation and Emerging Spirituality every Tuesday evening in room 109. She and Sam will soon be married and are excited about their future together in ministry.

JACOB BROWN has been asked by the new president of Flat Plains Bible College to head up the new Biblical Apologetics Committee.

MARGARET BROWN sews Scripture quilts and gives one to every teen who arrives at The Rock.

SAM GOLDSMITH has been chosen to be the new President of Flat Plains Bible College. He will be replacing spiritual formation with a program called Equipping this Generation with Biblical Discernment.

JONAS from Seattle has been hired at Flat Plains to coach a soccer team whose aim is to hold Christian soccer camps for inner-city teenagers.

FRANK JOHNSON resigned and was last seen in Mongolia.

JASMINE WINTERS was recently seen on the *Twila White Show* talking about her pilgrimage to India where she sprinkled the ashes of her great-aunt Bea on the Ganges River. Her position at Flat Plains Bible College has been terminated.

THOMAS THIESSEN is now a speaker for Merging Force and gives workshops on Christian Yoga and how to do your own Ekstasis experiential worship. His grandmother prays for him every day.

THE GIRL WITH BLUE HAIR from Earl's Electronics Shop came to the Lord after reading a Gospel tract that Katy Buckler had given her and is now volunteering at a large youth ministry in the Pacific Northwest that is rumored to have started in a church parking lot in Seattle.

NATHAN has been accepted into a Bible-based Christian college in the Rocky Mountain foothills where he has free room and board in exchange for working with the maintenance crew. He keeps in touch with Tessa through e-mail and phone calls. Rumor has it he sent her flowers . . . for no particular reason at all . . . but Gramps doesn't believe that. If he's guessed right, this young man will come courting soon.

THE FOXES couldn't afford to rebuild the The Quiet Place after it blew across the lake. They have since partnered with the interfaith society that helped replace it with a small hermitage cabin behind the lodge in the woods called The Hide Away. Business is booming.

TERESA OF AVILA trusted in spiritual advisors even when they had given her opposing messages. Teresa fell ill and died on October 4, 1582 at the age of sixty-seven. She was later declared a Doctor of the Roman Catholic Church for her teaching on prayer and is the patron saint of headache sufferers.

# GLOSSARY

## **In the words of our story's characters**

### ASHRAM

**The Foxes:**
Typically, it is a secluded dwelling of a Hindu sage and his disciples. We were actually building one at the lodge, a religious retreat center for yoga . . . uh, Christian prayer practices, that is. It was going to be beautiful. Then there was this storm one night. Did you know flood insurance doesn't cover wind damage?

### CENTERING/CENTERING PRAYER

**Thomas Thiessen:**
Just another term I've recently learned that has been rediscovered in the Christian contemplative heritage. It's a deep silent prayer where we can be rooted in God's presence. I've started taking twenty minutes to center myself on Jesus, before I get out of bed in the morning. I just repeat his name, and my head gets cleared. I know some websites out there call it New Age, because when some people excel at centering they reach alpha brain wave patterns and can even get into the thin place, but it's not New Age. Actually, the New Age stole it from Christianity. How else are you gonna get kids coming to youth group if they don't have an experience? It's the only way God can break through to them. So what if some of these guys teaching it are monks—we all believe in the same God. Besides, I learned this year that we left way too much behind when we left Roman Catholicism.

### CHAKRAS

**Katy Buckler:**
Chakra is a Sanskrit word that means wheel or disc. Those who practice Hinduism believe there are seven major wheels of light, or energy centers called chakras, within the body. This belief has been passed down for a thousand years before it was finally written down between 1200-900 B.C. Today New Agers also believe that during meditation

these seven energy centers open up, resulting in the kundalini effect. A very dangerous thing to be opening yourself up to, yes?

## CONTEMPLATIVE PRAYER

**Jonas:**

We were taught in Bible college that it was just another way to meditate on the Bible, but it's actually going beyond thinking with your mind by using repeated words and phrases to shut down your mind. I didn't know . . . I just didn't know . . . but I do know the Lord has forgiven me after I repented for allowing my youth group to practice it.

## CREATIVE VISUALIZATION

**Jacob Brown**

Over the years, I've noticed that many athletes have used this method to imagine in their mind what they want to happen. It's basically positive thinking or creating your own reality. Some say you can affect the world, and even your past and future, by your thoughts. It's bad enough the *Twila White Show* has been promoting this, now it's even being taught in Bible schools! This is not what God's Word tells us to do with our minds at all. What if this exercise with your subconscious mind connects you with spiritual guides from the demonic realm? To tell you the truth, I wouldn't touch it with a ten-foot pole!

## DESERT FATHERS

**Ms. Jasmine:**

Early Christians whose writings we treasure because they were the ones who first taught the practice of contemplative prayer. These writings are the heart of Christianity's traditions. Of course, some say they bear a strong resemblance to Hindu and Buddhist meditative techniques, but there is nothing wrong with borrowing from other streams of spirituality and rediscovering other traditions, as the Desert Fathers did. Just because some of them, such as Saint Anthony, frequently experienced strange and terrifying psycho-physical forces during prayer, doesn't mean we toss the baby out with the bathwater.

## EKSTASIS

**Thomas Thiessen:**

It technically means being beside one's self, but what it really involves is going beyond normal, boring worship and entering into an expression of body, soul, and spirit. It means abandoning yourself to go wild for Jesus, dying to yourself to reach a whole new level of experience. Of course, some say the rhythmic music induces hypnotic states and altered states of consciousness and invites deceptive spirits. But that's not true, although there was that one time . . . but no, my youth group loves it. They even bring their unchurched friends, and we have a blast. What better way to get kids to church?

## ECSTASY

**Tessa Dawson:**

It's what the Hindus call a state of higher consciousness, a "blissful" or euphoric state that mystics experience during meditation. Like the state of rapture where St. Teresa of Avila saw visions into the spiritual world. Definitely not of God. I know that now.

## ENERGY HEALING

**Nathan:**

They always have Mind–Body–Spirit posters for classes on this up on the library bulletin board. Supposedly, it's causing healing energy to flow through the body and activate the chakras or energy centers by using mystical techniques. You'll find energy healing being practiced in hospitals and spas, and even in some churches that say it's within the Christian traditions of healing. But it's a spiritual force that works on the assumption that man is God!

## JOURNALING

**Sam Goldsmith:**

This is basically opening your mind and being available to write down a flow of spontaneous thoughts or visions that you believe to be from God. The obvious danger is that the mystical inner thoughts might just be spirit guides speaking through your pen. It's also called automatic writing or channeling in New Age and esoteric circles.

## KUNDALINI

**Girl with blue hair:**

Dude! Kundalini is a term for the power force behind Hinduism. Don't you know it's called the serpent power? It's bad stuff. You see, there's this lady that has a shop across the street from where I work—she's got a snake tattooed on her leg. Anyway, she says she gets her serpent power from yoga and meditation. You should see her eyes! Bright green! Creeps me out, like especially that day I gave her this tract about God and she screamed at me and tore it up! Said her cards had warned her about me. But hey, I'm praying for her.

## LABYRINTH

**Jacob Brown:**

As I researched the labyrinth, I discovered it was a single path or universal tool for spiritual transformation. Of course, some are saying it's a tool to enhance right brain activity. In a way, they are right, it's a tool all right, a New Age one that Christians everywhere are embracing as a method to practice contemplative prayer and meditation! In fact, I know of one Bible college that . . . used to have one. The idea of the labyrinth is that as you walk toward the center of it, you also center your soul (get in touch with your inner divinity) by repeating a word or phrase.

## LECTIO DIVINA

**Frank Johnson:**

Yes. Lectio divina is derived from a Latin word that means "holy reading." It is one of the greatest treasures of our traditions. It is an ancient method of slowly reading and repeating the Scriptures in order to encounter the presence of God in the silence. I do this every morning now. It really helps me get rid of all the distractions going on in my mind.

## MORTIFICATION

**Margaret Brown:**

From what Jacob tells me, I understand this to mean one of the methods Roman Catholics use to train themselves in virtuous living. It can mean merely denying oneself certain pleasures and choosing a simple lifestyle, or taking vows of poverty, like the monks do. But Jacob said it can also mean causing self-inflicted pain and physical harm, such as . . . such as . . . do you mind if I'd rather not speak about it?

## SELF-FLAGELLATION

**Girl with the blue hair:**

Yeah, I read it in a Goth novel once. These mystics in the Middle Ages would use a whip or a stick to punish their own bodies. They'd even starve themselves and try to stay awake for days, and then they'd get into weird states of mind. Altered states, I think you'd call it today. Crazy, like, I used to cut myself, I guess it's like that. I was in bondage, but Jesus delivered me. Praise God!

## SPIRITUAL DIRECTOR

**Sam Goldsmith:**

Well that's obvious. A spiritual director is someone who has been trained to introduce a person or group to contemplative practices and awaken them to inter-spiritual traditions. They are being trained by the droves and showing up everywhere lately where you'd least expect to see them, even in Bible-believing churches and colleges here in North America!

## SPIRITUAL FORMATION

**Dr. Frank Johnson:**

This is the emphasis on traditions and practices based on the ancient writings of the church. These methods represent various streams of spirituality that we can profit and learn from, including contemplative prayer, disciplines, solitude, meditation, journaling and spiritual direction. Some fundamentalists have anxiety over these things based on fear and paranoia. My students often hear me refer to this illness as spiriformaphobia.

## SACRED SPACE

**Margaret Brown:**

Jacob told me this could be a physical spot where a person can go to engage in a mystical practice, like the prayer room in the Bible college that had to be remodeled in the Bible college after that unfortunate incident. They say it still has a strange smell. Jacob says it can also mean the actual silence or the state of being during a mystical practice. Isn't that right, JB?

## TAIZE

**Jacob Brown:**

Taizé is an ecumenical prayer service where participants achieve a contemplative state through chanting, singing, and silence. They use lots of candles. Jasmine would love it.

## TERESIAN PRAYER MODEL

**Tessa Dawson:**

The mystical stages of the steps of prayer based on the seven mansions of the Interior Castle of St. Teresa of Avila, a sixteenth century Spanish mystic and Roman Catholic nun. I got one hundred percent on that paper.

## THE SILENCE

**Nathan:**

It's the absence of normal thought. Going into the silence is like putting the mind in neutral or tuning the brain into another frequency. New Agers call it a thin place, sacred space, and ecstasy. Now we've got both New Age *and* Christian leaders telling us we must practice silence and stillness if we really want to know God, but it's a lie from the serpent. This practice is different than finding a quiet place (such as beside stream or in your house when you turn off the television and radio), contemplating (thinking on) God's Word with your mind, and praying. It's important to understand the difference.

# BIBLIOGRAPHY

**Note:** The books listed in this bibliography should not be considered a recommendation. The author of *Castles in the Sand* has used these books for research as well as for citing.

Teresa of Avila; *The Interior Castle.*
Hodder & Stroughton Christian Classics
Edited by Halcyon Backhouse, 1988

Teresa of Avila; *Selections from the Interior Castle.*
Harper Collins Spiritual Classics, 2004

Malone, Mary T; *Women and Christianity.*
Orbis Books Volume III, 2003

Osuna, Francisco de; *The Third Spiritual Alphabet.*
Paulist Press, Translated by M.E. Giles
The Classics of Western Spirituality, 1981, pp. 45-47

Dalton, Rev. John; *The Letters of St. Teresa.*
London: Thomas Baker, I, Soho Square
Translated from the Spanish, 1902, http://digital.library.upenn.edu/women/teresa/letters/letters.html

Teresa of Avila; *Life of St. Teresa of Jesus of the Order of Our Lady of Carmel.*
Translated from the Spanish by David Lewis
Third Edition Enlarged
With Additional Notes and an Introduction by
Rev. Fr. Benedict Zimmerman, O.C.D.
http://www.ccel.org/ccel/teresa/life.html

Foster, Richard; *Prayer, Finding the Heart's True Home.*
HarperCollins, 1992, First Edition, pp. 156-157.

**Note:** To learn more about contemplative spirituality, visit:
www.lighthousetrailsresearch.com.

# Photo and Illustration Credits

**Cover Photos:** Mike Bartlett, "young girl on horse," used with permission; Andrew Barker, "Bamburgh Castle," used with permission from 123rf. com; iloveotto (background image), used with permission from 123rf.com

**Flowered Border:** Alina Pavlova, used with permission from 123rf.com.

**Page 3:** Andrew Barker, "Bamburgh Castle," used with permission from 123rf.com

**Page 8:** Drawing by "Kristin," used with permission.

**Page 18:** Paul Hill, "St Theresa of the Child Jesus," used with permission from istockphoto.com.

**Page 28:** Chris Aquino, used with permission from 123rf.com.

**Page 39:** Heide Hibbard Reed, used with permission from 123rf.com

**Page 49:** Drawing by "Kristin," used with permission.

**Page 62:** Al Jorge, "Silhouette of a bell tower in Avila, Spain," used with permission from 123rf.com.

**Page 63:** Teresa of Avila, public domain.

**Page 69:** "Ecstasy of St Teresa" statue by Gianlorenzo Bernini, photograph by Adam Eastland, used with permission.

**Page 76:** David Hughes, used with permission from 123rf.com

**Page 79:** Matt Trommer, "The Iglesia de San Pedro in Aila," constructed in 1100s, used with permission from 123rf.com.

**Page 89:** Pierre Graffan, used with permission from BigStockPhoto.com.

**Page 93:** Hulton Archive, circa 1545, "Saint Teresa Of Avila," used with permission from istockphoto.com

**Page 99:** Drawing by Carolyn A. Greene.

**Page 109:** Hulton Archive, circa 1550, "From an engraved portrait in the 'Iconografia Espnola' of M Carderera," used with permission from istockphoto.com.

**Page 124:** Matt Trommer; used with permission from 123rf.com.

**Page 127:** Painting by Francois Gerard, 1827, "Saint Theresa," used with permission from Erich Lessing / Art Resource, NY.

**Page 175:** Jake Hellbach, used with permission from BigStockPhoto.com

**Page 210:** Drawing by Carolyn A. Greene.

**Page 212:** Teresa of Avila, painting by Peter Paul Rubens, public domain.

# FOR MORE INFORMATION—
## BY LIGHTHOUSE TRAILS PUBLISHING

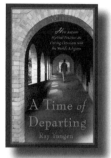

*A Time of Departing*
by Ray Yungen

*Faith Undone*
by Roger
Oakland

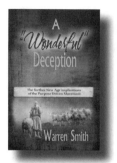

*A "Wonderful"*
*Deception*
by Warren Smith

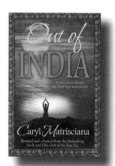

*Out of India*
by Caryl
Matrisciana

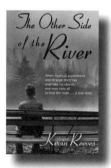

*The Other Side*
*of the River*
by Kevin Reeves

For a complete listing of Lighthouse Trails books and DVDs, please go to www.lighthousetrails.com or request catalog.

## BOOKS
*Trapped in Hitler's Hell*
by Anita Dittman with Jan Markell
$12.95, ISBN: 978-0-9721512-8-3

*Another Jesus* (2nd Edition)
by Roger Oakland
$12.95, ISBN: 978-0-9791315-2-3

*Things We Couldn't Say*
1st Lighthouse Trails Edition
by Diet Eman
$14.95, ISBN: 978-0-9791315-7-8

*For Many Shall Come in My Name* (2nd Edition)
by Ray Yungen
$12.95, ISBN: 978-0-9721512-9-0

*Tapestry: The Journey of Laurel Lee*
by Laurel Lee
$15.95, Hardcover, illustrated ISBN: 978-0-9721512-3-8

*Laughter Calls Me*
by Catherine Brown
$12.95, ISBN: 978-0-9721512-6-9

## DVDs
*Standing Fast in the Last Days*
with Warren Smith
$14.95, 57 minutes, ISBN: 978-0-9791315-9-2

*The Story of Anita Dittman*
with Anita Dittman
$15.95, 60 minutes, ISBN: 978-0-9791315-5-4

*The New Face of Mystical Spirituality*
with Ray Yungen
3 DVD lecture series
$14.95 each or $39.95 for set

To order additional copies of:
CASTLES *in the* SAND
Send $12.95 per book plus shipping to:

Lighthouse Trails Publishing
P.O. Box 958
Silverton, Oregon 97381

For shipping costs, go to
www.lighthousetrails.com/shippingcosts.htm

You may also purchase Lighthouse Trails books from
www.lighthousetrails.com.

For bulk (wholesale) rates of 10 or more copies, contact Lighthouse
Trails Publishing, either by phone, online, email, or fax. You may also
order retail or wholesale online at www.lighthousetrails.com, or
for US orders, call our toll-free number: 866/876-3910.

For international and all other calls: 503/873-9092
Fax: 503/873-3879

*Castles in the Sand,* as well as other books by Lighthouse Trails
Publishing, can be ordered through all major outlet stores, bookstores,
online bookstores, and Christian bookstores in the U.S. Bookstores may
order through: Ingram, SpringArbor or directly through Lighthouse Trails.

Libraries may order through Baker & Taylor.

For more information on the topic of this book:
Lighthouse Trails Research Project
www.lighthousetrailsresearch.com

You may write to Carolyn Greene care of:
Lighthouse Trails Publishing
P.O. Box 958
Silverton, OR. 97381
USA